**SAM CRESCENT**

# EVERNIGHT PUBLISHING ®

## www.evernightpublishing.com

Copyright© 2020

Sam Crescent

Editor: Karyn White

Cover Artist: Jay Aheer

ISBN: 978-0-3695-0273-5

## ALL RIGHTS RESERVED

# SAM CRESCENT

## *The Family, 3*

**Sam Cresscent**

**Copyright © 2017**

### Prologue

*Seven years ago*

Luiz Barone's heart was racing. At seventeen years old he'd seen so much crap that even though he was young, he didn't feel like it. He felt old, and right now, his very future was on the line. Rushing into his secret girlfriend's home, he saw the bodies of her parents across the dining room.

"No, let me go!" Lora's scream drew him to the back of the house, and he had his gun raised and ready.

*Fuck.* Lora was a civilian. She was under his protection, and nothing should have happened to her. He should have known his father would try to screw him over. No Barone was going to have a bastard out of wedlock, and that was exactly what Luiz had done. Christie, his little girl, was the best thing that had ever happened to him, and he couldn't let anything happen to her, or to his love, Lora.

Rushing toward the kitchen, he watched as the man slammed her face against the tiled counter and pushed her away. Luiz drew his gun, pointed, and shot. The man, whom Luiz didn't even recognize, looked completely shocked.

"Luiz," Lora said, gasping.

Firing the gun again and again into the man that had tried to take his new family away from him, Luiz didn't stop until his bullets ran out. Dropping the gun, he rushed to Lora's side and saw the blood pooling out of her stomach.

"No, no, no, no." Covering the wound, he tried to put pressure on it, but it just seemed to be constantly leaking.

"We ... were ... not meant to be."

"Shut up, Lora."

"You have ... to go."

"No."

"Yes. Christie."

"Did those bastards get to her?"

"She's with Raine."

Luiz closed his eyes. Raine was Lora's younger sister. She was fifteen but too damn mature for her age.

"I can't."

"You're going to have to. I'm ... dying."

"No."

"Face it, Luiz. We were not meant to be." She released a cough, gasping. "Love her ... for me. Let her know I'll always love her."

In his arms, Luiz experienced his first taste of unimaginable grief. Lora was his girl. She had driven away the darkness. The moment he was in her arms, he'd finally felt that he could live a normal life. A life away from danger, away from the threat of death.

Lora faded away, and he couldn't grieve. Not a

single one of his friends knew the truth. He had kept it from them in the hope of protecting Lora and Christie for the rest of their lives. That wasn't going to happen now.

"I'll always love you."

Getting to his feet, he ignored the blood and the death that surrounded him. Going upstairs, he passed Lora's bedroom, and went straight for Raine. When he didn't see her in the bedroom, he opened the bathroom door, and saw her outline in the shower curtain.

"You can come out now, Raine."

He saw the curtain shake a little as she opened it, drawing it back to reveal her. Her brown hair was pulled back into a ponytail. Her glasses perched on the bridge of her nose as she looked back at him. In her arms, she protected his baby girl.

"I wouldn't let them hurt her."

"I ... er ... I need you to come with me."

"Lora's out there. We need to get her."

"She's gone, Raine."

"What?"

"She's dead." He hated how damn hard it was for him to get those words out, but he did it. "I need to get you and Christie to a safe place."

"I'm only fifteen."

"I'll deal with that. I've got a friend who can keep an eye on you. You'll be safe with him, I promise."

\*\*\*\*

Raine had always been a little afraid of his sister's boyfriend. Luiz might have been seventeen, but if you stared him in the eyes long enough, she was sure you'd see the devil. She loved her sister, and her sister loved Luiz, so Raine helped. When Lora came home pregnant, Raine was happy for her. She'd finally be an aunt, and she would spoil her niece terribly. She'd loved Christie even before she first saw her.

Of course, her parents weren't too happy, but with Luiz paying them for the inconvenience, no one said anything.

"Xander will take care of you," Luiz said. "He's got the details. You can go to the local high school, and here are all your new IDs."

She took the card he held out to her. It was still so surreal that three days ago she'd woken up to gunfire. Lora had given her Christie and told her to be quiet.

"What do I do?" she asked.

"Go to school. Have a life. You don't have to worry about money. All I ask is that you take care of Christie."

"Of course I will. You don't need to question that."

She saw the pain in his eyes. For once he no longer looked like the devil but broken, rough around the edges.

"I'm going to be around a lot, or as much as I can."

"Will anyone else be coming to visit?" she asked.

"No. I've made it look like everyone in that house died."

"Oh."

"You can't go back, Raine. Not ever. If it ever got out, they will hurt you. I promised Lora I'd protect you."

"I'm a big girl. I don't need protecting."

"You do."

He shoved his hands into his pockets, and she watched as he made his way toward the crib that Xander had set up for her when they first got there. Christie had a chew toy in her hands and was shaking it around. "Hey, baby girl, it's Dadda."

She smiled, and slowly moved away from the room, giving him his moment.

Entering the kitchen, she looked over at Xander, who was pouring himself a coffee. "Am I going to have issues with you?" he asked.

"Issues?"

"Girl shit. Boys, and that kind of crap?"

"No."

"You going to be joy riding? Taking drugs?"

"Can it, Xander. She's not that kind of girl. You give her shit, and I'll make you pay, understand?" Luiz asked, coming up behind her.

"I told you. I don't like trouble, and girls tend to find it without even looking." Xander stared at her.

"It's fine. I'm not going to be any trouble. I promise."

\*\*\*\*

Luiz stood at the back, allowing all the parents to take front and center. He didn't even know why he was here. The last time he'd visited Christie, Xander had taken him aside and asked if he'd be coming to Raine's graduation. He'd not cared about his own graduation. Sure, he'd been there, but it wasn't exactly something he would rave about either. Luiz had also given Xander a warning as well. He'd watched the way Raine and Xander were together, and there was an intimacy between the two that he really hadn't liked. Of course, he'd been wrong. Xander had told him he didn't fuck little girls, even if Raine *was* getting to the age that meant she wasn't so little anymore. His friend saw Raine as a daughter, nothing else.

"She has no one, Luiz. No one, and she's going to be there without any of us."

So, instead of staying well away, he'd come to see Raine graduate. She was a beautiful woman, no denying that. In the past three years she'd matured in ways he didn't think was possible. Xander adored her, and they were standing together with Christie in between them watching as Raine walked up the steps. Luiz wished there had been a better future for her. One where she didn't have to take care of his little girl but in his world right now, he didn't have that luxury. There were more pressing problems.

"She's worked so hard for this," Xander said, leaning in close to whisper.

"She didn't have to do this. I could have made sure she passed."

"Nah, Raine isn't the kind that cheats. She loves to do everything properly. For the last year she's barely slept so that she can graduate today."

"Any boys you've had to worry about?" Luiz asked. He had expected Xander to complain a lot more about her.

"None. I'm a little worried actually."

"Why?"

"Well, she's a girl heading into a woman. I expected some kissing, or some sneaking around. Nothing. I've even tried to make her date."

"Make her?"

"You know, arrange for her to go on dates."

Luiz didn't like that. In fact, he found it really annoying. Why was he even worried about Xander being a problem when he was more worried about her being with someone else? "Did I ask you to make her date? She's got a job to do, and it's not screwing random guys."

"You wonder why you've got a problem with her dating?" Xander asked, raising a brow.

Luiz glared and picked his daughter into his arms. Another ten minutes and the ceremony was over. Raine made her way toward them.

"Auntie!" Christie squealed.

"Hello, sweetie, did you see me? I've finally got it."

Christie giggled and slapped Raine's hand. Christie tried to pull out of his arms, so Luiz let her go into Raine's arms.

"She stopped her from calling her 'Mom'," Xander said.

Luiz frowned. "I'm sorry."

"Christie kept trying to call her mom, but she wouldn't let her. There have been moments when it has been hard without … Lora."

"I can imagine."

"Erm, Raine?"

They all turned around at the question.

Raine turned, and the smile on her face was like a kick to Luiz's gut. "Todd, hey, congratulations."

"Thank you, and to you."

"This is Christie, my niece," Raine said.

Luiz was getting angry. Did she really want this fucking loser?

"She's beautiful."

"Of course. So was my sister." The smile disappeared from her face, and the reality came in.

"We've got to head out," Luiz said.

"Right," Raine said.

"Wait, I was wondering if you'd like to go to dinner with me?" Todd asked. "You know, to celebrate."

Before Luiz could shut him down, he listened to Raine do it.

"I'm really sorry, Todd. I can't. I've got to get going, and I'm sure the invite doesn't extend to Christie, so I've got to go."

"Oh, okay."

"Maybe another time?" she asked.

"I'll keep you to that."

Raine still held his daughter as they made their way toward the car.

"You could have gone with him," Xander said.

"No, it's not possible for me to."

"Why not? You've got a life, too."

"No, I don't. I've got to take care of Christie. It's what my sister would have wanted."

Luiz didn't say anything. He used the mirror to stare at Raine. She stared out of the window, and he recognized the yearning in her eyes. He wished that he knew what was going on in her head.

Later that night while Raine was having a bath, and Luiz was playing with Christie, Xander sat on the chair.

"What?" Luiz asked. Xander's gaze was full of judgment.

"Are you going to let her go through life always passing up opportunities?"

"She doesn't need to go on dates and shit like that. They're a waste of space."

Xander sighed. "She's eighteen years old. Other girls her age are out dating, messing around. She's taking care of her niece, and she's losing every chance she can."

Luiz didn't want to think of Raine dating someone else, or worrying about that shit. "She's not missing out."

"You're blind, and for whatever reason, you're determined not to see."

Raine came into the sitting room an hour later. Her brown hair was curled, and her face was nice and red.

"Are you heading out soon?" she asked.

"Yes." He watched as she took a seat across from him. Christie wriggled away, and sat between Raine's thighs, picking up toys, and shaking.

"I don't want you to bring boys back here," Luiz said.

"I wouldn't do that."

"Good. I expect you to put Christie first in everything."

"I do, Luiz. You don't have to worry. I'll always protect Christie. She will always come first."

Guilt swamped him, and he hated this. He didn't want to take from her, and yet he didn't want her to find someone else.

"I've got to go."

"Okay. Christie always loves it when you visit."

"I love coming here." He took hold of Christie's hand, trying not to say the next words, but he couldn't hold back. "What about you? Are you happy to see me visit?"

He looked into her eyes.

"Yeah, I like you visiting."

"There's something I want to tell you."

"What is it?" Raine asked.

"I don't want any of your boyfriends around Christie. The last thing I want is for her to feel confused by it."

"Luiz, it's the last thing you have to worry about right now. I'll not let anything happen to her. I promised my sister, and I will continue to promise you. In my world, in my life, Christie will always come first."

# Chapter One

*Present day*

"What are you saying?" Luiz asked.

"I'm saying that we were fools to think that we could clean up this mess and walk away." Donnie threw his pen on his desk, and rubbed his eyes.

"But this is what we agreed. The Family doesn't have to rule this city, Donnie." Tonio was pacing, and every now and again stopping.

"It's what I hoped. You don't think I didn't have a plan for myself, for Paige, and for my future? Fuck. I didn't want this. I never wanted to be some fucking ruler, or the head of this fucked up family."

"You are, and there's nothing you can do about that," Jake said. Jake sat in the corner of the office. His fingers were pressed together as he leaned back, staring at all of them. "Together we can do this."

"This isn't about *us* doing this," Luiz said. "Our plan should have worked."

"It didn't."

"Where did we fail?" Tonio asked.

"We failed in the fact that we didn't take into account the importance of The Family."

"Huh?" This came from Tonio.

Luiz understood instantly. "When there is one family at the top, they are the rulers of all others. Take away one family, another will rise up, and it may not exactly be the best decision for the city or even the country." He moved toward the window, rubbing at his eyes. He was so damn tired. Between this work, and trying to see his kid, he was just exhausted. In the beginning he had believed it was possible to be part of something bigger, something better. That belief was rapidly running away from him, and any hope he had of bringing Christie and Raine closer to him was fading fast.

"So that's it. We fucked up, and now we're screwed?" Tonio asked. "I've got George to think about, and Zara's pregnant again. I can't do this. I'm not going to allow my son to become what we were. What my father made me."

Luiz stopped and went to his friend. They were all friends. Putting his hand on Tonio's shoulder, he tried to offer him the comfort and strength he needed. "You will never be the monster that your father was. Believe me." Tonio's father demanded that he rape and kill for films. For sick bastards who wanted to get off on that kind of shit.

"I just, I can't. We all agreed that The Family had to cease to exist."

"I know. Even though we were mature for our ages, we didn't see the full truth. We can still turn this around."

"How?" Tonio asked. "We stay with The Family, keep it up and running. We're practically begging for death. Bullets, threats, our very lives will be at stake."

Donnie stood and rounded the desk. He leaned against it. "What about if we walk away? Do you think any family would let us four live? They would hunt us down and kill us. I can't have that. Not for George, not for Petal, and not for my little sister either. I can't do it."

Luiz didn't speak up. His friends didn't know that he had fathered a child. They didn't know about the hit his father had placed on Lora, on his kid, or that he'd kept her hidden for so long now. Too long. She was nearly seven years old, and asking questions all the time. He'd hoped to bring her back to him, to have a life away from the danger, away from the risk of death.

"What do we do?" Luiz asked.

"We have to make a choice."

"You're saying that we've got a choice?" Jake asked.

"It's a choice I'm granting each of you. *I* can't walk away. I know that now, and I accept it. Paige is pissed. Of course she is, but I'll deal with it. I'll deal with everything that comes our way, and I will protect our families the best way I can. I'm giving you the chance to walk away." Donnie reached onto his desk with an envelope. "Here are three passports, with different identities. I've not looked at them, to save you all. If you want out, and I know you do, take them, and start a new life. I don't want to know where, who, or why. Just start over."

Luiz looked at that envelope. It was the chance that he wanted. The only problem was he'd made a pact, a blood oath to his best friends. They were his brothers.

"What would you do?" Jake asked.

"I'll be here, of course. Trying to keep The Family together, tearing apart all threats, and hoping to save my very soul and Paige's love in the process."

"Then that's it, I'm staying," Jake said. "You couldn't organize your own pussy growing up. Paige likes me, and the way I see it, you're going to need some help with her and with Petal along the way. It's not like I've got my own woman waiting for me."

Jake had a crush on the girl, or the woman that Donnie's dad had stolen, and used for his own personal pleasure. The problem was, Charlene, the woman, was a lesbian, and she now had a lover of her own. Jake was still brokenhearted about that.

Tonio cursed. "Fuck! I wouldn't be the man I am now if it wasn't for us working together. You bastard. This isn't a real choice. I can't leave you behind. Zara would kick my ass. We've always had each other, and I can't let you face whatever shit you're about to face alone. It's now who I am, so I'm in. No matter what."

Luiz stared at the brown envelope and thought about his kid, and his kid's aunt. They deserved a life better than the one he was providing. He just knew it.

"What about you? You in?" Donnie asked.

"I'm in."

Christie and Raine were as protected as they were ever going to be.

"So what happens now?" Luiz asked. "I mean, nothing really has changed, is it? The only difference is we're the ones giving the orders now. No one else."

"We need to keep our show of force. I believe we'll be stronger if we each take a key lead in our areas."

"Then you need to handle the main legit businesses," Luiz said. "It's already in your name. You have the contacts, and it makes perfect sense."

"You think so?" Donnie asked. "This is where we can change what we want to do."

"No, Don, you've always been the lead of our legit business. I'm with Luiz on this," Jake said. "You're the only one that can do this. I'm going to take our drugs link. My dad was the one who organized the drug runs and the distribution."

"You think you can do that?" Luiz asked.

"It's what I know. It's what my father wanted me to take over. The drugs, and also the dealings with the soldiers. We'll be keeping soldiers for The Family."

"Yes," Donnie said.

Luiz listened as they all made their final decisions. Tonio was going to handle the guns and gambling, leaving Luiz with the girls and the fighting.

"You okay with that?" Donnie asked.

"Yeah, I'm fine with it."

"Right, I'm going to head out and touch base," Jake said, and left the main office of Donnie's home.

Tonio left next, and Luiz was heading out when Donnie stopped him.

"You hesitated," Donnie said, getting out of his chair, and rounded the desk to stand in front of him.

"It's not what I wanted, and I never pretended it was."

"Does this have to do with Maria—"

"Fuck no. Maria took her own life because she couldn't stand the bitch she had turned into. She killed my niece and nephew along with her. The last thing I want to think about is that bitch."

Maria had strung his friend, Jake, along. Even though she had been Luiz's sister, and he'd done everything he could to protect her, he wasn't stupid. Maria had been a bitch who was more willing to take a beating for a life of luxury than get out.

Jake had offered Maria a life out of The Family. She was more interested in a diamond necklace.

"What's going on with you, Luiz? Did something happen?"

"No. Fuck all has happened to me. We had a plan, which has changed, and now I have to deal with the change. I handle the underground fights, and the girls. It's not hard to do."

"There is a chance for us to have a good life, Luiz. I believe that."

Luiz burst out laughing. "You're fucking joking right? There's no way that you can have a good life and be part of the criminal world. This will probably bite us all in the ass in years to come, but there you go." He moved toward the door, wanting out of his friend's home.

"I have to think positively about this, Luiz."

"Donnie, look what this family did to Tonio, to Charlene, to everyone it touches. It's a fucking nightmare, and with every single death, there's less of a chance of us coming back from that. I know this, and you're a fool to think you can get away with it."

****

"I don't think I can do this," Raine said, her stomach churning.

"Sweetie, you're twenty-two years old, and you deserve to date at least once," Xander said.

"What about you? You're not dating, and you're getting old."

"Shut up about my age, and I do just fine," he said.

She knew he went and visited women whenever he wanted. Raine was happy that she and Christie hadn't cramped his style by living with him. The best thing about living with Xander was the visits from Luiz. Those were the ones she enjoyed the most, and no, she wasn't going to read too much into that.

"Luiz won't like this. He doesn't want to risk Christie, and I've never gone against him like this."

"You're not going against him now. I'm the one that has decided that you need to get out some more. You've never dated, and I've known you since you were fifteen."

"You didn't like me," she said, reminding him of how much of a bastard he'd been to her in the beginning. "My charming personality and Luiz's threats have helped with that."

What was with her constantly thinking about Luiz? It was driving her crazy. She even dreamt about him now, and no matter what she did to exhaust herself so she fell to sleep, nothing worked, and it drove her insane. Waking up aroused was something new for her as well.

"I thought I was going to have to deal with all of your messes. The women that come from The Family, they have a lot of baggage okay? I find women like to make more mess than they actually clean up."

"That's not me, Xander. I'm not part of The Family, not really. I just take care of my niece because it's what my sister would have wanted, and Luiz would have probably killed me for knowing too much."

Xander actually laughed at her words, and she rolled her eyes. Only he would find humor in a death threat.

"Luiz wouldn't have killed you."

"You don't have to try to make me feel better. I'm not a fool. I've seen the mafia movies. It's a good thing they didn't sell me into sexual slavery or something." She finished applying her lipstick, and hated the dark red color, but it was what Xander told her she should wear.

Would Luiz like the dark red? *Ugh, stop already.*

"Luiz is not like that. He's trying to find another way for The Family to work. I also know he's wanting to make a completely different world for you, and for Christie."

She didn't see the point in arguing with Xander. The moment he made up his mind there was no stopping him. For the past seven years, Luiz had been coming and going, seeing Christie, issuing his threats. She was starting to see his warnings as a little bit of a flirt, especially when he winked. Still, Luiz was untouchable, and she wasn't that big of a fool to think that she could win him over.

Not that she wanted to. No. She and Luiz simply had one small girl in common, and that was it.

How much of a liar could she be? She had a crush

on her dead sister's love, and that wasn't right, right?

"I can't believe you arranged a date for me with the guy from the local grocery store." She grabbed her jacket and bag.

"You wouldn't arrange a date. I was starting to see that you really weren't going to live your life, and being a martyr really isn't good, Raine."

"I'm more worried that Luiz is going to take this as a sign that I'm not fit to take care of my niece."

"You forget that I'm here, sweetie. I'm here to deal with Luiz, and to help you live your life. You're not supposed to spend the rest of your life helping her. What happens when she's eighteen? When she's twenty-two like you are now."

"I don't know."

"Well, it's time for you to know. I'm not going to be around forever, and you're going to be alone. I don't want you to have regrets."

"So Bradley the grocer is going to help me?"

"He's a college student who comes home every summer to help out at the shop. I've seen the way he looks at you, and I think you should give him a chance."

Xander saw her out of the house, and she took a deep breath as she found Bradley waiting for her outside near his car.

She glanced back at Xander, and he simply smiled. "Go, have fun, and for once in your life, stop worrying."

"It's easy for you to say. Do you know if Luiz is coming over tonight?" she asked.

"If he is, I'll deal with him. You can't keep making him tell you what to do. Live your own life."

"The threat to Christie's life?"

"I'll handle it, just like I've been handling all kinds of threats since you came into my life. Mostly that of filling my house with feminine products, and making me fat through your cooking."

She rolled her eyes. "Fine. I'll have fun, and you better not watch horror movies with Christie. The last time you two did, I had to stay up with her three nights in a row. My body cannot handle that much coffee, and so little sleep."

"We can amuse ourselves. I was just thinking of playing a few board games. The word being 'bored' as in boring."

Raine chuckled, and turned back to Bradley.

*I can do this. It's easy.*

Lifting her hand in a small wave, she tried not to cringe at Bradley's huge smile. This was all wrong, and yet if she didn't do this, Xander was never going to get off her back.

Stepping toward Bradley, she forced a smile. "Hey," she said.

"Hello."

"I'm sorry that Xander forced you into this. I'm sure you had a lot more fun planned for a Friday evening."

She saw that Bradley's cheeks actually went bright red.

"Well, this was my idea."

"Oh."

"I wanted to date you for a long time now. I've just never gotten around to it."

"Wow, erm, now I feel a little sorry. I, wow, I don't know what to say." She chuckled. "I guess I put my foot in my mouth."

"You don't have to worry about a thing." He chuckled. "I should have asked you. I got to Xander first because every time I tried to ask you, you were always so busy. I'm sure you don't even remember me all that much."

"Of course I remember you. You're always so sweet to me, and to Christie. You're the only guy at the store who'll offer to take my groceries to the car."

"Christie, is she yours?" Bradley asked.

"No, why? She's my niece but my sister..." Raine paused. This was not the topic that she wanted to talk about. "She's no longer with us, and I promised to always look after her. Do you understand?"

"Yeah, I do. Shit, I'm so sorry. This is not how I imagined our first date being."

"You imagined your first date with me?" she asked, charmed.

"Yes. I had to get the courage to ask you."

"Xander told me to go out on a date with you. You never got the courage."

He glanced at the ground, and then at her. "Raine, would you go out with me?"

"I'd love to."

Bradley opened the door of his car for her, and she slid inside. Her heart was racing. Ever since Luiz had brought her to this place, she'd avoided contact with everyone. She kept to herself, made sure friends were aware she wasn't available for anything. Her main priority had been keeping Christie safe, and living with Xander had been a lot of fun.

She had enjoyed proving him wrong, and making him a little guilty for some of the nasty words he'd thrown her way. Even before she moved in with Xander, she'd never been the kind to make friends easily. In fact, she had found it damn hard to connect to people all the time.

Her sister, Lora, had been the more outgoing one. She knew what she wanted, and the moment Lora met Luiz, they had been inseparable. Raine wondered if her sister would have ever regretted being with Luiz. It was still hard for Raine to think of Luiz as part of the mafia, as part of The Family. Ever since she learned the truth of who he was, she had researched him.

It was something she had to do to know what she was dealing with, what Christie was going to have to deal with as well. Of course what didn't help either were her growing feelings for Luiz. It made no sense, and yet at the same time, it did. He was a handsome man, or at least, she thought he was. There was no way she could think any differently seeing as he was the one she thought about all the time.

"You're back home from college. What are you studying?" she asked. She knew next to nothing about Bradley.

"I'm studying business with the hope of taking over from my dad when he's ready to retire. I want to expand the business."

"It sounds like you have a plan already in motion."

"Oh, I do. I can't wait, to be honest. I really want to get my hands stuck in. The only way to live is to keep moving forward. The world doesn't stay still. It's always moving, and we've got to keep up, or we'll die."

It was a morbid thought, and one Raine didn't want to think about. Her world had been moving for the past seven years, and she was tired of it. All she wanted to do was for it to slow down, so that she could have time to enjoy it.

"I'm sorry. I'm rambling."

"It's fine. Honestly. I like listening to your plans for the future." It certainly beat being worried about a certain father being pissed with her.

## Chapter Two

Luiz was tired, and instead of going home to pass out for the night, he needed to see his girls. He didn't know when he'd started to think of Raine as his, but he had. She was part of his world, and it was all his fault that she'd never be able to live a normal life.

Pulling up outside of Xander's house, he stared at the plain house. The point of Christie and Raine being here was for them to lead as normal a life as possible. With Donnie's latest revelation, their life wasn't going to change anytime soon. He couldn't risk bringing his little girl into his world. He hated doing this.

There was no other way for him to draw her into his world.

Christie didn't deserve it.

Neither did Raine.

She was too sweet.

Too innocent.

This was his battle.

Climbing out of his car, he made his way up toward the house. He didn't knock, knowing there was no need to. Xander told him he was family, and he was supposed to just enter.

"Anyone home?" he asked, calling out to be heard.

"Daddy!" Christie ran toward him and threw herself into his arms.

Pulling her close, he held her tightly. "Hey, baby girl. You had a good day?"

"I'm making brownies."

"With Raine?" he asked.

"No. Xander."

"Where's Raine? Is she sick?"

"She's on a very important date." Christie smiled

at him. "Xander told me so."

The pain that slammed into his chest was not what Luiz expected. "Date?"

"Yep."

He lifted her up into his arms, and walked toward the kitchen. Xander had on an apron, and was reading through a recipe, frowning.

"What the fuck does she do?" Xander asked.

"Language!"

He didn't like bad words around Christie. There were many reasons Luiz kept his little girl away from him.

"Sorry. I'm just wondering what Raine puts in these damn brownies to make them taste so good."

"I need to go to the toilet," Christie said.

Lowering her to the floor, Luiz watched her go, and turned back to Xander. "She's out on a date."

"Raine, yeah, she is."

"Why?"

"Do you have anything against her dating?" Xander asked.

"She's raising my child, and I told her not to go out. You said you didn't want the hassle of a girl constantly dating."

Xander held his hand up. "Stop right there. Raine didn't organize this. I did."

"What?"

"I made her go on this date, and don't worry, the kid is harmless that she's with."

Luiz felt betrayed. Xander had been the closest thing to a family for him, and yet he was betraying him.

"How could you do that? What about Christie?"

"What about Raine?"

"What about her?"

"Since she was fifteen old, she has been

helping me take care of Christie, studied hard, cleaned this place up, and done everything you asked of her without question."

"So? I promised to protect them."

"And in order for her to keep living, she has to forget the chance of her own life, is that it?"

Luiz frowned, not knowing what to say.

"Raine didn't want to go tonight. She wished I hadn't made her. She's twenty-two years old, Luiz. She's never had a boyfriend, or felt love."

"She has Christie's love."

"That's not the same thing and you know it."

Xander stood tall, placing a hand on his hip. "You're pissed off that another guy is with her."

"Grow up."

"I am, Luiz. *I'm* a grown ass man. What about you?"

"What does this have to do with Raine going out on a date?" He faced off with Xander, wanting any reason he could to hurt the man.

How dare he make Raine go on a date?

"What you need to think about is why it hurts you so much."

"It doesn't hurt me."

"You're lashing out, wanting to piss me off, Luiz. That's new, even for you. What the hell is going on? Just the other week you were telling me how the end of The Family was coming. You were prepared to take Christie into your life, and keep her there. What's changed?"

"The Family has changed. That's what."

"What do you mean?"

Luiz checked to make sure his baby girl couldn't hear him. "Donnie called us all into the office today. If we don't continue to take over, there will be others determined to take our place."

"So? Didn't you boys think of that?"

"I thought of it. I figured I wouldn't care."

"The only way someone will be able to take over from The Family, and to come to power, would be to hand over all four of your bodies. The moment you killed your parents, and slaughtered your enemies, you made yourself the target, Luiz."

"I know that now. I don't need this shit with Raine."

"You care about her?"

"She's my daughter's auntie. Of course I care."

Xander shook his head. "I'll let you be delusional. I don't have the energy to fight with you, and it's incredibly boring to do so. Just know that life is short, and you know what you want, Luiz. Stop fighting it."

Rolling his eyes, Luiz took a seat at the kitchen counter. "What's the kid's name?"

"Bradley. He's a good boy, and he's had his eye on Raine for a while. She was worried you would think she was breaking your rules."

"Only you."

"You're telling me that when you look at Raine, you don't feel anything?" Xander asked.

"What do you feel?" Luiz answered with his own question.

Seven years he'd been part of Raine's world. She was there to listen to him, to guide him when it came to his little girl.

"I feel protective of her. She has been amazing, Luiz. You should realize that."

"I know she has given everything up for herself. I appreciate that. I really do."

"You do?" Xander asked.

"Of course. Lora would want me to take care of

her."

Xander scoffed. "You're an idiot."

Luiz ignored the insult. "Can I stay the night?" He was only going to drop in, but now he wanted to stay, spend some time, and find out what the hell was going on with Raine.

"You know it is, and I know why you're staying."

"Bite me, Xander. I'm not in the mood."

"Go ahead. Go and get settled in. I'll try and not burn the sixth batch of brownies."

Leaving Xander in the kitchen, Luiz made his way upstairs, toward the back of the house where his room was. Christie and Raine's room was beyond his. He made sure they were together so that he would have time to deal with any threat. When he brought them here, he'd made Raine go through several practice runs in case they were ever attacked. There was an escape for her only, and he made sure it was hidden so no one could use it to actually get in. Pausing at his room, he glanced at Raine's door.

What could it hurt to go into her room? The house was his anyway. He simply allowed them all to live here. All the bills were paid by him. Even though the house was in Xander's name, everything came down to Luiz.

Seeing no reason to not go into her room, he stepped toward her door, and without another thought, opened the door.

Raine's room was a pale peach color, and the instant he entered, the scent of cinnamon filled his senses. She loved cinnamon, and used it in as much baking as she could.

He'd never been a big fan of the spice until Raine converted him with a coffee-style cake.

Closing the door, he moved toward her bed and

looked around. The room was bare of any personal touches. No posters on the wall, or photos. The only photo he saw was a single one by the side of her bed. He knew the photo as he had one himself, locked away in his safe back at home. It was a rare photo of all four of them taken one Christmas two years ago. Raine had wanted it taken so badly. She'd forced them all into a small spot, and they were all so happy to be there. Christie was on his lap, Raine perched on the chair, and Xander was behind them all, watching over them.

It was a powerful photo, even to him.

This was a dream he'd had many times.

All four of them, able to live in peace.

It would be so simple to take them all back to his world, but Xander wanted no part in it, not anymore.

Xander had once been his bodyguard when he was a baby. During an attack, Xander had lost everything, his wife, his kids, and nearly his life. If it hadn't been for Luiz finding him years later, without his father knowing, Xander would have probably been six feet under by now.

He shouldn't be in this room.

Luiz left, and he didn't want to think about Raine, or the pain that he was experiencing knowing she was on a date.

It was an entirely new sensation, and not one he liked.

**\*\*\*\***

Waving at Bradley, Raine wondered if he was disappointed with her. She hadn't invited him in for coffee, nor had she accepted the kiss he'd wanted to give her. When he had leaned in, about to put a kiss on her lips, she'd panicked, giving him her cheek instead. Kissing wasn't something that came naturally to her.

She'd never been kissed by anyone.

Maybe she should have let Bradley kiss her, and get over it. It would have made her life a lot easier. Entering her home, she locked the door, and heard some commotion in the kitchen. The scent of burnt chocolate was heady in the air. The smell turned her stomach.

Xander came out of the kitchen, covered in chocolate and looking a little frazzled.

"You've been baking?" she asked.

"I tried to bake thinking it would be easy. Guess what?"

"It's not."

"You make it look easy."

"My mom used to bake all the time, and I stood with her. It's what I love to do. How much chocolate did you use?"

"All of it."

"Wow, you went through all of my supply. The chunks, the chips, the bars?"

"Yep. I've got to go shopping tomorrow for you. No problem. I'll just include it with the flour, sugar, and spices. Oh, and Luiz is home. How was your date?"

"Luiz is here?" she asked. She would *not* get excited. The urge to go looking for him was strong, but she held back.

"Yeah. Bradley, how was it?"

Before she could answer Luiz was coming out of the kitchen. "I put Christie to bed."

"Hey, Luiz," she said, feeling a little sick. This wasn't good, and was the red lipstick still on, and did he like it or did he think it was silly?

Crap, this was not going to go anywhere.

"Xander told me you went on a date."

"He made me go."

"Did you enjoy it?" Luiz asked.

Why was it whenever he asked a question, she

felt like she didn't have a choice but to answer? It was so frustrating.

"I did. Yes."

"Where did you go?" Xander asked.

His excitement was infectious.

"The little Italian place in town. It has just opened up. They have the most amazing spaghetti with clams. So good."

"You like Italian food?" Luiz asked.

"Yeah, I do. It's my favorite. My mom was obsessed with it. Lora was more of a Chinese girl." It was a lot easier to talk about her sister now. The pain was still there, just not as bad. They walked back into the kitchen. "I had no idea you were coming tonight."

"We never know when he's going to turn up," Xander said.

She sat at one of the chairs near the kitchen counter, and smiled at Luiz. "I bet Christie was excited. I know she loves it when you visits, and hates it when you leave."

"It's not easy for me either."

"I'm just going to head to the bathroom to wash up. Do you think I can leave you two alone for a few minutes?" Xander asked.

"Of course." Raine never knew how amazing it felt to actually go on a date or be part of something like that. Bradley had been attentive, charming, and so sweet … but he wasn't Luiz. *Shut up!* "What brings you home? Good news? Bad news?"

"I just wanted to stop by and see everyone."

"So it's bad news?"

"Why does it have to be any kind of news?"

"You only come by unexpectedly when you've had some awful news."

"I come by all the time."

"Not all the time, sweetie." She touched his hand, feeling the prickle of awareness that his touch always created. Xander had to be right if she was starting to feel something more for Luiz. "Most of the time you plan your visits. A phone call or something like that."

He rolled his eyes, and she chuckled. "Something bad did actually happen."

"What?" She tensed waiting for the bad news.

"It's not so bad. You don't have to worry too much, baby."

Baby? He called her baby.

"Hit me with it. Will we have to move?"

"You want to be with Bradley some more."

She heard the disgust in his voice. "I went on one date, and it was at Xander's urging. If I need to move for Christie, I will. I'll do whatever you need me to do."

"You'll always do that?"

"Of course. I love Christie, and I'll do anything for her. So please tell me."

"Okay. That's good to know. Do you think you and Bradley will be a big thing?" he asked.

"I don't know. It was one date, and he asked me to go out again. I told him I'd have to see Xander first. Why don't you tell me what's going on?"

Luiz sighed. "I'm remaining part of The Family."

"I thought you said that you wanted it to be over. That you were making it easier so that you can have a life without threat."

"We were all fools. There's no way for me to walk away. If we walk away, we'll be the ones on the chopping block. Someone else will just come and take my place."

This was going to be her life forever. There was no getting away from the secrecy, from the fear. Even after seven years there were times when she heard bumps in the night that made her afraid.

She suddenly felt the overwhelming need to cry. Glancing down at her clothes, she released a sigh. "I've got to go and get dressed."

Without waiting for Luiz to say anything, she left him sitting at the kitchen counter. On her way to her room, she passed Xander.

"What did he say?"

"Nothing. He said nothing. I'm going to call it an early night, okay?" She kissed Xander's cheek, and quickly rushed toward her room. Closing the door, she collapsed against it, and pressed her face against her hands. Her chest was so tight, and she was hurting inside. There had always been hope that maybe one day this would all be over. She had wondered if Luiz was just being overprotective of them over the years. They had never been attacked here, but then he'd always taken care of everyone that even got close to them.

Moving away from the door, she grabbed her stuff, and went to the bathroom. Washing away the night, and the illusion of a future, she changed into her pajamas, and walked back to her bedroom, brushing her hair.

She gasped when she caught sight of Luiz on her bed. He was sitting, staring down at her bear. She still had a bear that she enjoyed, sue her. This was nothing like any of her sexy dreams where Luiz was completely naked, and wanting her.

"What are you doing in here?"

"I don't want you to be upset."

"Did Xander send you up here?"

"No. I came here because I know you were really upset."

"I can't do this right now. There's nothing I can say to make you feel better, Luiz."

"I'm here for you, Raine. Not for me."

She moved toward him, and took a seat. "It's nothing that a good's night sleep won't fix."

"You've given up so much for Christie, and I really appreciate it."

"Don't worry about it."

"You were hoping for a future though, right? A future of your own." He took her hand. "You can tell me."

"I'll never give up Christie. I promise I'd never do anything to hurt her, but, she's not going to be a little girl forever. She's going to be eighteen and twenty-one, wanting to go to prom, to have some fun, fall in love, go on dates."

"That's what you want?" he asked.

"I didn't know what I wanted until tonight. It's amazing what one date can do." She chuckled, but it was a forced sound, not natural.

"You've never been on a date?"

"Never been on a date. Never kissed a guy before, and I didn't think it mattered, but it does. I'll be thirty-three when Raine's fifteen. I'll probably still be a virgin." She shook her head. "Can we leave this? I really don't want to talk about it with you."

She didn't want to be talking about her virginity, or how she was reading dirty books at night, or that she craved being touched. When she took Christie out, or even if she went by herself, she watched couples, and craved the easiness that they all had, and it just wasn't fair.

"You can come to me for anything."

"No, I can't. You cannot just drop everything for us, and I get that. I know you're busy. I'm just being a girl, so ignore me." She forced herself to look at him, and groaned when she saw the pity in his eyes. This was not what she wanted.

"A guy has never kissed you?"

"I've always kept my distance, Luiz. My first and only priority has been Christie."

Luiz cupped her cheek, and ran his thumb across her bottom lip.

"What are you doing?"

"Something I should have done a long time ago."

Before she could question him, Luiz pressed his lips against hers, shocking her still.

## Chapter Three

Raine's lips were softer than Luiz imagined. She was tense as he kissed her. He didn't know why she was so surprised, and why he hadn't thought of them being together until now. It made total sense. They were both young, free, single, and they had Christie in common. He'd dated her sister, but Lora and Raine were nothing alike. Raine was bigger than Lora ever was. She possessed way more curves, similar to Paige in size. Cupping her cheek, he tilted her head back, and became aware of two things. One, he was hard as fucking rock, and hadn't felt this alive in years. Two, Raine was as tense as a board.

Pulling away, he saw she was frowning at him, looking a little confused. "What's the matter?" he asked.

"Why are you kissing me?"

"I want to."

She took his hand, moving it away from her face. "I don't feel comfortable with this." She spoke while getting up, and moving away from the bed.

This was a new experience for him. He wasn't used to being pushed aside, or ignored. He was Luiz Barone. An equal ruler in The Family. Every woman wanted to bed him, or to wear the title of being with him with pride. He didn't see the problem.

"Why?" she asked.

"I figure what's the problem? You want to experience stuff. I don't like the thought of you dating someone, and putting Christie at risk. I can give you everything you're looking for."

She scoffed. "Seriously?"

"Yeah."

"What about love?" She folded her arms over her breasts.

"What about it? It doesn't exist."

"Wow! Get out."

He frowned. "What is the problem? You want to experience this kind of stuff. I'm your guy."

"I mean it, Luiz. Get the hell out of my room."

"Technically, it's my room."

She moved toward him, grabbed his shirt, and shoved him toward the door. In one quick move she had the door open, and him pushed out. He didn't fight her hold as he didn't want to hurt her. Raine said nothing else as she slammed the door closed, and didn't even look back at him.

"What did you do?" Xander asked, making Luiz jolt.

"I thought it would be convenient for her to use me for what she needs."

"You mean instead of her dating someone else?"

"Yes. I can't believe I've not thought of it before, but it will work."

"Luiz, sometimes you're the biggest asshole on this planet, and a blind one." Xander didn't elaborate, and went back to his bedroom.

Luiz was completely baffled. Entering his own room, he took a quick shower, and after thirty minutes, he still didn't get it. What had he done wrong? She wanted something. He could give her whatever she needed.

Grabbing his cell phone, he dialed the only person he would know who had the answer.

"Who the fuck is calling you?" Donnie asked.

"I don't know. Hello?"

"Hi, Paige it's me."

"It's Luiz," Paige said.

"Why is he calling you?" Donnie asked.

"Maybe because I'm a lot nicer to him than you

ever are. What's the matter, Luiz?"

In the background he could hear Donnie making threats.

"I want to ask you something, as a woman."

"Okay. I'm awake."

Sitting up, Luiz stared at his reflection in the mirror opposite his bed. He let out a breath. "If a guy offers a woman the chance to be with him, shouldn't she be happy about that?" No one knew about Christie and Raine. He wanted to keep it that way.

"I have no idea. It would depend if the guy is an idiot."

"He's … lovely. How about this? The girl has never been kissed, a complete virgin, and he's just offered her everything."

"Luiz, why are you asking me this? You're confusing me."

"I just. I had a dream, and I was just curious about it."

"You have weird friends, Donnie. Ugh, I don't know how to answer this, Luiz. It would depend on what the woman or girl wanted. Does she just want sex? What does she mean to you? What's she like? No woman is exactly the same."

"Okay, what if it was you, and I offered you sex, and it was before Donnie?" he asked.

"I really don't feel comfortable answering this."

"Please."

"Fine. I wouldn't have been interested in you, Luiz. I'm not attracted to you."

Luiz wasn't attracted to her either. "Okay, fine. How about this? Say the girl is the younger sister of the girl he was actually with, and he had a kid with this girl?"

"The younger sister?" Paige asked.

"No, the older sister, only something terrible happened. Younger sister has been watching the kid, and she was too young to know better, and I, I mean he, offered her everything."

"Sex?"

"Yes."

"What is the younger sister like?" Paige asked, yawning.

Donnie was going to be on his case, but he just needed advice, and the only person he knew who could give him that kind of advice was Paige.

Luiz smiled as he thought about Raine. "She's smart, sweet, loving. She's dedicated to helping to raise my—I mean his—kid."

"Are we talking about you, Luiz?"

"No, it's my dream."

"Look, I don't know who this dream girl is, and frankly, I think it's cruel to keep her from finding her own chance at love. You're offering yourself, or your dream you, or whatever, is making yourself seem like it's a sacrifice to be with this person. That's not fun for anyone, nor is it fair."

"What—"

"Luiz, it's late, and I'm really, really tired. You're confusing me, and I don't think I can help you. This doesn't sound like a dream to me."

Before he could stop her, she had already hung up the phone, and he groaned. *Great, just great.* He was back to square one again, and there was no way he was going to get any damn answer.

He didn't like Raine going on a date, and he didn't care how nice the guy was. She belonged to him, and he wasn't very good at sharing. He wouldn't share her.

\*\*\*\*

Entering the kitchen, Raine saw that Luiz was already at the coffee pot. The music was on, and someone was belting out an old classic. Luiz hadn't heard her yet, and he was dancing, which she had never seen before. She couldn't recall if he'd ever been in such a good mood to dance. Leaning against the doorframe, she folded her arms, and watched him as he sang into the spoon.

His voice was awful. She looked down his body seeing him in a pair of jeans, and green shirt. It shouldn't have worked, yet it did. The clothes suited him, and he looked somewhat normal. Again, it was a strange thing, but she could live with it.

"I wouldn't quit your day job," she said, entering the kitchen. She went toward the cups and pulled one down.

"I didn't hear anyone come in."

"That's fine. Christie watching cartoons?" she asked.

"Yeah. She came and got me up, jumping around excitedly."

She chuckled. "That's Christie. She loves it when you come around. She misses you."

"I miss her, too. All the time."

Spooning some instant coffee into her cup, she tried to ignore the tingles that rushed through her entire body from being close to him. That kiss last night had made her cry, but she was attracted to him, and that made it harder for her. He was only trying to keep her in line, and she didn't want that. Luiz didn't feel the same for her as she did for him, and she had to live with that. She had already been living with that.

"Have you ever thought of taking her with you?" she asked.

"I can't do that."

"The threat is always going to be there, and she misses you. She's seven in a few days, Luiz. She should be with her father." Pouring hot water onto the coffee, she gave it a stir, and took a seat at the counter.

"You're not going to add milk?" he asked.

"I can do without the calories." After last night's dinner, she had made a new vow to go on a diet. She had been self-conscious last night. Not that she would ever tell Xander or Luiz that. Her love of food had never changed, not in the past few years, which sucked.

"You're fine."

"Thanks." Great. She was fine.

He'd forced himself to kiss her, and she didn't want to think about what else he actually planned to make himself do, to keep her in line.

"I can't bring Christie into this world."

"Your father tried to kill her."

"And he took your whole family."

"You're her father, and I think you need to consider that future for her. She's going to want answers. She's not going to be the adorable little girl for much longer, who likes a toy, and she'll shut up. One day soon, she's going to want answers. What are you going to do then?" she asked.

She had tried not to think about it, but Christie's questions were becoming more prying. Where did her daddy go? Why did Daddy have to go? What did Daddy do? Why couldn't she have friends over?

"Raine's right," Xander said. "We didn't really think this through, and if we're not careful, it's going to bite us in the ass."

"No one knows about you, and that's the way I want it to stay."

Raine sighed. "If that's what you want."

She took her coffee, and walked into the sitting

room, taking a seat on the sofa. Christie was sitting on the floor, eating some cereal, and watching the cartoons.

"*Do you love him?*"

"*Of course I do. He'll take care of me, Raine. I'll be protected.*" Lora touched her stomach. "*I'm so happy.*"

A flash of pain rushed through her. She would do anything for her niece, anything.

"I've finished," Christie said.

"Take it into the kitchen, and then go and get dressed."

Sipping the dark liquid, Raine wrinkled her nose at the bitter taste.

"I think we should talk," Luiz said, coming into the room.

"There's nothing for either of us to talk about. You don't have to worry about me thinking you're offering anything." She smiled at him, even though it was the last thing she felt. There was no happiness, not really.

They were all waiting for Luiz to come back, to pay a visit for their lives to move on. Only now it wasn't going to move on. They were all going to stay in the same world forever. Waiting for him to arrive, and play with them, until he grew bored.

It was how it was starting to feel.

"I've got to head back."

"Of course you do." And that didn't hurt at all. *Liar!*

"I don't want you to go on another date with Bradley."

"I'm sure you don't." She didn't know why she felt so angry, but it was so strong, and so instant. Gripping the cup tightly, she gritted her teeth, and tried to think of the good this was all doing. Christie was growing up in a semi-normal environment. Wasn't she?

"It's good for Christie."

"Please, leave me alone, Luiz. Go back to your life, and we'll be waiting here for our next lot of instructions. That's what you do, right? Instruct, order? Stuff like that."

"You're pissed at me."

"Wouldn't you be at me?" She shook her head. "Forget it."

"Talk to me, Raine."

"No. I don't want to talk to you. You'd just brush my concerns away. Go, and do whatever you need to do. Xander and I, we can fix it. Believe me." They had been doing it for so long that it was almost second nature. "Go!"

Luiz hesitated for a second, and then turned to go. She closed her eyes, waiting for the door to close, and of course it did, like so many times before.

When the car was gone, she went back into the kitchen to find Xander sitting at the counter.

"You okay, baby girl?" he asked.

"I'm fine." She poured the coffee down the sink, noticing that her hands were shaking. She didn't want to think about how fucked up this whole situation was. "He's going to fuck up, and all of this is going to bite him on the ass. You know that, right?"

"I know it. You know it. He doesn't think it will happen. We've just got to keep doing what we do best."

"And what's that?"

"Picking up the pieces every time he leaves." Xander opened his arms, and she went into them. Every time Luiz went away, he took a part of her with him, and he didn't even know it. Xander could clearly see that she had feelings for Luiz, and hiding them was the hardest thing she ever had to do. When Luiz was around, he made her forget about all of her troubles, and made her believe for a short time that her life could go back to being normal.

"Will it ever get easier?" she asked.

"I hope so, kid, for your sake."

## Chapter Four

*Three weeks later*

"You've been acting weird," Tonio said.

Luiz ignored his friend, and looked over the books from several of the brothels and fighting rings they had in town. Nothing had changed, not really. The only difference between now, and seven years ago was the fact he didn't have to answer to his father, and people were now afraid of him.

"Donnie told us about your late night call," Jake said.

He didn't know why his friends had descended on him this late Friday night, but he was intent on ignoring them, getting the books done, doing the rounds, and then making his way toward Christie and Raine. Three weeks had already passed since he last saw his little girl. Raine had avoided him as well, which he hated. He didn't like this tension between them, and it was all his fault.

"Do you have a girl waiting around for you?" Tonio asked.

"Can nothing be fucking sacred anymore?" he asked, glaring at his two friends.

"Not when you've been different," Donnie said, entering the room, and turning off his cell phone.

Jake turned his cell off.

"Seriously? How old are you two?"

"Old enough to know something is wrong with our best friend, and you are. You're at least one of our best friends," Jake said.

"I'm not in the mood for this. I've got a lot of work, and I've got somewhere to be."

"It has been three weeks, and even Paige is mentioning how absent you've been," Donnie said.

"What's wrong, man?"

Luiz wasn't interested in talking.

"I've got work to do."

"It's going to be there for you tomorrow. What's wrong?"

He closed his eyes and tried to stem the anger that was building inside him. He was so angry. So pissed off. Infuriated.

Thinking about Raine's face, the anger in her eyes, and how heartbroken she'd been, it tore him up inside.

"Back off, Donnie."

"All you're doing is working, man. We're worried," Tonio said. "This is not like you. You've not visited us, or hung out."

"I'm busy."

"Too busy for your friends."

He'd had enough. "You want to know why I'm not hanging around?" he asked. "It's because nothing has fucking changed." Slamming his hand down on the desk, he stood and glared at Donnie. "We had a plan, Donnie. We had a big fucking plan, and guess what, we're not going to get a chance to see it through. We were fucking fools."

"We can still live our life the best we can, Luiz."

"Bullshit. We can't do anything, and you fucking know it." Picking up the file, he threw it at Donnie, and papers fell out, covering the floor. "We're always looking over our shoulders. There's always a threat of someone taking from us, threatening us. This is why we can't lead normal lives, we're always waiting for the next fucking threat, and I didn't sign on for this shit."

"You think any of us signed on for this? You think we want to be constantly in this fight? I've got a family, Luiz. So has Tonio. We all know the risks, and yet we're still fighting today, to keep on working, to keep on living to make sure we can still have a fucking life." Donnie reached down, grabbing the paperwork. "We were born into this life. We are the ones that drew the unlucky straw here, and I get it. I do."

"You don't get fuck-all."

Luiz walked around his desk, and headed toward the door.

"Where are you going?" Donnie asked.

"I'm going to work, because right now I think I'll say something I'll regret." He stormed out of his office, and released a breath as he got into his car and was able to shut out all of those doubts.

Pulling out of the office, he reached out to his cell phone, and dialed Xander's number as he drove toward the first brothel. There was no chance of him going to his little girl. The last thing he wanted to do was to go to Christie when he stank of sex and desperation. He didn't want his job to touch her.

She had to stay innocent for as long as possible.

"Hello," Xander said.

"Hey, how is everyone?"

"They're fine."

"Christie?" he asked.

"She's … fine."

"What's going on?"

"She's upset. She had hoped that you would be at her school today as it was 'bring your father to school' day."

"Fuck, I completely forgot that. I'm sure there were other kids that didn't have a dad there."

"Actually, there weren't. She's a little upset."

"Will you put her on the phone?" Luiz asked. He should have been there. He was missing everything, and as he thought about what he'd missed, he hated what he was doing. Raine was right.

"She doesn't want to come, Luiz, I'm afraid."

"Crap. Can you tell her how sorry I am?"

"Yes, of course."

"This is happening, isn't it?"

"Again, what did you expect to happen?" Xander asked. "It seems that you're always making decisions here, Luiz, but you're never here when it actually matters."

"I know. Fuck, I know. Is Raine there?"

There was silence, and then he heard some muttering. "Raine can't come to the phone right now."

"Why the hell not?"

"She's busy washing her hair. I'm sorry, Luiz. I've got to go. We're having a movie night."

"No more dates for Raine?"

"She's been on a couple because I've asked her to. I've got to go, Luiz. Bye."

Before Luiz could say anything, he cursed, and slammed his hand against the steering wheel. He was so pissed off and angry at himself, and at Raine. She didn't need to go with anyone else. He was right here for her. Didn't she realize that? He was happy to give her whatever she needed, and it didn't have to be awkward.

Pulling up outside of the first brothel, he stared at the building, which had men going inside and coming out. His cell phone went off again, and he checked the screen to see that it was Donnie.

Picking it up, he ran a hand down his face. "What's up?" he asked.

"I know you're pissed off. I know you're angry with us. With me."

"It's ... nothing. I should have known we wouldn't be able to do this. It's fine. It really is."

It wasn't. He was struggling between his

responsibility with his daughter, and his best friends. He had to make a decision.

The more he actually thought of having Christie and Raine with him, it sounded like a really good idea. He couldn't think of having one without the other. Raine was just as important to him as Christie was, and having one without the other was out of the question.

"I need you to be focused, Luiz. I hate to be an asshole here, but our enemies are always there."

"I thought we killed all of them."

"That's the thing about enemies, they are everywhere, and it's next to impossible to get rid them all. Someone will get through the cracks, and we all have to be careful if that ever happens."

"We can never leave, can we?"

"No, we can't. We have a job to do. All of us have a responsibility here. We were young and foolish to think we can walk away. Death is our only way out," Donnie said.

"What about our families, Donnie?" he asked. None of them knew that he had just as much to lose as everyone else.

He had a little girl who was almost taken from him before. He didn't want to think of life without her.

"We protect them together. Unlike our parents, we band together. We know our parents only put up with each other. We're partners in this. We'll fight to the bitter end."

"You make it sound so easy."

"I'm supposed to, right? It's what I'm trying to do."

For the first time Donnie sounded tired, weary, and fed up.

"You okay?"

"Yeah, I just, I don't want to be fighting with my

best friends for this to work, you know? I love you guys like you were my own brothers," Donnie said.

"You'll always have us, that I can promise you."

"You sure you don't need to talk to me about anything? I'm here if you need me."

"I'm sure. I can handle everything, I promise."

After another few minutes, Luiz closed his cell, turning it off. They had enemies everywhere. Was there a chance that any of them were watching him? Watching his family? He'd killed everyone who knew about Christie and Raine. There wasn't a chance of them being killed, he hoped.

****

*One week later*

Raine laughed at Bradley's joke. Xander had arranged for her to go out again, and of course they had both gone to the fair. She wished she had been able to bring Christie, but neither of them wanted to cause any trouble with Luiz. He had every right to have a say in his daughter's upbringing. She had done everything she could to forget about the one kiss she'd had with Luiz. It didn't help that the kiss had fed her erotic dreams, and now it always went further in her dreams.

"You're funny."

"Not really. Just stating a fact. You know, Xander and Christie could have come as well. We could have made this a whole family thing."

"It's fine. Christie's ... not feeling well."

"Oh, I'm sorry."

Christie hadn't been feeling well since her father had forgotten to go to her school. She hated seeing her little niece all heartbroken, and it was Luiz's fault.

"It's fine. Xander said he'd watch her, and he pretty much shoved me out of the house. I'll take her some candy, and when she's better, she'll be fine."

"You're a really good auntie."

"Thanks. I only do what I'm sure a lot of other people do. Take care of family."

She sipped at her milkshake, as they walked around the fair. Bradley was a really sweet guy, only she saw him as more of a friend than anything else. Her body didn't come alive when he was close, nor did she mind if she never saw him again.

"They're all character traits that are strong."

"Great, I have strong character traits."

"It's not a bad thing. Crap, I'm ruining this date."

"You're not ruining anything. Don't worry. Everything is fine, more than fine. It's really good. I'm having a lot of fun."

"Good. I do want you to have fun." He stepped in front of her, and she really didn't like the look in his eye. The way his gaze kept moving to her lips, and going back up again. She wasn't an idiot, and knew what was going on in his mind, and yeah, she wasn't going to deal with that, not yet, not today.

"Look at that, a giant teddy bear. How is your shooting?" she asked, rushing past him to look at the ghastly giant bear. The thing was huge, and ugly, but it had stopped him from kissing her.

*Why make him stop?*

*Let him kiss you, and then you can stop thinking about Luiz's kiss, and think about something far better.*

*If Bradley's kiss is far better, which it probably isn't.*

*Shut up.*

"My shooting isn't that great. Let's see what I can do."

Providing no more kisses happened, she was happy.

"You can do this," she said, tapping his arm.

*Smooth, Raine. Real smooth.*

For the next hour she kept Bradley busy trying to win as much as he could. She won a few bears, and other than that, he wasn't the best shot. For a second she wondered how good Luiz would be. With his line of work, he had to be good with a gun.

Bradley pulled up outside of her home, and she was so relieved to finally be there. "This is me. I had a really great time," she said.

"I want to take you out again."

"Wow, so soon," she said. "Aren't you bored with me?"

"I like you, Raine. I really do."

"Oh. That's nice." She was really killing this. "Tell you what, how about I call you when we can go out again. I really want to make sure Christie is okay." She was going straight to hell for using her niece to get out of the uncomfortable predicament.

"Of course. I'm so sorry."

She climbed out of the car, grabbing her goodies. "See you later," she said.

This time she didn't linger on a goodbye, and she rushed into her home, slamming and locking the door.

"Have fun?" Xander asked.

"No, not really. It was a fucking nightmare to be honest."

"Wow, cursing as well."

"I'm done with the whole dating thing. I keep expecting Luiz to show up. Hey, is he good with a gun?"

"Bradley?"

"No, Luiz."

"Of course he is. He's the descendant of the mafia, sweetie. Guns are his life."

"Figures." She dumped the bears on the chair and walked into the kitchen. "I need hot chocolate. You want one?"

"Love it."

"How was Christie?"

"She's … sad."

"Still struggling with her dad?"

"Yeah. The kids are calling her names at school, and asking if she really has a daddy."

"Kids are such bastards."

"Your language is showing through."

"I know. I'm just having a really bad couple of days. You know how it is. I seem to be on stress overload."

"Does this have anything to do with Luiz?" Xander asked.

"Yes. It has everything to do with him. Don't you see that? We're stuck here in this little rut, waiting for him to come to us so we can move on with our lives. Now I'm starting to sound like a baby. Tell me I'm not, please, please." Replaying the kiss with Luiz was going to drive her insane.

"You've got a right to be pissy and childish. It doesn't suit you though."

She stuck her tongue out, teasing him. "Spoilsport.

Xander laughed, and stood near the window, looking out. "Luiz said he might be able to stop by tonight."

"Oh." She glanced over at the clock to see it was a little after eleven. "That's late."

The sound of glass breaking had her turning to Xander.

"Xander," she said. The window had a perfect circle in front of it, and there was blood coming from his arm.

"Get out, go," he said.

More gunshots were fired, and she screamed, going behind the counter. "Xander, what is going on?"

"You've got to go. Get Christie now."

"What about you?"

"I'm expendable. I've got to protect you." Xander had moved crouching behind her. She watched as he opened a couple of drawers, ones he'd told her to never touch. "Go get Christie. You protect her. This is what I've been asked to do."

She stared at his bleeding arm. This couldn't be happening again. Her parents, Lora, and now they were being attacked again. He handed her a gun. "Go."

"Luiz will come."

"Not in the next couple of seconds. Try and call him, go!"

She ran as fast as her legs would carry her, trying not to scream as gunshots rang all around her. Christie was at the top of the stairs, holding her bunny, and Raine didn't wait around. Pulling Christie into her arms, she ran to the end of the corridor going toward her room. She could hear the gunshots, the shouting, everything just like she had seven years ago.

"Xander?" Christie said.

"It's fine, sweetie. He's going to be fine."

She closed her door, locked it, pulling a dresser in front, and then moving toward the escape door.

"I need you to be very quiet."

"We can't leave him," Christie said.

She pushed her hair out of her eyes, and knelt down to look at Christie. "This is what he wanted, sweetie."

"We can't leave him."

"We've got—" The sound of a door handle rattling filled the air. Pressing a hand to Christie's mouth, Raine listened.

Whoever they were, they were closing in, and she had lured them upstairs to Christie.

*Fuck! Fuck! Fuck! Where is Luiz? Would he be able to get here in time? Crap, don't think about him. Xander is down there. He needs you, and so does Christie.*

"Sweetie, listen to me. I've got to go out there, and stop him from getting to you. I want you to get out, and go to Mrs. Ruth's. You know where it is?" She whispered the words.

"I don't want to go without you."

"I know, sweetie. I know, but you've got to do this for me. Okay? I love you so much. I'll be with you soon." She kissed Christie, held the gun, and left the room, making sure the door was locked.

She could do this. There was no choice. This was the only way to protect her family.

Xander had taught her how to shoot, how to fight, and how to protect herself. All the time she had trained with him, she'd thought about Luiz, and how she'd be able to protect herself and Christie. She really needed to stop thinking about Luiz right now. Thinking about him wasn't going to help what was happening.

The gun was loaded, and the safety off.

*You can do this, Raine.*

*For yourself, for Christie, and for Lora.*

Moving into the main bedroom, she stood away from the door, containing her screams as the door handle was shot off. The door was shoved open. Raising the gun, she fired, and the man fell back. Grabbing the pair of scissors from the dressing table, she launched herself at the man, and started to attack him with the pointy end of the scissors, embedding it into his flesh.

"Die. Die. Die. Die." She just kept repeating the same word. The moment he was dead, she looked up in time as another guy tackled her to the ground. He landed a blow to his face, and she kneed him between the thighs.

He paused in his attack, giving her enough time to grab the gun. Just before she fired, she let out a little scream as his head exploded.

Turning toward the direction of the bullet, she saw a very bloody looking Luiz. His white shirt was covered in blood. He had a split lip, and even from here, she saw his knuckles were also covered in blood.

"We've got to go," he said.

"Christie?"

"Is in my car. I saw her running, and I put her in the backseat. I'd bought her a gift. A DVD player, and I made her watch it."

Pushing the guy off her, Raine got to her feet, and rushed past Luiz. "Xander!" She shouted her friend's name in the hope that he would answer.

There was no answer.

Her heart was racing, and she was panicking. She couldn't lose anyone else. He was her best friend.

Xander wasn't in the kitchen. There were a couple of bodies, and she found Xander curled up, bleeding, pale, and she knew without a doubt that he was dying.

"Hey, sweet girl," he said.

She went to her knees, grabbing his hand. "No, no, no, this can't be happening." He was the only father figure she had. She trusted him, and he was dying.

No, too many people had died in her life. She couldn't lose someone else.

"It's fine."

"No, it's not."

"This is what was supposed to happen."

"I don't accept that, Xander. You should live."

"It's okay. I'm fine with this. I promise. You've

got to take care of our little girl now, Raine. You can do this."

"Not without you."

"You've been doing it without me. Luiz will take care of you."

Tears fell down her face, and her heart was breaking. This couldn't be happening again. No, it couldn't. She wouldn't be able to survive another like this.

"I love you," she said, meaning every single word. It was the love of a good friend, of a father.

"Being with you, and with Christie, was the best thing ever. I'm honored to have spent all this time with you."

He stroked her face and died in her arms.

## Chapter Five

*Hours later*

Luiz stared at his friends, and he didn't know how to say the next words, but he did. "I've been lying to you guys for seven years."

Donnie, Tonio, and Jake all tensed. Paige held onto Donnie's arm, calming him, and Zara did the same thing to Tonio. This was the harsh world where their lives were nothing more than pawns to many.

"What the hell are you talking about?" Jake asked.

"Seven years ago, I met the most amazing girl. I fell in love, and I got her pregnant. I was seventeen, and I thought I could handle everything. I thought I could keep her safe, that I could keep us all safe."

"What happened?" Donnie asked.

"My father knew everything, so he ordered a hit on the family. It was his punishment of me, for thinking that I could have a life away from The Family. To live with happiness, with an outsider. Lora, she was the shining light in my life, and so was Christie. Our little girl." He licked his lips, which were dry. For seven years he'd wanted to tell his friends the truth, but he'd been afraid, trying to keep them all safe. "I found out too late that my dad had ordered the kill. He wanted all of her family slaughtered, and my little girl." He ran a hand down his face, remembering the chaos he'd walked into the moment he went to protect her. "The guards that were on my side were all dead, and so were her parents. Lora was dying, and I was too late to save her."

He looked up to find Paige and Zara crying.

"Lora had a younger sister, Raine. She'd made her take Christie into the bathroom, and try to protect her. I saved them from being killed, and since that day, I've been protecting them."

"Who did you have with them?" Donnie asked.

"A guy called Xander," Raine said, coming out of the backroom. She was covered in blood, and hadn't washed yet. Neither had he. He'd been more focused in getting his friends here for them to know the truth. "He was Luiz's old bodyguard, and he was our friend." Her gaze met his, and he saw the pain inside her eyes. She was hurting really bad.

She'd screamed at Xander to come back to her.

Luiz had had to pull her away against her will to stop her, and to protect them all.

"Christie asleep?"

"Yes, she is."

"Your daughter?" Paige asked.

"She's seven years old."

"In a couple of weeks she's seven," Raine said. "Xander and I were going to take her out to the mall." She stopped, and he saw the tears flowing down her cheeks. "Do you know who did it?"

"I'm getting to that now."

"Excellent." She pulled out a chair, and took a seat.

"What are you doing?" he asked.

"I'm waiting to see who you think it is. I take it you're going to exact revenge, right? Make them pay."

"I don't think you should be here."

"You think you're going to stop me?" she asked. If looks could kill, he'd be dead by now just from the look shooting at him.

"I don't want to get into an argument with you."

"Then save it, Luiz. I've been living with your decisions for far too long. You think bringing me here is going to help the way I feel? I've seen the security this place has. You're surrounded by friends, and by people who respect you."

"Raine—"

"You don't get to tell me what to do anymore. For seven years I lived with Xander. I put up with your instructions because you thought you knew what you were doing."

"I did."

"Xander is dead!" She yelled the words.

Everyone else fell silent, listening to them.

"I know."

"He died in my arms, and if we had been here, surrounding by your damn friends, he could still be alive. Your thoughts, your beliefs are total bullshit, Luiz."

"You're not thinking straight."

"I watched my family die. I had to hold Christie, your little girl, while I listened to my family die. Tonight, I've just done the same thing, and if you think for one second that you can dictate to me, think again. I'm not fifteen years old anymore, Luiz. I won't be stopped. Not now."

Silence filled the room.

"I like her," Tonio said.

"Me too. We could totally be BFFs. What do you think, Paige?" Zara asked.

"Totally. I'm Paige, by the way."

"Nice to meet you," Raine said.

The fight didn't once leave her, and when he threw one of the IDs that he'd gotten at Donnie, he waited for his answer.

"Wait, he was connected to Maria's husband, who we put in the ground."

"Rafael?" Luiz had killed his sister's husband as he was a fucking wife-beater, one of the foulest creatures to ever walk the planet. Months later, Maria, his sister, had killed herself, and her unborn child. "What do you think it means?"

"When Rafael died, his entire estate went to a long distance relative. I was dealing with a lot of shit at the time that I didn't look into it. This man, he was on Rafael's guard. I recognize him. He served my father many times." Donnie threw the ID into the center of the table.

"Why would someone from your past want to kill us? Kill Xander?" Raine asked.

"To take over from The Family," Donnie said.

"I thought you guys were supposed to be dangerous? Feared?" Raine looked at each of them without even flinching. Luiz admired her spirit. He only wished it hadn't come at the loss of another person she held dear.

When she had told Xander that she loved him, he'd been struck by jealousy, and he hated that. His friend had been dying, and even though he looked at peace, Luiz had hated himself. Xander was a good man, a troubled man, and now he was gone, not knowing how much Luiz loved him and respected him.

"We are," Donnie said.

"Clearly not that well for some distant relative to have a go," Raine said. "You take out all threats."

"How much do you know about us?" Donnie asked.

"Everything. Xander told me everything. He figured my life was fucked up enough that I had a right to know what I was getting myself into." She grabbed the ID, and he saw the hatred in her eyes. "When you find these people, I want to be there."

"No," he, Tonio, Jake, and Donnie said in unison.

"Why not?" Raine asked.

"You're a woman. We can't allow that."

"You're being sexist now?" Zara asked, looking at Tonio.

"We don't want her getting hurt," Tonio said.

"I'm fine. I can handle myself."

"Your face is bruised, and you were struggling," Luiz said. "You could have easily been killed. I told you to go with Christie. To run, to get out."

"I made sure she was safe, but by the time I got there, someone was already trying to get in, Luiz. It wasn't a good plan."

Luiz turned to his friends. "I'm sorry that I've kept this part of my life secret. I need some time to talk to Raine."

"We want to meet her, Luiz," Donnie said. "You didn't have to keep her from us."

"Raine is right. We could have protected them all here. Xander would have had backup."

"See, even your friends agree with me."

Luiz hated that they were all right. He'd fucked up, and miscalculated. All he'd wanted to do was protect them, and instead, he'd gotten his friend killed.

After seeing his friends out, he entered the kitchen to find Raine breaking into his stash of whiskey.

"Do you think that is wise to do?"

"I'm covered in blood. My face hurts. I've been attacked, almost killed, and I just had a friend die in my arms. Yeah, this is the most sensible and *wise* thing I've done all week." She poured herself out a shot, and downed it in one gulp. "Are you ashamed of us?"

"What? Where the fuck did that come from?" he asked.

"I'm just curious. Your friends seem nice. Understanding and they like me. I was wondering if you were ashamed of your past. Of me and Christie, or of all of us." She put the glass down on the counter, and turned toward him. "Well?"

"I'm not ashamed of you."

"Then what the fuck is it, Luiz?"

"Language."

"Right now, I really don't care if Christie hears me. We've been through hell tonight. I'm covered in another man's blood, and that of Xander. Nothing about tonight is all right. Don't you get that?"

"What can I say to make this all right?"

"Nothing. That's the thing. There is nothing for you to say, or do that is going to make this okay," she said.

"I'm not ashamed of you."

"Really? Because right now I'm starting to think that you are. You had a kid when you were a teenager, Luiz."

"I'm not ashamed of Christie, okay? I'm ashamed of myself."

She frowned.

Seconds passed, and she folded her arms. "Now you're going to have to explain that shit," she said.

"I fucked up. I'm no good for you. Don't you see that? From the moment I was born I had blood on my hands. I'm not good for you, for Christie, or for Xander."

"That's crazy."

"Is it? Look at me, Raine. I can kill a man, and I don't care."

"*I* just killed a man!"

"Yeah, and you're shaking. You look fucking crazy, Raine. You're not like me." He reached out, grabbing her arms. "You're good. I'm not."

She shoved him hard.

Luiz took the pain, wanting her to lash out at him. He would ruin her if given the chance. The more she hit him, the more he embraced it.

"You killed him!"

"I did. I did this, Raine, and I can't let you get away from me." He grabbed the back of her head, holding her still as he slammed his lips down on hers.

She tasted heavenly. He felt like a drowning man, and she was his fountain of water.

****

One second Luiz was kissing her, and the next, he was carrying her through his bedroom toward the en-suite bathroom. Raine slammed her fists against his back, wanting him to put her down.

It was all just too much.

Xander was gone.

Her best friend, her second father, was completely gone, and she didn't know how to handle that. Then Luiz was kissing her, and she wanted those kisses more than anything. She craved the feel of his lips against hers.

"Let me go!"

"No, never." He put her down after he'd shut the bathroom door, and she fell, landing in a heap at his feet.

"Ugh!"

"You can argue with me, bitch, moan, and even use your claws on me, but I will take care of you."

"Fuck you!" In her heartache, Raine struggled to gain any control over her language. She was hurting, and it was all because of Luiz.

"One day, you will."

For a few seconds she didn't know what he meant, and when he looked her body up and down, she glared. "You're not going to touch me."

"Oh yes I am. You'll let me as well, so don't even for a second pretend that it's not something you want."

"I don't want you near me."

"Right now I accept that. You and I, this was

meant to be, and now I know what Xander was talking about the past couple of years."

She frowned. "What?"

"You'll see."

"What are you going to do about his body?"

"Xander died over fifteen years ago, Raine. I can't do anything more."

"The cops? His body. He has a right."

"They won't find his body."

"What?"

"I've already put a call to it. His body will be cremated, and I'll collect his ashes. That's all we're going to be able to do."

Raine stared at the floor. The pain was consuming, and it hurt her chest. She rubbed at her heart, needing some respite from the pain. "Did he know that?"

"Yes. He never wanted a big funeral. He always thought he'd be burying me long before he was gone. Always told me I was reckless."

He reached out, grabbing her shirt and tugging it open.

She let out a little squeal and tried to swat his hands out of the way. "Stop that."

"We've got to get clean, and get rid of these fucking clothes."

Raine didn't know why she was fighting. Seconds passed, even minutes, and they were both naked.

Luiz dumped her into the shower, and the shock of the cold had her screaming and trying to get away.

Too much.

Everything was too much, and she couldn't handle it anymore. Wrapping her arms around Luiz, she didn't fight him. She held on as sobs took over, and she couldn't contain the pain.

He held her tightly, his hand pressed against the

base of her back.

She felt nothing but the comforting heat of his body. "He's gone."

"I know, babe."

Raine looked up and saw Luiz was crying right along with her. "You're crying."

"I lost him as well. Xander meant so much to me."

She dropped her head to his chest, and held him as they both cried for a fallen friend. Raine had felt this pain before, and she hated it. She wanted it to stop.

"We'll get through this."

"Are you going to dump me with another friend?"

"No. I really thought I was doing the right thing."

"And now?"

"I fucked up, and I don't know how to apologize enough. You were right. I should have brought you all here."

Raine shrugged. "We can't change what happened."

"No. I can make it better." He stroked her cheek, wiping away the tears. "Please don't cry."

"I can't help it."

"I can't stand the thought of you crying, let alone seeing it." He cupped her face, looking into her eyes.

Every second that they were staring at each other, she felt him strip another layer away. She wanted to hate him, to put him out of her mind so she could find an excuse to move on. At the same time, this was everything she had ever wanted, and had been dreaming about. This was such a cruel twist of fate right now.

"I'm so sorry."

She bit her lip and nodded. "We can't change it."

"I know, and I fucking hate that. I want to change it." He wrapped his arms around her, pulling her close. "I want to make you happy, Raine. Please."

Raine took hold of his hands, and stared at them.

This was all surreal to her. She was completely naked in the shower with Luiz, the father of her sister's child.

"You can't keep me in the dark anymore."

"Fine."

"I also want to do something with my life."

"Spend time with Christie, Paige, and Zara."

She shook her head. "Christie needs to go to school."

"No, I can't."

"Make it happen, Luiz. She is going to have a normal life. You've taken so much already. Give her this, otherwise I walk, and I take her with me. You'll never find us together."

"You'll never hide from me."

"Want to bet? The only reason you've been able to find us is because Xander wanted you to. He taught me everything he knew, and I know a lot. That's all I ask."

"If I give you this, let Christie have as close to a normal life as possible, then you have to belong to me."

"What the hell does that mean?"

"No more dating, no more finding someone else. You come to me. I'm your guy. You belong to me, and that's for everything."

"You're blackmailing me to stay with you?"

"Yes and no. If you want Bradley, then you can go to him. I'm offering you a life with me."

"No one else for either of us? No cheating?"

"I won't cheat. I'm not going to lie to you, Raine. I loved your sister, but that was the love of a seventeen-year-old. I care about you, and laying my cards on the table here, I didn't like you going on that date. I think it killed me to know you were having fun, and it didn't involve me. I bet that was what Xander was counting on."

"Why?"

"So we could be together. We share a lot of history together, Raine. We're perfect for each other."

"Great, so now you're going to sacrifice your chance to find love."

"No, I'm not."

"I don't want to just be together because a bunch of people thought it was a good idea. I want love, Luiz. I want the chance to have children, and a family of my own. Not right now, but someday I hope to have that."

"I can give you that."

"Really. You think you can fall in love with me?" she asked.

"Yeah, I do."

Okay, that made her pause. She bit her lip and stared at him. "You're just saying that."

"You've known me long enough to know that I don't just say shit that I don't mean. I can fall in love with you. I care about you, and I already feel jealousy at any guy who looks your way. They don't deserve you. I do. I know I can make you happy."

He grabbed the soap and started to run it over her body. She didn't fight him as he touched her, cleaning away the blood. Staring down at her feet, she watched the water tinted red run down, and away from them.

"I can't believe I killed someone."

"Why didn't you run with Christie?" he asked.

"I heard someone coming upstairs, and I'd locked my door, pushing my dressing table in front of it. I messed up because he was getting in. I wanted to be a distraction in case I wasn't able to get Christie to safety before he found us. I'll always do whatever it takes to protect her."

"I know. I'll do whatever it takes to protect the two of you. When I saw that guy over you, I wanted to murder him with my bare hands, but I knew I wouldn't get over to him fast enough. I can't lose you, Raine. I can't lose you or Christie. I don't want to."

"You won't." She finally made herself look at him. "I'm not going anywhere." There was nowhere else for her to go. This was the life she'd picked the moment Lora went with him.

"Thank you. I promise to you that I won't fuck this up."

They finished washing in the shower, and once they were back in his room, she grabbed a robe, and went to check on Christie. She was asleep in the spare bedroom, and right now, Raine didn't want to think about where she was supposed to sleep, or what she was supposed to do. Her life was crazy. Leaning against the doorframe, she folded her arms, and watched as Christie slept. She held on tightly to her bear, sleeping soundly.

Raine was thankful that she wasn't having nightmares, or worried about people coming to get her.

"She's sleeping safely. We've got men in the hotel, and they're on our side, wanting change for The Family," Luiz said, coming to wrap his arm around her.

"I trust you," she said, looking at the small child in the bed. "There are times she reminds me of Lora."

"She was a little bossy."

Raine smiled. "Even when we were kids. I'm tired. Do you have another room here?"

"No. You're sleeping with me, and I'm not going to have you argue with me on this."

"I'm not going to have sex with you."

"I've not said sex, yet. I just want us to be together, okay? I want to hold you. Nothing wrong with that."

She nodded. She partially closed Christie's door and stepped away, following Luiz into his room.

They both wore robes, and even as they lay down, neither of them said anything, and she stared across at the wall, wondering what her future was going to be. She liked Luiz's arms around her, and she finally fell into a deep sleep.

## Chapter Six

"So you have a kid," Donnie said the following day.

"Yes."

"And you've had a whole other life?" Tonio asked.

"Yes." Luiz looked toward the kitchen where Raine and Christie were making pancakes together. Paige and Zara were at the kitchen counter, talking.

Raine wore one of his shirts and a pair of his boxer briefs. They were the only things that were close to fitting her. He'd need to get her some clothes, and he wasn't going to let her go back to the house in case there was someone watching to see if they went back.

"Why didn't you say anything?" Jake asked. "We tell each other everything."

"Do we? Tonio didn't tell me about his relationship with Maria."

"You fucking knew!" Tonio glared at him.

"You didn't tell me. Look, I met Lora one night in the damn diner. I loved her. She was everything this world isn't. My dad didn't have a clue, or I didn't think he knew, but he did. He knew what I'd done, and he made me pay."

"Did you face him?" Donnie asked.

"After I got Raine and Christie to safety, I went to face him. He didn't have a clue that I'd gotten there. I'd saved my little girl, and her auntie. He didn't know, so I vowed he would never find out."

"Did you ever visit her?" Jake asked.

"When I could. Since we took our parents out, I've been able to visit them more often. Someone followed me, and decided to finish what my father started."

"Rafael is dead."

"I know, but clearly someone wants to take our place, and what better way to do it than to go after us one by one?" Luiz said.

"We're going to need to tighten security," Donnie said.

"I'll do that," Jake said. "I'm the one handling the soldiers. I'll make sure we have double security in this building by the end of the day."

"Daddy," Christie said.

Luiz turned to find his little girl holding a small plate. "What is it, sweetie?"

"I made you a pancake. It's really tasty. I hope you like it."

He took the plate from her, putting it down on the table, and lifting her up onto his knee. "Christie, I want you to meet some of my friends. Would you like that?"

"Yes."

"That scary-looking guy there is Donnie. There is Jake, and this weird dude here is Tonio."

"Hello, everyone."

Luiz watched as his friends smiled at her, showing their softer side. "Why don't you go and thank Raine for the pancakes? Will you do that?"

"Yes."

He let her down, and glanced up to see Raine smiling at him.

They were going to make it work. He was more determined than ever before about making a go of this life with them.

"She's sweet," Jake said.

"Thanks."

"Her mom's dead?"

"Yeah. I didn't get there in time to save her, but I got to Raine, and that's what Lora would have wanted."

He took a bite of the pancake and closed his eyes. Raine was a damn good cook.

"What's going on between you and Raine?" Tonio asked. "Are you together in raising the child or not?"

"We're together. I want more, but like all things, it's going to take time. I can't expect something to happen overnight. It doesn't work like that." No matter how much he wanted it to.

Waking up this morning, he'd taken his time to look at Raine. She'd been curled up with one hand underneath her face. In sleep she had been so peaceful. He'd finally gotten the chance to look at her, to see how beautiful she was. Her brown hair was long, thick, and glossy. There had been many times over the years that he'd wanted to run his fingers through the full length. He'd always held himself back, never wanting to cross that imaginary wall.

"Do you know any of Rafael's contacts?" Jake asked.

"I do." This came from Tonio. "We killed them all. That's what's so confusing about this."

"The guy's ID that I got. I recognized him. He worked with Rafael, and with our father. He was a soldier, a very loyal one. When the shit hit the fan when we took over, he fell through the cracks. I don't remember every single soldier we've hired, and I don't recall us keeping an entire file of everyone in our pocket either," Luiz said. "That's a paper trail, and they only used that if they wanted to hurt the person they were after. Bribery, blackmail, you name it."

"That's got to be something that changes," Jake said.

"Do you think soldiers would want that?" Donnie asked.

"Who gives a shit what they want?" Tonio asked. "This is what *we* need. We need to be able to keep an eye on our businesses, our families, everything. None of us want to be constantly looking over our backs. Let's face it, we could have every single Tom, Dick, and Harry walk through that door, and not one of them work for us. This is what we need to do to survive in this world. There isn't any other way. We've tried it other ways, and it doesn't work."

"This is what I think we have to do. There's a paper trail, but it ends with us. We have one file, we review it every week, remove and destroy who was lost." Jake pulled a piece of paper out of his pocket. "I decided to do an example to see what you guys think."

After Tonio and Donnie looked, Luiz picked it up. The example was of Jake. His picture was on the left hand side, along with his physical description, past jobs, and current status, including contact information.

"One single sheet with the relevant details. No one can get caught for that. It could be anything, and we have officers on the force who'll see that stuff like this gets lost," Jake said. "This is our safest option."

"I like it," Donnie said. "There has to be a whole new level of security around here."

"We can do it for everyone," Luiz said. "The girls, all of the legit employees. We have the files, and we secure them. They have our word that they won't go into the wrong hands."

"We're all in agreement?" Donnie asked.

"Yes." They all spoke in unison.

"We have to stay in this world, and I don't see a reason why we can't make it work for us. I don't know about you guys, but I'm tired of working to *their* ways. This is our Family, our lives, and we should be the ones to choose how we live it." Luiz felt stronger, more in control. He was doing the right thing. He knew he was.

Glancing over at Raine, he watched her talk with the other women. With his friends by his side, and Raine in his life, he could do anything. Handle every single threat that came his way.

"We need to get started right away. No new employees," Donnie said.

"How are we going to set it up?" Tonio asked.

"We start tonight," Jake said. "Each of us takes one building, one set of employees, and write the file. We can do this, and I reckon within a month, we'll have what we need."

He made notes of what they wanted to go onto the employee paperwork, and once breakfast was finished, his friends and their women left.

Christie rushed to her bedroom, leaving him alone with Raine.

"Business went okay? You look happy."

"I feel happy. I'm hoping it went okay. I don't know if it did or not."

"Do you want to tell me about it?"

Jake had left the example of what he wanted to do. Luiz went through the same process with Raine.

"What do you think?"

"It sounds good. You'll always be able to identify them on a database as well. Not just on paperwork."

"We can't have too much of a trail that brings them back to us."

"You don't have to. There are people out there that can work on security. Xander knew this guy. What was he called?" Raine frowned. "Keyboard. He called him that. Said the guy was the fastest guy on a keyboard, and that's what he named him."

"How the hell am I supposed to find a guy like that?"

"I don't know. Check Xander's records. He was always preparing for the next stop, the next attack. You'll find him, if he's out there wanting to be found."

"Thank you."

"I decided I'm not going to judge you, and I'm going to do my best to help you."

"What brought this change of attitude around?" he asked.

"Paige and Zara. They're strong women, and they help their men when they can. I really like that, and it's what I want to do. I want to help where I can. So, I've already found a new school for Christie." Raine held up her cell phone. "I know you don't want her going too far. This is fifteen minutes away. It's expensive, but it also guarantees safety. They have a lot of high profile clients. Celebrities' kids, politicians' kids. People like that."

"This is normal life?"

"No, this is a compromise for the two of us. I want us to have as close to a normal life as possible for all of our sakes. This school means we can pick her up every day, drop her off, and she's protected always. What do you think?"

He took her phone, and started to read through some of the points that were raised. It looked like a good school, and it was indeed a compromise. "Let's do it."

****

"How are you finding life with Luiz?" Paige asked.

"It's good." Raine put away the last of the clothes that had just been delivered that very morning. She had been with Luiz a full week, and the change in life had been crazy. Xander's loss still hurt her. She had been with him for seven years, and he had meant the world to her. His ashes were on the mantelpiece in the sitting room in the corner of the television. She wanted him to be able to watch his favorite programs, even though it felt silly. He wasn't there anymore. It didn't stop her from hoping he was with them in spirit.

Christie got into the private boarding school, and life was … okay. Her nights were in Luiz's bed where he held her. Nothing else had happened since their naked shower together. Just having Luiz's arms wrapped around her made her feel safe and secure. The world was one scary place, and with everything that happened, knowing he was there helped.

Raine didn't mind that they hadn't done anything more since they had been naked in the shower. There were times she missed him, like today. He was out a lot of the time, leaving her to fend for herself. There was always Paige and Zara close, but again, it wasn't the same. Not really.

Paige and Zara didn't always live in the apartment blocks. They had homes, families of their own. Paige was pregnant with her second child. George and Petal were also in school. Life was interesting.

"Good? That's it? Good?" Zara asked, walking in with a carton of ice-cream.

The most thrilling thing Raine had done since she'd gotten to the apartment was to go grocery shopping. Luiz didn't know how to cook, and it showed. He had cans of beans, and ramen noodles. There were some ready meals in the freezer, and some blue-looking cheese, that was completely moldy, and in no way edible.

Other than that, she'd not put any of her special touches to the place. The apartment wasn't hers. She'd done her best to make Christie's home more comfortable, but again, there was only so much she could do.

Putting away the last of the shoes, she nodded. "It's good. I don't know what more you want me to say."

"Are you two together?" Zara asked, talking

around a mouthful of food.

"I think so."

She left her room, and went into Christie's room. The room was a mess. Opening the curtains, she let in a little fresh air by opening the window as well.

With more light inside, she made Christie's bed, and gathered up her stray clothes. They had been in a mad rush last night. After picking her up from school, she'd gone to the park, after which they had a quick takeout burger, and did her homework. It was past nine by the time they got home. After a quick wash it was after ten, and they both were exhausted.

She was trying to distract herself as every day after school, she didn't want to come straight back to the apartment. It hurt too much as memories of Xander just took over, making it next to impossible to breathe.

Picking up toys, she gathered the clothes, and walked into the kitchen. The apartment had its own washing machine, and she was grateful.

"What is going on here?" Paige asked.

"I don't know what you mean." Raine put the laundry into the machine, and turned to face the two women.

"We're trying here. Both of us are staying close, trying to help you in any way that we can, and you're doing everything you can to push us away. I don't know about Paige here, but I'm feeling a little hurt."

"I'm sorry. I'm not used to this. It's nothing personal," Raine said.

"What are you not used to?" Paige asked.

"This. Friends. Talking about boys."

"We know that you lost someone, Xander," Zara said. "That must have been tough."

"It was tough. Really tough. I don't even want to think about it right now, and it's easier, okay? It's easier to keep Christie busy, and to be completely exhausted so that by the end of the day, I don't have to think. I don't want to think. I just … I want to move on."

Luiz was rarely around. Nothing had changed, not really. He joined her late at night, and was gone most mornings. Life was the same. The only difference for Raine, was she didn't have Xander to keep her company, to help her.

Every day without fail, Xander would take them home, and they'd do homework. It would be a fun game where they all helped each other to learn. She would make dinner, and Xander would pretend to help. They were a family.

"I can take this from here," Luiz said, startling them all.

She hadn't heard him enter or join them.

Paige and Zara said their goodbyes, leaving them alone.

"Hey," he said.

"Hello."

She left the washing machine, grabbing a dust cloth, and getting to work on making the apartment totally clean.

"I heard what you said."

"Those words were not for your ears."

"Did you want me to close them up?"

"I'd appreciate it if you didn't listen to something that wasn't yours."

Moving the coasters off the coffee table, she sprayed it with the polish spray, and started to use the cloth.

"Raine?"

"What?"

"Look at me."

She didn't stop wiping the table, but she turned

her head to look at him. "What's the matter?"

"I want you to talk to me."

"I don't want to talk. If you'd been listening properly you would know that. You would know that I don't want to talk about anything!"

"I miss him, too."

"No! You don't get to talk about him. Do you understand? Not right now." She stood up, and threw the cloth on the table.

"He wouldn't want you to be hurting."

Tears filled her eyes as she looked at him. "You're nothing like him."

"I know."

"Xander cared. He wanted to be there for the two of us. He was there. You're never around, Luiz. Christie is growing up without a father, and now she doesn't even have Xander."

"I'm sorry."

"Why? What are you sorry for? Sorry that you're a waste of time? Sorry that he's dead? What the hell are you sorry for?"

"I'm sorry for everything. For fucking this up. For trying to control everything. For killing one of my friends. Xander, he was the best thing I ever did. Saving him, making sure he was protected. He made me believe I could be a better person, and I'm trying here, Raine. I don't know what I'm doing. I don't know how to be a father."

"Then try."

"My own father sold my sister off to the highest bidder because she was a girl. He used her to make sure his wealth stayed intact. The father I knew beat the living shit out of me every single day to make me a better man. A stronger man. A man who would one day be feared, and he did that. I don't give a shit about the amount of blood that is on my hands. I've killed so damn easily, and that shouldn't be okay. I shouldn't be able to look in the mirror, shave, and do all the normal shit that everyone else does." He slashed his arm through the air. "I know I'm the biggest fuck-up, and that I should be ashamed for the fact that I've even had kids. I'm a monster, and I'm doing my best. I am."

Raine saw the turmoil in his eyes, the pain that he tried to hide.

"I can help," she said, giving into the pain that she had felt for so long.

*"He's so cold. How can he love Christie?" Raine asked, wiping away her tears.*

*"Luiz has a good heart. He's loyal, Raine. The love he has for Christie goes beyond anyone's understanding. He doesn't show it, nor is it easy for him. You've got to give him time, and we can show him how to be a good man, a better man, and to trust in his heart."*

Xander was always the guy full of wisdom.

"What?" he asked.

"I can help you be the father you want."

"You can?"

"Yes, of course I can. Xander always believed that you had a lot more to give than you ever gave us. You've got to agree to be around us more, though. No more coming in late, or leaving before we get up. You've got to be part of Christie's life."

"I will. Does this mean you're going to be home as well?" he asked.

"What do you mean?"

"The past week I've gotten home by four. You've never been here. I've waited as long as I can, and you're never here. I figured you needed time for yourself."

She ran fingers through her hair. "I had no idea. I've avoided coming home. Crap, I'm so sorry. I guess

I'm as much to blame as you."

"How about we both pick our girl up from school? Would you like that?" he asked.

"Yes. I would. She'd love to see you, Luiz. Her birthday is tomorrow."

"I got her a birthday present."

"So have I. Well, I did have it. It was back at the old house." The smile fell from her face, and she no longer felt so happy. "I'll get over this. I did when it was my family. I will do the same with Xander."

She glanced over at his ashes, and sighed. One day at a time.

## Chapter Seven

Until getting Christie from school, Luiz had never thought that his absence would affect his girl so deeply. When she ran toward him and flung herself in his arms, he knew without a doubt that he had fucked up. He should have been there for her long before now. By trying to protect her, he'd screwed up. She wanted him in her life.

Once they were back at home, Raine left him with Christie to do homework while she made dinner.

The scents coming from the kitchen were amazing, and both he and Christie had rumbling stomachs. They finished her homework together, and he told her to go wash her hands to get ready for dinner. Inside the kitchen, he watched as Raine pulled the casserole out of the oven, and placed it on the stove.

"How did you find that?" she asked.

"I suck at math, and I don't know if I'm so thick I don't get it, or the way they're teaching it now is so complicated."

"They're always trying to advance teaching. You'll get the hang of it always changing. Did you send her to go and wash her hands?"

"I did. She's a good girl, isn't she?"

"Yes, and I can certainly say that with a hell of a lot of pride." She smiled at him. "How do you feel about chicken casserole with buttermilk biscuits?"

"Love them."

"Great. Do you want to set the table?"

Luiz grabbed some cutlery and plates, heading to the table to see Christie already sitting on one side.

"Are you hungry, sweetie?" Raine asked.

"Yes. It smells so amazing."

Raine put the casserole on the center of the table,

and tucked in, serving them all a piece.

Luiz watched as Christie put her hands together, and said a little prayer. "Xander said it was important to say a little prayer. There are others who won't be getting a meal tonight."

"He's right."

Picking up his fork, he took a bite, and moaned. "Your aunt is one great cook."

"I know. You should try her brownies. They are nice."

Raine's face went a pretty shade of pink. "I like to cook."

"Xander always said it helped you deal with frustration." Christie stumbled over the last word.

"He didn't?" Raine asked.

"Yep. He said you need to learn to chill."

"Damn that man. He always thought he was right."

Luiz … liked this.

He'd shared dinner before, only it hadn't been like this. Throughout he'd spoken with Xander, never giving the girls a thought.

Christie talked about her day at school as they ate. Once dinner was finished, Raine came out with some ice cream.

The food, the conversation, everything, was so good. "Why don't you guys go watch a movie or something?" Raine said. "I'll clean up this mess."

Luiz took Christie's hand, and got a movie set up.

"Daddy," she said.

"Yes, princess?"

"Do you love Raine?" she asked.

"I care about her."

"I love her so much. She's my mommy. Jessica at school told me her mom slaps her bottom when she's bad. Raine puts me in time out, but she never tells me I'm useless. I don't want a real mommy when I can have Raine."

He held his arms out to her, and Christie walked into them. "I'll make sure she never leaves us. Okay?"

"Yes."

"I'll go and see how she is doing."

Putting Christie onto the sofa, he walked into the kitchen. "Do you want some help?"

"What about Christie?"

"She's a good girl and can watch a movie for a few minutes without us."

"Yes, she can. She's a real darling, isn't she?"

Grabbing a towel, he started to dry the dishes. "I didn't even know that I owned all of this."

"You didn't," she said with a chuckle. "I had to go and buy everything. I didn't spend too much money though."

"Money is not, and will never be, a problem." They finished drying their duties. He wiped down the counter while Raine put away the last of the dishes.

Luiz stood in the doorway as Raine looked around.

"We're all clean. We can go join our little angel," she said.

That was the truth of it. Christie was their little angel, no one else's. Raine stood in front of him with a slight frown on her face. "What's up?" she asked.

"Nothing. Have you ever had moments of clarity, where something makes sense that has seemed so odd before?"

"Yeah."

"This is one of those moments." He stepped closer, keeping hold of her gaze. "I'm going to kiss you now."

"Luiz?"

"Not because you went on a date, or to teach some lesson. I'm going to kiss you because I really want to."

"Do you think this is a good idea?"

"Yes. I do."

Cupping her cheek, he tilted her head back, and slammed his lips on hers. She released a little moan, and he took advantage of that, sliding his tongue inside her mouth, tasting her, touching her. As he stroked his thumb across her cheek, they both moaned.

Raine's hands moved up his chest. She didn't push him away.

Up and down.

Up and down.

Her hands stroked over his chest.

His cock swelled, wanting more than anything to bend her over the counter, and take what he wanted.

Luiz stopped himself, and simply ravished her mouth.

Pulling away, he stared into her eyes, seeing the twinkle back inside them. "I kissed you because I want to, and I'm going to keep on doing it because I love the taste of your lips." To emphasize his point, he licked his lips. "Let's go and see how the movie is getting on."

Taking her hand, they walked into the sitting room together. Christie was sitting in the same place that he'd put her. She really was a good girl.

Raine sat on one side of her, while he took the other. Not once did he stop touching Raine.

He craved her touch, needed it. The past week had been hectic, rushing from one brothel, to the fighting rings, and documenting everything. He'd also reached out to Keyboard, real name Jamie, to get him to work for them.

Jamie wanted nothing to do with The Family, but he would help a friend of Xander's. A deal was struck, protection guaranteed, and their new life was emerging.

None of them could walk away, but they could make it so they didn't need to run.

When the movie finished, Raine got the bathroom ready, and by eight o'clock they were able to get Christie to sleep, together.

It was the first real taste of family he ever had, and he wanted to hold onto that.

Partially closing Christie's door, they headed back into the kitchen. "Do you want a beer?" Raine asked.

"Yes."

He watched as she opened a bottle of wine, pouring herself a glass. She handed him an open bottle of beer.

"Do you want to see the cake I made?" she asked.

"Yes."

She pulled out a doll cake, and he saw the dress was made out of frosting. "What do you think?"

"It's beautiful."

"I love practicing. One day I hope to be really good."

She put the cake back into the fridge.

"I have something for you," he said.

Luiz walked to the sitting room. There on the coffee table was the box of stuff he'd taken from the house. He'd finally gotten around to getting it. He'd gone through the whole house, taking what he felt they could keep.

"You went back?" she asked.

"I did. You can tell me what you want to do with all of this stuff."

She pulled out the photograph of the four of them

together. "Can I have this in your room?"

"It's just as much your room. Any pictures you want to put up, do so. I want you to find this place a comfort. This is your home now."

"I'll try." She put the picture down, and took out several more. "Thank you for the clothes."

"The clothes?"

"The ones you got me. I finally put them away."

Luiz nodded. He'd gone through a website, picking everything he thought she might like. "I want you to see this as your house, too."

"I will. Thank you."

He watched as she found the present she had gotten for Christie.

"What is it?" he asked.

"It's a dress she wanted. It probably seems silly. I remember my mom always buying us a special birthday outfit. If we weren't in school we could wear it the whole day. I miss them."

"It's not silly."

"I want to pass on similar traditions to Christie. Her life will never be like mine, but it doesn't mean she can't have little things."

"Together we can make her life shine, Raine. Together we can do this."

"I love the faith you suddenly have."

"Dealing with loss, it can help. Paige and Donnie invited us back to their place tomorrow. Is it okay for us to throw her a little party?"

"Yes. Of course."

"That's what I want to do."

"I'm more than happy with that."

Luiz had the urge to kiss her again, so he did. They were making progress. Small steps. He didn't need to rush anything.

They had the rest of their lives.

\*\*\*\*

"This cake is so beautiful," Paige said. "Would you do something like it for Petal?"

"Erm, sure."

Raine slid the cake inside the refrigerator. Christie was out in the back yard, running around with several kids that she didn't even recognize.

"We called some of the other women in The Family. The ones that wish to make a change. I hope that is okay?" Paige asked.

"I don't mind. I just want Christie to have a good time. This is the first time she's been able to have her father with her all day."

Christie had loved the princess dress Raine had brought her, and refused to do anything until she had it on.

Luiz got a load of toys, and promised a special vacation for Christmas.

Looking out of the kitchen window, she saw Christie still had Luiz's hand, and was making him dance around all the kids. Tonio was there doing the same.

"Your house is lovely."

"This was Donnie's parents' house. We've been redecorating, and wiping their memories from the place."

"Didn't you have your own place?"

"We did. There's a reason this place was the headquarters though for dealing with The Family. It holds many secrets."

"You're happy about that?"

"I knew what I was signing up for when I went with Donnie. In the beginning, I didn't want anything to do with him though. I tried to stay clear of him."

"They were step-siblings," Zara said.

"My mom decided to marry Donnie's dad. To cut

a long story short, they're both dead, and I'm now married to Donnie. My dad was a soldier of The Family. I never knew all the real connections until Donnie took over. He tells me the truth," Paige said.

Raine looked at Paige, then at Zara. She had seen the other women with men who worked and fought for The Family. Some of them were just outside, enjoying the sunshine, and the scents of the grill.

"How do you deal?" she asked.

"Deal?" Paige and Zara asked at the same time.

"I think Luiz wants to make it work between the three of us. How do you stay sane with the threat of constantly being attacked? Doesn't it bother you?" she asked.

"It bothers us. We have to go out, knowing that someone there wants to make a name for themselves, and we're the easy target. We have a target on our backs all the time. It's hard at times," Zara said. "I know Tonio freaks at the thought of anything happening to me. I hope nothing ever does. You've got to live your life otherwise you're going to spend the rest of your life worrying about something that may never happen."

Zara left the kitchen taking out another tray of burger buns.

"I know it's hard. I grew up in The Family, without even knowing it." Paige smiled. "There are times I can't sleep at night for fear of what could happen. I've got Petal, and another on the way." She touched her stomach. "It would be easier to give up, I imagine. To run away, and pretend nothing bad is happening. I'm not that kind of girl. I love Donnie. Living with him, and this is easier than living without him. You've got to make the decision about you. Not about us." Paige touched her arm. "I'll always be here."

"You're very open to new people," she said.

"There are not many friends here, Raine. Once you realize that some would take your spot easily, and would happily put a bullet in your head, you see the good and bag eggs. If you know what I mean?"

"What am I?"

"You're a good egg. You'd die for your family, and you gave up your whole life for your sister's kid. That takes a lot, don't you think?"

"I've never thought of it like that."

"Maybe you should. To me and Zara, you're one of the good ones. You'll get to meet Charlene in a moment, and little Darla."

"Little Darla?" Raine asked.

"She's Donnie's younger sister." Paige wrapped her arms around her, hugging her tightly. "I hope one day you can find some trust in me."

Paige moved away and headed outside.

Raine released a sigh, and watched everyone enjoying the party. There were people she didn't know, didn't trust. Luiz, he looked happy, even if he was carrying a gun. Rubbing at her temples, she moved away from the window, and gasped when she fell against a hard chest.

"I'm so sorry," she said, looking up into a scarred face. She had seen him at the apartment block.

"It's okay, Miss Raine. You should be outside enjoying the party."

"Do I know you?" she asked.

"I helped you with your groceries the other day."

"You did. Thank you."

"I'm the security detail at the apartment building, and I wanted to promise you that I will do everything in my power to make sure you and Christie are protected."

"Thank you, Mr...."

"It's Reese, Miss."

"Please call me Raine. Is Reese your first name?" she asked.

"Yes. Reese Turner."

She held her hand out for him to take. "It's nice to meet you. I'm sorry I didn't get your name earlier. Do you work for Luiz?"

"I work for The Family."

"Oh."

"I work for The Family under their ruling, yes."

She didn't know what the difference was. "Do you like them as bosses?"

"Yes. Soldiers were nothing more than minions. We were considered expendable and sometimes killed just to make a statement." He pointed at his scarred face. "This was also a statement."

"What do you mean?" she asked.

"Our enemies decided to take several soldiers, and held us all for ransom. I was standing next to Donnie's father at the time. To make a statement, he got me, and hacked my face and body, letting me fall to the floor in my own blood. If it wasn't for Donnie, Luiz, Tonio, and Jake, I would be dead. To their fathers we meant nothing. Anyone could be a soldier, and we could all die whenever they deemed it was right."

"I'm so sorry."

"Those four men out there, they're making everything different. The dangers are still there, but the men are more than willing to die for them."

"Why are you telling me this?" she asked.

"I overheard your conversation with Paige and with Zara. This world is hard, but you are surrounded by allies."

Raine understood. "Thank you. That means a lot to me. It really does."

Reese nodded, and left her alone.

Heading out into the garden, she waved at Luiz and Christie. Luiz made his excuses, leaving Christie with Jake as he walked back to her. "You've got a smile. Are you okay? Was it something I've done?" he asked.

"It was something you did a long time ago," she said. "I spoke to one of your men, and he, erm, he put some insight into something."

"And now?"

"Now I can deal with everything a lot easier. You're doing good here. You may not see it every day, but there are men here that count on you. I bet there are women, too. They need you all."

"It's why we can't give it up, even though I wanted to."

"Why did you want to give it up?" she asked.

"To make a better life for you, for Christie. I promised you something, and I don't like failing."

"You've not failed me, Luiz. I just want you to be a good father to Christie, and to be there."

"I will. You're going to help me." He placed his arm around her shoulders and pulled her close.

She didn't fight him, and melted against his warmth.

If Paige and Zara could handle this, she could. Not just for herself, or for Christie, but for the men and women who needed Luiz and his friends.

During the afternoon, she danced with Christie, watching as Luiz's friends teased him about his secret life. She met little Darla, who was a couple of years younger than Christie. Her parents used to have barbeques all the time, and Raine remembered enjoying them. This was no exception. She didn't know everyone, but it seemed like family.

Luiz made sure she stayed at his side, and even as Christie passed out with all the excitement, he didn't let

Raine miss a moment.

If she wasn't careful, she was going to fall in love with Luiz, and that wouldn't be very good.

Would it?

\*\*\*\*

"Hey, Jake," Charlene said.

Jake looked behind him to find who he thought was the most beautiful woman, standing behind him. She was wearing a denim skirt and white shirt. Even now, she was stunning.

"Charlene," he said.

This woman had broken his heart, and he didn't know what the hell he was doing anymore. He'd wanted to protect her, had offered her everything, and in return, he'd gotten shut down. She was a lesbian, and never wanted to be with a man. Donnie had tried to help him, even getting Paige to try to set him up with as many women as possible.

"How have you been?" she asked.

She locked her hands in front of her, and he saw she was nervous. "What's wrong?"

"Nothing. I just wanted to make sure you were okay. You've not called recently, and you seem to be avoiding me."

"With all due respect, Charlene, I made a fool out of myself when it came to you, and I'm not doing it again."

"You weren't a fool."

"No? I thought you were the most beautiful woman in the world. I still do, and you can't stand me."

"I tried to tell you many times. I want us to be friends, Jake. I don't want you to cut me out. Please."

"There was never a chance, was there?"

"No. I know what I like, and who I love. I'm moving on, and I think I'm in love," she said.

"At least one of us is."

Charlene moved toward him, and took his hand. "Please, let us be friends. I don't want to lose you. You've always been there for me, and I know this is horrible to ask this, and I hate that I cause you any pain." Tears filled her eyes, and he saw how much she was hurting because of what she was saying, and what he was clearly feeling.

"You're not going to." He squeezed her hand, knowing he'd rather be her friend than lose her.

## Chapter Eight

"Do you know who organized the hit?" Luiz asked.

Donnie finally had the information that he'd been waiting nearly a month for. One month and Luiz still hadn't avenged his friend's death. Every week Raine asked if he knew more. "Everything is in there, Luiz."

"Is it someone we know?" he asked.

"No. This is a new player. Francis Bracken. Ever heard of him?"

Luiz took the file and flicked it open. The picture showed a businessman, and according to his stats, he was well over six feet.

"No, I've not. Have you?"

He looked at Donnie, and watched as his friend nodded. "Yes, I remember him. He was once a soldier to my father."

"Oh."

"Why do I feel you're about to tell me a story I'm not going to like?"

"Bracken was the head of security for my father, Luiz. He was the best of the best. Knew his weapons, and how to defend our family if in the event of an attack." Donnie got up from his seat and rounded the desk. "The men who joined to become part of our security, joined to train with Bracken. His very name commanded respect, and people he'd never known, gave it to him. He was a good man."

"What happened?" Jake asked.

They were all there to hear about their next enemy. Donnie sighed. "My father was jealous. Not only was Bracken good with everyone in The Family, but my mother and brother adored him. He could do everything. Slay our enemies, and make pancakes. So my father decided that he was … a waste of space. It was time to show that a soldier is just a soldier."

"This is not going to be good," Tonio said.

"It's not. My father, during a live feed, had Bracken tortured, raped, and beaten, and left him to rot in the streets. No one heard from him again, and another man took his place."

"This is the guy who ordered the death of my family?"

"Luiz, Xander was one of the men who took part in the beating."

"No. No. Xander was a lot of things, but he wouldn't have done that."

"Not long after Bracken was taken care of, Xander was next. Think about it, who do you think they were after? The men who attacked that house were after Xander, I'm telling you," Donnie said.

"Can anyone else say that the plot is constantly thickening?" Tonio asked.

"What the hell do you want me to do with this?" Luiz asked.

"There has been no attack on any Family members that didn't have anything to do with that. The only soldiers that have gone missing are the ones that helped to hurt Bracken. I think I need to arrange a meet," Donnie said. "He could be an ally."

Luiz shook his head. "No. One of those men was hurting Raine. He killed Xander, and he was a good man."

"Not always," Donnie said.

"Think about it, Luiz. You have to see sense right now," Jake said.

"Anyone connected to The Family has had to do things they're not proud of. We all have," Tonio said.

Luiz felt sick to his stomach. Xander had been his

friend. He had trusted him.

"I can't. No. You're not going to do this, Donnie."

Donnie shrugged. "It's the next step I think we should take. We're nothing like our fathers, and reaching out, we can make our lives easier. The Family is not about being closed off, accepting only deals in flesh and blood. It's something more than that."

Luiz was shaking with anger. "I promised Raine that I would deal with the man who killed Xander."

"You killed them," Jake said. "Job done."

"They were minions, Jake. I can't believe you are wanting me to agree to this. Xander was my friend. I trusted him not only with my life or with Raine's. I trusted him with Christie's life. He wouldn't do anything so vile."

"He wasn't being held at gunpoint, Luiz. You need to consider this, but I understand this is hard for you. We're here when you change your mind," Donnie said.

Luiz stared at the file, and then at his friends. It couldn't be true. He wouldn't accept this kind of shit. It was wrong, all of it.

Storming out of his friend's office, he left Donnie's house, and got into his car. He didn't even think of where he was heading until he was at the edge of the forest. There were several people around, hikers and explorers. He parked the car, grabbed the file, and headed down the long path. The only place for him to think was to be surrounded by nature, so that he could have some time to focus on the revelations.

The thought of Xander doing something so awful wasn't right. It was out of place, and no, he couldn't believe it. Not now, not ever.

Finding a large rock, he sat down on top, and

took several deep breaths. Anything to clear his mind.

If Donnie thought it was a good idea to have a meeting, then Luiz had no choice but to find out everything he needed to.

Opening up the file after a good five minutes of hating it, he stared down at the details before him.

It was a nightmare.

Bracken had been perfect. The best soldier they had to offer. Their fathers had seen to his destruction, and in doing so, they had ruined him. Now he wanted revenge.

Luiz's cell phone started to ring, and he closed his eyes. He couldn't handle this shit right now, and didn't want to deal with it.

Turning off his cell, he read through the file. Only when he'd forced himself to read through every single piece of paper did he leave the comfort of the forest, get back into his car, and drive back home.

There was still time before they had to worry about Christie.

Entering his apartment, he saw Raine near the window with the phone in her hand.

"I've been trying to call you." She placed the phone back into the cradle. "Where have you been?"

"I had to think."

She paused, and he stared at her. Raine, everything pure and good. He'd brought her into his world.

"What is it?" she asked.

"I've found the person who killed Xander."

"You have."

"Yeah, I've found him." He stared at the paperwork, and handed it out toward her. "He wasn't after you, or Christie."

"What do you mean?"

"It's all there. The truth about what Xander did to him. This was about Xander, and revenge."

Raine frowned and flicked open the file.

"Beaten, knifed, raped, what the hell is all this?" she asked.

Luiz took a seat and urged her to do the same.

"You're scaring me."

"It kills me to have to tell you this. We both know Xander. The good inside him." Going against everything he knew, Luiz explained to her everything that he had come to see.

"No. No. Xander wasn't like that. He was a sweet man. You know him."

"Before he was almost killed, he was a monster." Like every single person in The Family. No one was left unharmed by their surroundings.

"I can't believe this."

"It's all there, Raine. Everything." He took a deep breath. "Donnie wants to meet him, join forces."

"What?"

"This was a revenge mission for Bracken. Donnie believes we can be stronger by partnering up with him, controlling The Family together. We're not like our fathers. We didn't do any of that shit to him."

"He killed Xander."

"He killed the man who raped and beat him."

"No!" She yelled the word, and threw the file away. "I don't give a shit about what that says. It's lies. All of it is lies. I don't believe it. I won't."

She stormed toward the window, wrapping her arms around herself.

He released a breath. "I'm sorry."

"You can't be serious about this. We knew who Xander was. You promised you would get revenge."

"The Family has to come first."

"You and this stupid family. Does that mean more to you than your real family?" she asked, turning on her heel and rushing toward him. "Xander, Christie, me, we're your family. We're the ones that have cared for you through everything."

"Donnie, Tonio, and Jake have been there forever for me."

She shook her head. "I can't ... deal with this. You're going to face the man who ordered his death." She pointed at the urn. "Why don't you just throw the ashes in the trash?"

"Stop." She was hurting, exactly like him. He held her arms and pulled her close. "Please, baby, I don't want to do this."

"Then don't. Don't let them win."

"I have to do what is better for The Family." He ran his hands up and down her arms. "Please, Raine, trust me."

She stared at him, and all he saw was the pain. "I've got to get dinner in the oven."

Luiz watched her walk away. He had to find a way to reach her, to stop her from reacting rashly. Reading all the shit inside the file, he'd known that Xander wasn't an innocent man. He'd been brutal, and even had a reputation of his own.

Xander had asked him for a chance to make amends for all the wrong in his life. He'd done what he thought was right.

Now he had to wonder if this was just another one in a long line of bad decisions.

****

"This is ridiculous. I don't know why I'm even going out," Raine said a week later.

Paige was in her room, fixing her hair into ringlets.

"You and Luiz have never gotten out before, and it's time. You've got that connection."

"I don't want to spend any time with him. Not right now."

For the past week they hadn't avoided each other. They had simply ... not spoken to each other.

"Donnie told me what happened. How are you coping?"

"You mean, how am I coping with the fact that the guy who I've lived with for the past seven years could have raped and beaten another man, and got killed from it? Or do you mean how do I feel that *The Family* wants to meet this guy, and join forces?"

"All of it?" Paige asked.

"I'm struggling." Raine found the whole situation a nightmare, and it made her feel sick to her stomach. The one thing that hadn't changed was her feelings for Luiz.

"I don't want to think about it. All I want to do is forget it ever happened."

"Did you read that file?" Paige asked.

"I did." After Luiz had left to pick up Christie, she'd gathered the file, and read every single word. "I can't imagine the guy I was living with, who I joked with, and loved as being that horrible."

"What I've come to see with The Family, they are all doing a job. It's not personal to any of them. They have all done something they hate or regret."

"I don't think I should know this stuff about Xander."

"Do you think, even just a little, that it could be true?" Paige asked.

Raine's throat was swollen from all the tears she had shed. "That's what I hate. There is a small part of me that thinks it's true." There were times that Xander would be thrown into a terrible depression. He wouldn't be able to smile. She'd take him a cup of hot chocolate, and sit with him. It would help a little.

*"Tell me what's wrong, Xander. I hate to see you like this."*

*"There are many things in my life that I regret, sweet girl. Some days it's harder to forget than others."*

She didn't want to think of him being a monster, or there being even the slightest chance of him doing those things to a somewhat innocent man. Bracken hadn't deserved what was done to him.

It had been an act of jealousy. This life, it was dangerous, and she couldn't believe her sister hadn't even thought about it.

Knowing Lora the way she did, she'd probably thought it was really exciting.

"You can't let the tears get to you, Raine. What happened, happened, and it's not your fault."

"It's hard though. If Xander did those things, shouldn't a small part of me hate him for it? He was never like that with me or with Christie." She sighed. "He was the perfect father figure to be honest."

"Then be pleased that you were able to give him a small feeling of being normal. Of being accepted. You've got to remember one thing," Paige said.

"What's that?"

"He was acting on orders. It wasn't his choice."

"He could have told them no, Paige. Xander, he was a bad man, and I have to accept that. He changed, but he was still a bad man before." She couldn't argue with the facts that she had seen. Luiz was the one that was helping her to make sense of everything.

"There, you're done, sweetie. You look beautiful."

"I feel silly. After everything that has happened,

don't you think we should just stay in? Watch a movie?"

"Donnie and I are going to look after Christie. You've got absolutely nothing to worry about. Go out, have some fun. Enjoy your time. It's important."

"Is this what you do?"

"All the time. You've got to learn to separate the good with the bad. This is a bad point, and you will get over it in time."

"You sound like you know."

"Of course I do. I'm married to Donnie. We've had our bad moments. A hell of a lot of good but there are bad ones. Like in any marriage. Just because we're young doesn't mean we don't have a lot of problems. Enjoy tonight." Paige leaned down and kissed her cheek. "You look beautiful."

"She really does," Luiz said.

Raine turned to find him leaning against the doorframe. "I didn't hear you come in."

"You were talking. It's nothing to worry about."

Silence fell between them.

"I'm going to go. Donnie is waiting for me. I want you both to have fun. That is an order!"

Raine smiled, watching her go.

They waited for the sound of the door to close, and Luiz was the first to talk. "You okay?"

"Yeah, I think so. You?"

"I am. If you want to stay in tonight, I'm happy to do that."

Raine looked down at her clothes. She wore a beautiful red cocktail dress and heels. For the first time, she felt like a woman.

"Nah, I'd like to go out. It's the first time I've gotten dressed up." She stood, pushing her ringlets over her shoulder. "How do I look?"

"Beautiful. I always think you look beautiful."

When she went to grab her purse, he told her not to bother.

"I've got this, baby. Tonight, is all on me."

"It seems a little surreal. You and me, going on a date."

"I know." They locked up their apartment, and made their way down to his car in the parking lot.

"Has there been any news about Bracken?" she asked.

"Donnie told me that tonight I can't talk about anything. I've got to focus on you."

"You're going to do as he ordered?"

"No. I'm going to do what my friend advised me to do. Donnie's not my boss. We're all friends, and we had hoped to build a better world. I had hoped that with time, we could come away. We put targets on our backs, and for that, I'm sorry."

"I promise I won't talk about anything to do with your work."

"So, tell me about your day."

Raine told him everything, from cleaning Christie's room, to dealing with the apartment, to even baking an assortment of cookies. "That's what I do. Take care of the kids, clean house, and bake."

He chuckled. "I was going to ask, would you like to finish college? Go to college? Do some work, or something?"

"Xander told me it was against the rules."

"It's not. Making you stay at home all day is a waste of time. I want you to be happy, Raine. This is what this is about. Making you happy." He took her hand, and pressed a kiss against her knuckles.

She couldn't help the sudden indrawn breath or the tingles working all over her body. He made her feel so much.

Her mouth went dry, and words failed her.

"I feel it, too," he said.

"What?"

"Whenever I touch you, I feel awakened once again. It ... makes the entire world feel amazing."

She smiled. "Really?"

"When Xander told me you were on a date, I wanted to slaughter the guy. I didn't want him to have a chance to prove to you that you could have a great life away." Luiz sighed. "I've been keeping you safe for myself."

"What do you mean?"

"At first, you were young, and I was hurting. Christie was alive, and you were there. You were way too young, but I saw how sweet you are. How caring. That has never changed. Lora told me you were too sweet for your own good. Had a temper on you at times, and could be prone to bad language, but completely good."

Raine smiled. She missed her sister.

"You grew up, and every time I walked away, it was harder for me not to look back and have a second look. You were always smiling, always so innocent. Your cheeks would heat at the slightest flirtation. I knew you weren't ready, and then there was the fact that I am who I am."

"Being part of The Family, does it really bother you?" she asked.

"It can. It can be damn hard at times. I know this life is not for everyone, and I don't want to pressure you."

"I'm safer with you than we are apart."

"That's not why I want you to stay."

"It's not?"

"No. I want you to stay because you want to. I'll

always protect you. I hope you know that."

"I'm here because I want to be here. There's nowhere else I'd like to go."

"Good."

He rode toward the city, and she watched the passing scenery go by, loving every how busy everything was. It was a complete change from the life she remembered, which to her wasn't a bad thing.

"Italian?" she asked when he pulled up outside of a very posh-looking restaurant.

"I had to do better than that guy."

"Shoot, Bradley. I completely forgot. What should I tell him?"

"I already took care of it. He knows you've moved away."

"When did you see him?" she asked.

"When I grabbed the rest of your stuff. I should have told you."

Raine stared at him, and waited for him to say anything more. He didn't. There was nothing more to be said.

"Stay here," he said.

She frowned, watching as he climbed out of the car, and stopped the usher, or whatever he was called, from opening her door. Luiz held open her door, and offered her a hand. "Would you care to join me?" he asked.

"Yes, I would."

Taking his hand, she climbed out of the car, and smiled at the man as Luiz handed him the keys.

"What was all that about?" she asked.

"Simple. This is my date, and I'm not having another guy help you out of the car."

"This is a date? Like a real date?"

"Of course, and I do expect to get my kiss at the

end of it."

Her stomach filled with butterflies. She was nervous yet excited about what was to come. The night was only getting started.

## Chapter Nine

No expense had been spared this evening. Luiz wanted everything to be perfect. He'd gone to Paige and to Donnie, asking for their help. He wasn't above begging either. The tension between him and Raine was unbearable. He didn't like it, and tonight he intended to end it.

The private booth was romantically lit with two long-stem candles either side of them. The pristine white tablecloth was beautifully offset by the dim lighting. A beautiful red wine was already breathing beside him.

"Wine, miss?" the waiter asked.

"Not right away. Water, if that's okay."

"Certainly."

The waiter left to bring her some cool water. Luiz decided to take the cool water as well. This night had to go perfectly. He didn't want to be outdone by Bradley. His own jealousy surprised him.

Once they were left alone after their drinks, Luiz took her hand across the table. "Do you like it?"

"It's certainly very intimate. You've picked a very romantic place, Luiz."

"I want you to feel special."

"Right now, I can safely say that I do, and it's all your doing."

"I hope that's a good thing," he asked.

"I think it is. At least, I hope it is." She chuckled. "Ignore me. I'm just being silly."

"No, you're not. Tell me. Help me improve."

"What is this, Luiz? I mean, seriously. Is this trying to make me happy? Is this so I won't go on any other date? What is it?"

"I was hoping it would be the start of something more for both of us."

"How do you mean?"

"We share a bed, Raine. One day, I'm hoping we can share more than each other's warmth. I want you. I know I shouldn't, but I can't help what I want, and I want you."

Her cheeks had already gone a delicate shade of red. Like all the other times, he found it utterly charming.

"Sex?" she asked.

"That as well."

"I want love, Luiz."

"Do you think you can't love me, or learn to love me in time?" he asked.

"It's not just about me. What about you? Can you learn to love me?"

Luiz squeezed her hand. "It's not something I need to learn. I know I have feelings for you already, baby. I want to give you everything, and make you happy. I've got a past, you know that. I'm hoping you can see past it to give me a chance to prove to you that I can be something worth fighting for."

"Never doubt it. You're worth fighting for."

"Even with this Bracken problem?"

She sighed. "Even with this Bracken problem, and with you being some mafia lord, and with you saving me and my niece. I've never hated you, Luiz. Not once. You've annoyed me. Made me really frustrated and angry. I've never hated you."

"You've told me you had."

"That's emotions talking. It's not real, and please don't take it personally. I tell everyone," she said with a chuckle. "Can I ask you a question?"

"Anything."

"What was your sister like? I didn't even know you had one, but you mentioned her the other day, and I've been curious. You don't own any photograph albums, or have any pictures of your family."

"Maria. That was my sister's name. She was a couple of years older than me, and she liked to play pretend."

"Pretend?"

"It's what I refer to her behavior as. She used to pretend that she didn't know what this life was like, or what it entailed. She pretended to be the damsel in distress, much to Tonio's pain."

"Why?"

"Tonio and Maria had an affair when they were younger. He wanted to run away with her, start a whole new life away from The Family. There was a time I thought he could do it. Where we could run and hide, pretend we weren't who we were."

"What happened?" she asked.

"Maria pretty much laughed at him. She didn't want to start a life, risk having to work for a living. Dad had her married off within the year, and she had to start earning her living by taking a beating. She had a chance to have a normal life with my best friend, and she chose pain and greed over happiness."

Raine held his hand tightly. "Where is she now?"

"She couldn't deal with the guilt, and killed herself. She's dead."

"You don't seem cut up by it."

"I wasn't. To be honest I always saw her as a pain in the ass. Someone that I had no choice but to deal with because she was too much of a fucking pain."

"I'm really sorry you felt that way."

"Yeah, well. We can't exactly get the family we chose, can we?"

"No, we can't." She released his hand, taking a sip of water. "So, moving on. If it wasn't for your current position, what would you have liked to be?"

"I'll ask you the same question," he said.

"I know."

He leaned back in his chair, thinking about it. "A doctor."

"You'd like to help people. Cure them?"

"Yes. Spilling blood is a job I don't want to have to do. I've been born to do it, nurtured to do it. I have no enjoyment in it."

"I'm sorry."

"You don't need to be sorry. I knew there was no turning back for me no matter how much I wanted it." He stared into her brown eyes. "If I wasn't taking lives, I'd want to help them. Take care of them, and fight the illness within their body for them."

She released a breath. "That's really sweet, did you know that?"

"I can be a sweet guy sometimes. Take away the crap with The Family, and what I'm forced to do. Look at me. Think about me, and what do you see?" he asked.

"You want me to answer?"

"Yes."

"I see a very confident, sexy guy," she said.

"Sexy, I like that, Raine. Want to know what I see when I look at you?"

She averted her gaze, and shook her head. "No."

"I see a beautiful woman. An innocent woman who wants to get out and explore but can't. I can help you with that."

"I'm sure you say that to all of the girls in your life."

"Only the good ones."

She fanned herself. "You're talking dirty again."

"I've got to find some way of getting you naked again."

"Yeah, I still can't get over the fact we're sharing

a bed, and we've shared a shower. We're doing this whole dating thing backwards."

"Give me a time and a place, and I can really blow your world."

Her mouth parted, and he saw all the dirty thoughts playing inside her head as they were playing in his, too.

"First, tell me, Raine, what would you like to be when you grow up?" he asked.

"A lawyer."

"Oh, that does surprise me."

"Why?"

"I don't know. I imagined you saying you wanted to be a chef, or a nurse, or a hairdresser."

"Wow, talk about a little sexist there."

"I've never known you to have a love of the law."

"I don't have a love of the law. Before my parents were killed they were in some kind of legal battle with the neighbors. I don't know what it was or why. They were stressed about it all the time, and I remember thinking to myself that I could help them. If I knew the law, and knew what the hell I was doing, I could have found a way to help them. The law is about being understood, challenged, adapted, changed. I like a challenge. I also love cooking, but that's what I'd have loved to be."

"I'm so sorry."

"Don't be. I took an online course, and law is complicated. Scarily so. It was crazy what I learned, and I realized that I didn't have a place in law. I could want all I wanted." She smiled. "I'm not cut out for that cutthroat world. I guess I'll be a nurse or a hairdresser."

"Why not the chef?"

"I like to cook for myself. I couldn't deal with all of these people, and changing everything just to suit their needs. I'm not good with that stuff." She shrugged. "We know a little more about each other."

"We do."

"What do you hate most about being who you are?" she asked.

"You're really hitting with the questions tonight."

"You can ask me anything. Whatever you want to ask, go right ahead." She held her finger up. "After you answer mine."

Luiz stared at the blank table. They would have to order some food, as he was getting hungry. Taking a sip of his water, he thought about it.

"The shame."

"Shame?"

"Of knowing what I do, of what I'm forced to do. The Family, as you read, had to set examples. Some of them weren't very good ones. I've been forced to hurt innocents, kill people for no reason other than they wanted to get out. They wanted freedom from the control." Luiz ran a hand down his face. "There are times that I'm ashamed to look in the mirror because the man I see is not the man I wanted to become. This life, it has a great deal of advantages. When a drugged out whore is sobbing at your foot, begging for her life, and your father has a gun to your temple, telling you to end her ... it takes time to come back from something like that."

"I'm so sorry."

"Each of us, Donnie, Tonio, and Jake, over the years at our fathers' hands, we lost something of ourselves. I believe that everyone has a natural way they are. Whether it be kind, or cruel, or helpful, they are destined to be those people. I think I was destined for something else, but fate put me in this path."

"That's really deep," she said.

He snorted. "It's the truth."

"I'm not going anywhere, Luiz. You don't have to worry about that."

"Good. Now, can I ask you some questions?" he asked.

"What is that look in your eye? You're planning something, aren't you?" she asked.

"I'm planning something that I'm more than sure you're going to enjoy."

"Okay, ask away. I'm listening."

"You've never had sex."

She swallowed her water and immediately started coughing. Placing the glass down, she covered her mouth. "That's what you want to ask me?"

"I'm curious about you, about what you want."

"This is going to be embarrassing, isn't it?"

"No. Not at all. It's not my intention to embarrass you."

She took a deep breath, and nodded. "Go. I'm ready for them."

"The kiss we shared. Was it your first?" he asked.

"Yes. It was."

"What else have you done?"

"Nothing. You know that. I've spent all of my life with Xander and with Christie. There wasn't time for anything else." She pushed away a stray curl.

Paige had done wonders with Raine's hair. She really was a beautiful woman, and he was a lucky guy.

"Have you touched yourself?" he asked.

"No. I've not. I've been on a couple of dates with Bradley, and whenever he went to kiss me, I always turned away. I didn't feel comfortable. Can we change the subject?"

"Would you like to have sex? To play around. To have fun."

She blew out a breath. "Yes, I would."

"Good."

\*\*\*\*

The date with Luiz had been insightful, and at times sad. Raine knew more, and understood him a lot more now than she ever had before. Riding back to their apartment, she was aware of the mounting tension between them. Every time he touched her, she felt awakened. His questions had been as bad as she imagined they would be.

Yes, she did want sex.

She wanted to know what it was all about.

Why there were so many books about it? Was it as good as they made it out to be?

She was twenty-two years old, and still a virgin.

Pulling up into the parking bay, she didn't wait for Luiz to get her door. Raine climbed out, and by his side, they walked toward the elevator.

Christie was spending the night with Paige and Donnie.

The elevator doors opened, and she bit her lip. They stood together, and she watched him in the elevator to find his gaze was on hers. Neither of them was touching, and yet to Raine, it felt like he was stroking her with his gaze. The lust, the promise emanated from out of him, and she found it hard to ignore.

She licked her lips, and Luiz moaned. "I really wish you wouldn't do that," he said.

"Why?"

He moved suddenly, and had her pressed against the corner of the elevator. Luiz cupped her face, and ran his thumb across her bottom lip. "So fucking plump, and so beautiful. You make me think of how good these would look wrapped around my cock, baby. I want you to suck me while I lick your sweet pussy."

"Luiz?"

"Don't be afraid. I'd never do anything you didn't want, and I'm not hiding who I am anymore, what I want. I hid because I didn't think you could handle me, but I know you. I know you're strong, and you can handle anything, even me."

Luiz pressed his thumb against her lips, and slid inside. She sucked on his thumb, and moaned as he thrust his whole body against her. The hard ridge of his cock pressed against the front of her stomach, showing her exactly how hard he really was.

The elevator doors pinged open, and he pulled away. This time, he grabbed her hand, and took her toward their apartment. The moment they were inside with the doors shut and locked, he had her pressed up against it. Her hands above her head as he plunged his tongue into her mouth.

Raine closed her eyes, unable to fight his dominance, nor did she want to. She was completely surrounded by him, needed him more than she needed anything else.

Heat flooded her panties, and she tried to press her thighs together to create some friction and to ease the pain.

He wouldn't let her.

Luiz inserted a leg between thighs, stopping her.

"Is your pussy nice and wet for me, baby?" he asked.

She nodded. "I think so."

He kept her hands above her head, locked under one of his. With his other, he stroked down her body, gliding down her arm, over her breasts past her stomach, to her thigh. Using his fingers, he gathered up her skirt until he felt flesh. The moment his fingers touched her, she gasped out, unable to deny the eruption of pleasure from his touch.

"You make me want to do some crazy things to you, baby." He slid his hand between her thighs, and she cried out. His thumb pressed against her slit, rubbing across her panties and her swollen clit.

"Your panties are soaked, baby. You want this, don't you?"

"Yes."

She'd never felt anything like it, and didn't want it to end.

With one yank on her panties, they tore, and he threw them away. "I think I like the thought of you not being allowed to wear panties again." He cupped her once again, and his finger this time slipped between her folds.

Luiz added a second finger and began to stroke her clit, rubbing her between the two digits.

"I want to taste this pretty pussy. I want you to keep your hands up there, understand?" he asked.

She nodded. She would do anything he asked just so long as he didn't stop touching her. Her body was no longer her own, or at least it didn't feel like it, not right now.

Luiz released a hold on her body, and she watched as he sank to his knees before her. He lifted up one leg, and then his lips were on her body. She cried out his name, unable to believe the kind of pleasure that was coming from his lips.

His tongue swept over her clit, going down to circle her entrance, and back up again. "I'm going to take that cherry, baby. I'm going to own it."

She believed him, and never doubted him for a second. He had complete control over her, and she let him have it as well.

"So pretty," he said. "So perfect."

Closing her eyes, she moaned as he sucked her

clit into his mouth, using his teeth to create just enough pain to make the pleasure to the point of being unbearable.

"Look at how swollen you are, and so wet. You're all mine, Raine. You always were."

She knew he was right. There was no one else she could imagine being like this with.

"Please," she said.

"Do you want to come, baby?"

"Yes, I want to come. I want you, please, Luiz."

He used his fingers and his tongue, attacking her clit with both kinds of pleasure. It was too much, and she splintered apart. If it wasn't for Luiz holding her, she would have collapsed.

Luiz wouldn't stop even as she begged him. Only when he was ready to stop, did he do so. He stood up, and she saw his lips glistening with her cream.

"You taste amazing," he said.

"I want to have sex," she said, blurting the words out. She hadn't had any wine with dinner, or before, nor after.

Raine had a clear head, and knew there was no such thing as a perfect time. It simply didn't exist.

"Are you sure?" he asked.

Cupping his face, she kissed his lips, tasting herself on his tongue, and not caring. "I'm sure."

She let out a scream as he picked her up. "I can walk."

"I know you can. I want to carry you."

He entered their bedroom, and he placed her on the edge of the bed. She watched as he stood back, and pulled his shirt apart, spraying buttons everywhere. "I'll pick them up later," he said.

"Oh, you'll pick them up?"

"We'll have some fun picking them up together,

how about that?"

"I like that." She wondered what kind of game he could have in mind. Then, she stopped thinking altogether. Luiz removed his gun, and placed it on the chair, before coming back toward her with his shirt completely off. "You keep throwing clothes in the trash, we're going to be completely broke."

"I'll worry about money. You just focus on me."

"If that's what you want."

"It is, and you know it is." He took her hands, pulling her back up. Luiz turned her to face the wall, and in the mirror across from the bed, she saw them both.

"You're so beautiful," he said.

"You're not so bad yourself." She didn't know how to handle his compliments, or if she even believed them. She wasn't the prettiest woman in the world, and she didn't mind that, not at all.

The sound of the zipper at her back echoed around the room. It was almost deafening, giving her the chance with every second that past for her to put a stop to what was about to happen.

She didn't want to stop it.

This was what she'd been craving for so long. Luiz's touch. His arms wrapped around her.

"You can make me stop at any time," he said.

"I don't want you to stop."

He pushed the dress off her shoulders, and eased it down her body. She closed her eyes as the weight of the dress fell at her feet.

Luiz banded his hand around her stomach. His lips grazed her shoulder. "Open your eyes."

She wasn't slim, or smooth. She had lumps, bumps, and curves that drove her crazy. Dieting always failed. She'd put weight on rather than lose it. After so long of hating her body, she'd finally grown to love herself. She wasn't perfect, nor would she ever be. She was just herself, and she was happy with that.

Opening her eyes, she stared into his. There was no mistaking that he liked what he saw. His cock pressed against the base of her back, and in the mirror she watched as his hands moved up to cup her breasts. "Do you have any idea what you do to me?" he asked.

He sucked on her neck, and she whimpered.

Her body erupted in goosebumps at his touch.

Luiz cupped her breasts, and he tugged down the cups of her bra, exposing her tits to the air.

"So pretty. So beautiful," he said.

This was so much better than anything she had imagined.

## Chapter Ten

Raine's tits were larger than he remembered. They spilled out of his hands, and her nipples were large, begging to be sucked. Her body was fuller, rounder, designed to take a man as big as he was. His cock was so damn hard that it was hurting him.

All he wanted to do was throw her to the bed and ravish her body. Take what he wanted without a second thought. He forced himself to hold back. He needed to take his time. Raine was a virgin. He'd already given her a couple of firsts. Her first kiss. Her first orgasm. He was going to be the first man to make love to her, to fuck her, to take her every which way he could, and to give her even more.

They were bound together, and there was no chance of them coming apart. This was their future. He didn't find it a curse, but a relief.

Staring in the mirror, he watched as her head fell against his shoulder, and she moaned.

"Do you like that, baby?" he asked.

"Yes."

"I'm going to take off your bra."

"What about you?" she asked. "I'll be completely naked."

Luiz flicked the catch of her bra, and removed the offending item. He wanted her completely bare without anything between them. Stepping away from her, he watched as she turned toward him, and he kept his gaze on hers, and removed his pants.

He winced as he moved the zipper down past his cock.

"Have you hurt yourself?" she asked.

"No. I'm just hard, baby. It makes it a little difficult." The moment he removed his pants, he felt a lot better.

Raine's eyes went wide as she looked at him. He stared down at his stiff cock, seeing that the tip had already started to leak pre-cum. Wrapping his fingers around the length, he covered the head in the cream, and slicked the rest of his cock.

"Does it hurt?"

"No. Touch me." He took her hand and wrapped her fingers around his length. Gritting his teeth, he tried to control the pleasure that was rushing through his body at her touch alone.

Never had he felt such an instant connection to someone, and yet with Raine, everything felt so natural to him. It was clearer than anything he'd ever experienced.

"Do you feel that?" he asked.

"Yes. I do. Is this normal?"

"I don't know. I only know how much I love having your hands on me, and I don't want you to remove them." He groaned as her thumb flicked over the tip, taking his pre-cum. He watched as she put that same thumb to her mouth, and licked the cream off her finger. It was one of the hottest things he'd ever seen. "Do you want to taste me?" he asked.

She nodded.

Stepping closer, Luiz held his cock with one hand, while with the other he cupped the back of her head. "Don't use teeth, just your lips and tongue."

Raine nodded. She didn't shove him in her mouth. Instead, she flicked the tip of his cock with her tongue, tasting more of his pre-cum. She covered the head of his cock and sucked a little. Getting his length nice and moist, she lowered her mouth over his dick until he sank to the back of her throat. She pulled up with only the tip inside her mouth, and did the same thing all over again.

"Oh fuck, that feels so good, baby."

He pumped inside her mouth, watching as his slick cock appeared and disappeared inside her mouth. Her saliva coated his flesh, and the warmth of her mouth was sheer heaven.

Tugging on her hair, he pulled her off his length.

Her lips were plump and red. "Was I doing something wrong?" she asked.

"Not at all. You were doing everything right, baby."

She smiled.

"I can't last long with your mouth."

He liked being her first. She was his to train, to teach her how to enjoy everything he had to offer.

Leaning down, he took possession of her mouth. At the same time, he got her to move backward on the bed until she was near the pillows. Pressing her down, he broke away from the kiss, and started to kiss down her neck, sucking over her pulse. He drove her wild, seeing her body's response to his touch. Her nipples were rock hard, and her chest was flushed, not to mention her pupils were dilated.

Moving between her thighs, he reached over to the drawer, and took out a condom.

"Are you ready for kids?" he asked.

"I love children. Do you want kids?"

He nodded. "Yes. I'd love for Christie to have a little sister or a brother to boss around. We don't want to make it too easy for them."

Raine smiled. "One day."

Just not today. He wouldn't mind if she was pregnant soon though. This was a new stage for the pair of them, and even though they both had Christie, he didn't want to screw anything up. There was no chance of their life ever being simple, but he could make sure their life was perfect together.

Tearing into the condom, he slid the latex over his cock, and moved between her spread thighs.

"Will this hurt?" she asked.

"I think it does for you. I'm going to take this really slow, okay?"

"Yeah. This is weird, right?"

"It is weird, but I'll do anything to make it good for you." He gripped his cock, pressing the tip against her entrance. Staring into her eyes, Luiz slowly started to ease inside her, breaking through her hymen.

Immediately Raine tensed up.

He stopped, waited, and then pushed a little more.

She frowned, and he stopped again.

For several seconds or even minutes, he started and stopped, not getting very far inside her. She hated the pain, and he saw that in her eyes. He didn't want to cause her any kind of pain, and yet that was exactly what he was doing.

Gritting his teeth, he slammed every inch of his dick inside her, and finally claimed her for his own.

She cried out, and he wrapped his arms around her, holding her close. He didn't move, and stayed still inside her.

"I've got you, baby. I've got you."

"Ouch."

"I know. I know." He kissed her shoulder, and closed his eyes, counting to ten to try to stop himself from feeling any arousal. Her pussy was incredibly tight, and warm, and fucking perfect. He didn't want this to end, not for a second.

He lifted up, and stared into her eyes that were filled with tears. "What's the matter, baby?"

"That hurt. You're not small. If you were small it

wouldn't hurt."

"And I wouldn't be able to satisfy you. Something tells me you're going to be a handful."

"You're not moving," she said.

"I don't want to hurt you. This is about the two of us, not just what I want."

She licked her plump lips. "How does it feel to you?" she asked.

"You're tight, and warm." He closed his eyes and moaned. "It's hard for me to not just take you. This is amazing. Does it still hurt?"

She shook her head. "Not as much."

"At least you're not cursing me anymore, and you're not threatening to kill me. I'd say that's a good thing in my book."

Raine chuckled. He stroked his fingers down her cheek.

Luiz eased out of her body, and watched as her eyes grew wide. They weren't filled with pain.

He knew Raine. He knew her better than she knew herself.

Slowly, he took his time, making love to her body and showing her exactly how good it could be between them.

Reaching between them, he held himself deep inside her, and stroked over her clit, drawing another orgasm from her body. Only when she had come a second time, did he find his own release.

When it was over, he pulled out and lay beside her, pulling her close to him.

"That was beautiful, thank you," she said. Tears were leaking out of her eyes, and he frowned.

"Did I hurt you?"

"No, not like that."

"Raine, you shouldn't be crying. I hurt you,

didn't I?" he asked.

"No, you didn't hurt me. In the beginning you did, but after that, you didn't. It was wonderful, Luiz. I never thought it could be."

"Why are you crying?" he asked.

"I don't know? I'm twenty-two, and I've never felt like that, not with anyone. I'm a bit emotional. First orgasm, first sex, give me a break," she said with a smile.

"I'm sorry. It has been so long ago that I didn't even think about what it would mean to you."

"Was your first time with Lora?"

"No. My first time was because my father decided that it was time for me to be a man, and the only way he thought I could be a man was for me to kill someone, and then fuck a whore."

"Oh."

"This, between us, meant everything to me, Raine, and I'll treasure it for the rest of our life together."

He meant it.

This wasn't about him clutching at a way of getting away from The Family. He accepted this was his place, and where he was going to stay. Raine accepted that. She accepted him, and he'd do everything he could to make her proud.

\*\*\*\*

*Two days later*

Raine watched as Christie slept, completely content in her new world. She loved school, loved hanging out with her dad, and loved spending time as a family with them all. Closing the door, all the way this time, Raine entered the sitting room to find Luiz sitting on the sofa, legs spread, drinking a beer. The last couple of days had been heaven, and she knew without a doubt that it was about to come crashing down on them.

"Hey," she said. "Christie's asleep. Swimming

took it right out of her today."

"She was yawning all through dinner, and you made her favorite, lasagna."

"This school is fantastic for her. Her teachers challenge her in ways the other school didn't." She took a seat beside him, lifted her feet beneath her body, and rested her head in her hand. "What's wrong?"

"Nothing."

"You don't need to lie to me. I've told you for a while now that I can take whatever you need to tell me."

"Are you so sure about that?" he asked.

"Why don't you try me and find out."

"Bracken," he said.

She turned to look at Xander's urn. His ashes were still waiting to be spread, and she knew that The Family wanted to do something about Bracken. Time never stood still for any of them.

"Don't worry about it."

"Tell me, Luiz. I need to hear whatever has to be said." She took his hand, locking their fingers together, and kissing his knuckles. "Trust me to not freak out."

He nodded. "Donnie has arranged a meeting for tomorrow. We're going onto Bracken's territory, and we want to make a deal with him."

"What kind of deal?" she asked.

"We want him to come out of hiding. To take his place with us, and to promise no more retaliation."

"I thought you said the men who hurt him were all dead?" she asked.

"We believe they are. If we're wrong, we want to help him."

"What about Xander?"

"They want me to overlook it."

"Oh." She didn't know what to think. "What do you want to do?"

"I don't know. I want to punish him for taking Xander away from me, from us. Then I think about that damn file, and I wonder if killing one for the other would do any good. It was an old score, one we don't have any say in."

"So you want to leave it alone?" she asked.

"What do you want me to do?"

"I want you to do whatever you need to do for The Family. I do trust you, Luiz, and I know this is important. Donnie wouldn't have said it was, if it wasn't."

He tugged her so that she was over his lap, straddling him. "Thank you."

"What for?"

"For being understanding. For not kicking me in the balls, and for giving me a chance to figure this out."

She wore a skirt, and she smiled as he began to pull it up her body. To surprise him, she wasn't wearing any panties. Reaching into her bra, she pulled out a condom. "How about you make it up to me another way?"

"I'd like that. I'd really like that."

This time, she tore the condom open, and shuffled back onto his legs as he took his cock out of his sweatpants. He was already rock hard, and she saw the tip slick with his pre-cum. Working the condom over his dick, she took his hands, and followed his direction. As she sank down onto his cock, they both moaned. He was so hard, and even though she was a little tender, she loved the feeling of him filling her.

Sitting on his cock, she held onto his shoulders, and started to rock against him.

"Babe, do you have any idea what you're doing to me?" he asked.

"The same as what you're doing to me." She

wrapped her arms around his neck, licking his earlobe before sinking her teeth into the tender flesh. "Driving me crazy." She whispered the words against his ear, and they both moaned.

Luiz grabbed her ass, and started to lift her up and down on his dick. Pulling the skirt up to her waist, she watched them together, his cock filling her.

"Touch yourself," he said.

She slid her fingers through her slit, and like Luiz had showed her the other night, she started to stroke her clit. Staring into Luiz's eyes, she knew it was too late for her. She had fallen for this man. He was dangerous, at times annoying, but to her he meant everything, and she wouldn't have him any other way.

Regardless of what happened with Bracken, she trusted Luiz more than anything. He wouldn't do anything to hurt her. He'd protect her, just like he had done in the past.

Slamming her lips down on his, she only hoped that it would be enough for her.

****

"A security office? Is this guy for real?" Luiz asked, looking up at the building. Bracken's base was on the top floor near the roof. The only advantage to that that Luiz could see was throwing his enemies to the ground below.

"Maybe you should stay behind," Jake said.

"What? Fuck off. I'm here, and you've already taken my guns away from me. You don't have to worry about me freaking out, and you know, killing him." He didn't know how he felt about actually being here. Xander had died because of this man, and yet he was willing to work with him.

Raine hadn't spoken much to him today, even though he'd spent most of last night making love to her.

It wasn't like Raine to be silent, and he knew it had to do with him being here today.

"He's right," Donnie said. "We're here together as a team. I'm not going to worry about him trying anything. He shoots Bracken, we'll get trouble. He doesn't shoot Bracken, we could still face a great deal of trouble." Donnie shrugged. "We're here together in good faith, nothing more."

They climbed out of the car, and several guards came along with them.

Donnie held them back at the door.

"If you hear anything, we all want you to go. No questions asked. You leave, and don't look back," Donnie said.

Luiz saw that all the guards wanted to argue with him. They were loyal, and didn't believe in leaving anyone behind. Entering the main building they all walked toward the elevator.

"Zara invited you all over for pizza," Tonio said.

"Saturday?" Luiz asked.

"Yes. She's willing to do any of your toppings that you want."

"Buffalo chicken?" Donnie asked.

"Yes."

"Rock on," Jake said.

Zara used to work in a pizza shop, and had learned everything from her father. She was the master at pizza making.

Tonio didn't order takeout. He called Zara and got her to cook one for him.

"So assuming we survive, we can look forward to a weekend of food," Luiz said.

"It would be a good time to invite Bracken as well. Providing everything goes well today," Tonio said. "It was Zara's idea. She believes that food makes the world go around."

"It does," Donnie said.

The elevator pinged open, and Luiz tensed as they met a wall of guards. He didn't recognize any of them.

"Gentlemen," a man said in the center of the group.

Luiz wanted his gun, and he wanted it now. He didn't like being faced off with men who were pointing guns at him.

Four men parted, and Luiz paused when he saw the man they had revealed. Bracken was huge, well over six feet tall, and muscular. He wore a suit, and it was tight over his arms. His face was scarred, and down his neck. There were three scars across his cheek, from his ear down, and from the looks of it, one going from his forehead down. Whoever had made that, had been sure to miss his eyes.

"Wow," Jake said.

"It has been a long time since I last saw you boys," Bracken said. "I believe you were still in diapers."

"I wasn't that young," Donnie said. "I remember the rumors about you. Thought you were dead."

"I was, or at least I thought I was. A couple of the men who were loyal to me, and no one else, they helped me. They got me to the hospital, and made sure I survived."

Luiz stared at the man's face, and knew without a doubt that he had suffered, and not in a good way. This was who had sent men after Xander.

"Shall we?" Bracken asked, and pointed behind him.

"You think we're going to trust you?" Tonio asked.

"You're the ones that reached out to me. Not the other way around. I have to say I was surprised that you wanted to meet me. The Family did everything they could to get rid of me."

"In case you didn't hear, The Family has undergone a change in leadership," Luiz said.

"I heard, and I was shocked. Their own sons went after them."

"They had to be stopped," Donnie said. "No one else had the balls to do it."

"Or they weren't fucking stupid. Taking over from them requires a great deal, are you sure you're ready for that?" Bracken asked.

"Haven't you heard? We've been doing this for over five years. Believe me, we can do this, and we're going to keep on doing it," Jake said.

"I've heard a great deal, and you don't need to feel threatened by me. I have no intention of killing you." Bracken held his hand up. "Please, I have coffee waiting, and you can even test it if you like."

Luiz walked beside his friends, knowing that Bracken might look like a monster, but he wasn't one.

There were four seats near the door, with one right in front. The desk was behind the chairs.

Bracken took a seat.

Luiz wasn't the only one who was struggling to deal with the changes. Most businessmen stayed behind the desk. It was a place of power.

"I see my methods confuse you," Bracken said.

"Do you even know what you risk by talking to us?" Donnie asked.

"I risk nothing. I've been living in the same place as all The Family. You wanted to find me, and if I wanted to find you, you'd know about it."

"You came after my family," Luiz said.

Bracken turned his attention back to him. "Excuse me."

"Just over a month ago, you sent a bunch of men, and one of them belonged to Rafael." He pulled out the ID and threw it at Bracken, who caught it with ease.

Bracken glanced at it, and nothing happened to his face. No frown, nothing to give him away. Luiz stared at him, waiting.

"I lost several muscular nerves in my face. I struggle to pull facial features. That was what you were waiting for, right?"

"I'm sorry."

"Don't be. You're not the first person to struggle to read me." Bracken sighed. "I sent the men to kill someone who had made sure I looked like this. I was settling an old score. I had no intention of harming your family."

"Xander was a good man. When you knew him, he may not have been, but the last years of his life, he was a good one."

"And for that I'm sorry. Some scores need to be settled. I have nothing against you, or your family. I hope Christie and Raine can forgive me in time."

Luiz's hands fisted at his side. He didn't want to hear any more apologies.

"Why did you have some of Rafael's men?" Tonio asked.

"They were good men. They had served a man they didn't respect, and wished to make amends. I'm not above that."

"So long as you kill those that hurt you?" Luiz asked.

"I don't anticipate you agreeing with me. I know who Xander was to you. If there was any other way, I'd have wanted it to be different. He should have known that I was coming for him."

"How could he have known?" Luiz asked.

"Because he told me he'd wait for me to exact my revenge after he helped me."

They all paused.

"Wait, you're saying Xander helped you, and yet you killed him?"

"He told me to come after him, Luiz. Xander and I, we had an agreement. If he helped me, then I had to do something for him. Tit for tat. You know how it is. He said that when the time came, he would let me know what he wanted. Xander craved death more than anything. This was what he wanted. The Family, the only way to get out is with death." Bracken reached back, and handed him a piece of paper.

Luiz took it, and right there was the evidence.

"He wanted to die, Luiz," Bracken said. "Always had, but he wasn't the kind of man to point the gun at his own head. He needed someone to do that, and to pull the trigger."

Xander had done what he needed to do, and wanted Bracken to exact his revenge. His good friend had wanted to die, and begged for it. Luiz had been too preoccupied to even notice.

This changed everything.

## Chapter Eleven

"We're supposed to believe this?" Raine asked later that night, dropping the email onto the coffee table. Christie was sitting at the table doing her homework.

Sitting down next to her, Luiz pulled her into his arms. "We have no choice but to believe it. This is what Xander wanted. He'd done what he needed to do."

"And what was that?" she asked.

"I don't know if you're going to like this."

"Try me."

"He set me and you up. It's what he wanted me to realize."

"What do you mean?" she asked.

"I have feelings for you. I love you, Raine. I have for a long time, and Xander knew it. He was trying to get me to realize it myself, and of course, I did. He never told me something I didn't earn. He wanted me to earn the right to tell you that I love you."

He looked into her brown eyes, and saw that he had shocked her.

"You love me?"

"Yes, can you ever doubt it?"

She nodded. "I thought you put up with me. I'd hoped that you could one day fall for me like we talked about the other day."

"I've loved you long before now, Raine. Maybe even from the moment I saw you holding Christie, protecting her. How could I not love you? You'd give your life for me, and I would do the same for you." He cupped her face, and swallowed past the lump in his throat. "I really don't want to fuck this up."

She chuckled. "You won't."

"I'm not good with sweet words. I never grew up with having to learn to say something nice." He felt his own tears start to build inside him. Tears were a weakness, and he wasn't allowed to show any kind of weakness. He'd been beaten black and blue, tortured by his own father to learn there was no excuse for giving up. "I've got a past that I don't like. I wish you were never tainted by that shit, I swear." He pressed a kiss to her lips. "I'm not a good man. I'm a fucking monster. I've killed men and women, and I've done it for no other reason than I've been told to. I'm asking, no, I'm begging, please, Raine, don't leave me. Stay, give us a chance, and I know I can make you the happiest woman alive. I swear." Tears ran down her cheeks, and he wiped them away. "Don't cry, baby. Please don't cry."

"I never thought you'd tell me that you loved me." She smiled even as she cried. "I love you too. It's probably wrong, and I'm going to hell, but Lora told me to take care of you as well. She said that she would accept anything that happened between us."

Lora knew him even if he didn't know himself. She'd seen that he craved a life away from The Family, for someone to accept him for who he was but not to hold it against him.

"If you come home covered in blood, I will do what you need me to do with your clothes. I will wash you down, and be here if you need to talk. If you just want to hold me, I'll be here for that, and so much more. All you've got to do is ask."

"Thank you, baby." He took her lips again, sliding his tongue inside, and she melted against him. "Let's take this to the bedroom."

Raine didn't fight him as he led them into their room. He closed the door, and turned toward her.

"Do you trust me?" he asked.

"Yes."

"Will you prove it?"

The smile that danced on her lips gave him so much hope. There wasn't a chance in hell that he was ever going to let her go.

"What would you like me to do?" she asked.

He went to his drawers, and removed a blindfold. Holding it up, he let her see.

"You're into kink?" she asked.

"No, not at all. What I like is the chance to explore my woman, and with her to give herself completely over to me by wearing this. You don't take it off, and you listen to every single instruction I give you."

She ran her thumb across the fabric, and took a deep breath. Presenting him with her back, she nodded. "Yes, I trust you."

Luiz's cock was so hard at how willing she was to belong to him. He'd give her everything. All she needed to do was ask.

He placed the blindfold over her eyes dropping a kiss to her neck. "Thank you." Ever since he'd learned the truth about his friend, he'd been worried about telling Raine. They all knew Xander for the man he had become, not the man he was when he'd been ordered to do something awful. That was how they were going to remember him.

"Are you going to make this worth my while?" she asked.

"Yes." Running his hands down her front, he cupped her large tits, running his thumbs across the beaded nipples. She still had her clothes on, but he knew her body. She wanted him. "I bet your pussy is soaking wet."

Pushing his hand down the front of her jeans, he slid his fingers inside her panties, and touched her soaking wet slit. She was drenched. Thrusting two fingers inside her, he felt how tight she was, how hot and how desperate. "Do you want me to lick this sweet pussy?"

"Luiz, please."

"Who do you love?" he asked.

"You, Luiz. Always you."

He couldn't believe that by almost losing her, he finally realized how much he loved her. It was a love that had been growing for seven years, not instant. She'd been the light in his life, the love that he wanted to protect.

Pulling his hands from her pants, he licked his fingers with a moan. "So tasty."

"Luiz?"

He didn't answer. Rounding her body, he started to remove her clothes, revealing her naked body to him.

"You're so beautiful." Throwing the clothes in a pile, he removed every single layer until she stood naked before him.

"What about you?" she asked.

He moved behind her, and pressed every inch of his body against her back. "I'm already naked." It never took him long to get naked. He wanted her.

Wrapping his arm around her middle, he moved her toward the edge of the bed. He made sure she was sitting comfortably before sinking to his knees. Tilting her back until she was lying spread open, he stared down at her juicy cunt.

"Raine, I'm going to want those kids," he said.

"I want them as well, and a nice house with a garden for them to play in."

"That's what I want as well." Opening the lips of her pussy, he stared at her swollen clit. Her cunt was so slick. Sliding his tongue from her entrance up to her clit, he rounded the delicate nub, and moved down to suck her clit into his mouth.

She was perfect for him.

She tasted amazing.

Sliding his tongue down to her entrance, he plunged his tongue inside.

"Yes ... please ... Luiz."

"I've got you, baby. You don't have to worry." He grabbed her ass and ate her pussy. Luiz licked, sucked, and swallowed down her sweet cream. Running his hands up her body, he cupped her huge tits, pinching the large nipples, and giving them a little twist.

She cried out his name, and loved hearing her sounds. Eating her pussy, he focused on her clit, and after a few seconds, she called his name as her body was thrown into orgasm. He loved the sounds, and was thankful he had thick walls so they couldn't be heard.

She rode his face, and he continued to lick her pussy, refusing to release her until she hurtled into a second orgasm.

"No. No more." Seconds passed, and her demands changed. "Please, don't stop."

Flicking her clit, he felt her body go into a third orgasm, and he smiled against her pussy. She just couldn't resist him, and that was a damn good feeling.

Licking her pussy one final time, he got to his feet, taking her hand. Climbing on the bed, he moved her so that she was straddling his hips. Grabbing a condom, he tore into the packet, and rolled it over his dick. "I want to be inside you bare one day soon," he said.

"Yes. Can I take the blindfold off?" she asked.

He slapped her hands away. "Not until I'm ready."

With his cock covered with the condom, he eased her over his cock, and they both moaned as he slid inside her. She was still incredibly tight. Her cream made it easy for him to slide deep inside her until he was seated to the hilt.

Leaning forward, he took one of her nipples, unable to deny himself the taste of her. Placing his hands on her hips, he started to move her so that she rode his cock. He held her tightly, staring at her body, and watching as his cock drove inside her.

"You're so fucking beautiful," he said. "Have I told you that recently?"

"Every single day. I love you, Luiz."

"I love you, too, baby, and I'm going to make you so damn happy."

Driving deep inside her pussy, he fucked her hard. When he couldn't take anymore, he flipped them on the bed so that he was the one on top. She let out a little squeal, laughing as he remained inside her.

When he could no longer stand to not look into her eyes, he removed the blindfold, taking possession of her lips.

"I love you," he said, and kept on kissing her.

"I'm never going to get tired of hearing that."

He thrust inside her, filling her pussy, and riding her even harder.

"Touch yourself. I want to feel you coming around my dick. Give it to me, baby. Let me feel how hot you are."

Raine slid her fingers between them, and even as he rode her pussy, he felt the moment she touched her clit. Her cunt tightened around him, and he rode her harder. His own arousal was building, and at the same time that Raine started to come, he found his own release, flooding the condom.

She belonged to him, and that was the way it was going to stay.

\*\*\*\*

"Are you sure you're going to be able to handle

this?" Luiz asked as they drove in to Tonio's driveway. It was a Saturday, and they were going to enjoy the last of the sunshine as there was starting to get a chill in the air Christie was sitting in the back, really excited to be hanging out with some of her friends.

"I can handle this. Don't expect me to talk to him though. I don't want to deal with that. I still can't believe you agreed to this."

"It will be good for The Family."

"Have there been any attacks?" she asked.

"Not recently. We've upped our security, and are implementing new ways."

She nodded. Over the past couple of days Luiz had been attentive, and even though she believed his feelings for her, she couldn't help but feel a little lost. The man who had ordered their friend's death was going to be paying a visit, and she didn't know how she felt about that.

Her love for Luiz was true, and there was no denying her feelings. She loved him, and there was nothing she could do about that. Every time he came into her life, he always took a little part of her with him.

"We can head back home. I don't mind. This is asking a lot."

"It's fine. I want to hang out with the girls, and it's good for Christie. You love hanging out with everyone, don't you, sweetie?"

"Yes! Zara makes the best pizza in the world. She told me she even did one with lots of chocolate and caramel sauce. I can't wait."

Raine laughed.

"Are you sure?" Luiz asked.

"Yeah, I'm sure." She had every intention of ignoring him.

She wasn't going there to meet Bracken, or to

have anything to do with him. The last thing she cared about was having any dealings with Bracken. Xander had told her she needed to learn to live her life, and that was exactly what she was doing. She was going to live her life, and forget about all the crazy shit with The Family. When Luiz needed her support, she would give it to him.

Carrying the wrapped carrot cake, she climbed out of the car, and opened up Christie's door. Taking her hand, Raine watched as Luiz took her other, and they made their way toward the front door.

Tonio answered with George on his hip, and hugged his friend. "It's so good of you guys to come."

"Hey, Christie," Darla said.

Before long, they were out in the backyard. Raine had a glass of wine, which Paige handed to her.

"Thank you."

"How are things with you and Luiz?" Zara asked.

"It's good." Raine took a sip of her wine. "He told me that he loved me."

Paige and Zara smiled.

Zara spoke first. "How do you feel?"

"Good. Happy. Good."

"We know about Bracken," Paige said. "I asked Donnie what he thought, and he said that he couldn't find fault with him. He's a good man, Raine."

"So was Xander. We have to deal with the problems thrown our way, and this is just another big problem, and I'll get over it. There's nothing else I can do." She sipped at her wine, and watched as her man talked with his friends. She noticed Charlene was sitting on the ground with the kids, building sandcastles.

"It's such a shame she doesn't want Jake, you know. He'd be so good to her," Zara said.

Jake still looked at Charlene with such longing. It was a shame to see, but they hoped he'd find someone else.

The sound of the door going again made Raine tense. Zara placed a hand on her arm, and she knew without a doubt that Bracken was going to be there.

Tonio and Zara both left. "Are you okay?" Paige asked.

"Peachy. I need to use the bathroom. Is it okay if I go?"

"Yeah. I'll let everyone know."

Raine didn't wait around, and made her way straight to the toilet. She locked the door, and went over to the sink to grab the counter.

"You can do this, Raine. It's fine."

Accepting Luiz's love had been easy to do. She loved him. There was no doubt for her when it came to her feelings.

"I wish you were here, Xander. You'd be able to give me some advice." Even as she spoke to the empty sink, she knew he'd be having a go at her. He'd be telling her how strong she was, and that she needed to learn to see past the current problem to the solution below.

There was a knock on the door. "Who is it?" she asked.

"It's me, Raine. Will you let me in?" Luiz's voice was clear.

Releasing a breath, she made her way over to the door, and flicked it open. "I'm not going to do anything crazy. I just needed a minute."

Luiz entered the bathroom, and closed the door. "Talk to me, babe."

"I'm just having a moment. Gathering my composure. Am I allowed to do that?" she asked.

"You know you are."

She nodded. "I'm sorry. I don't mean to sound like a bitch. It's just tough, you know?"

"I know it is."

"Is he down there?" she asked.

"He is, and he's brought a couple of guests as well. Everything will be fine." Luiz held her arms, rubbing up and down. "Do you trust me?"

"You know I do. Without a doubt. It's ... Xander wanted to die."

"I know."

"That's what I'm having a hard time seeing. He loved life, Luiz."

"What I've come to know about Xander is I never really knew him. He was always happy telling me one thing, while doing another. He wasn't a simple guy, babe. There were many parts to him, and some of them I never even found out myself."

"I miss him."

"I know. I miss him, too." Luiz pulled her into his arms, and she breathed a sigh of relief when his lips brushed across her neck. "This isn't easy. It's hard. Every time I look at him I think of Xander. Of the way he was with you, and how he always had something to say no matter what."

"He wouldn't want me to hide."

"No. He wouldn't."

With their hands locked together, they made their way downstairs toward the backyard. She saw several men and women were there. None of them she recognized, but she spotted Christie first. There was a girl that looked about Christie's age, and they were chatting animatedly.

"Bracken has a wife. A family. You see the woman by his side?" Luiz asked.

"Yes."

"That's Tulip, his wife." The woman was beautiful. Long blonde hair, blue eyes, and a curvy figure. She was dressed in a long shirt that was designed to cover her swollen stomach. Even from where Raine stood, she saw the smile in the woman's eyes, and from the looks of everyone, she was kind.

"I had no idea that he was married," she said.

"Neither did we. By bringing his family here, he's showing us that he trusts us. When he worked for The Family, he never brought any of his family to see us. This is a big show of trust for everyone."

"That must be nice."

"It's nice not to have to worry about everything all the time. I want a place for you, Christie, and any children we have to be safe."

"I have every faith in you."

When they couldn't stay back any longer, Luiz took her forward for the introductions. Staring at the man who had ordered the kill on Xander was hard. Being forced to be polite and shake his hand was even harder. What she hated even more was how damn nice Tulip was, and her kids.

Tulip and Bracken weren't a recent couple. They had a twenty-one-year-old daughter, Emily.

With everyone playing nice, Raine took a seat at the edge of the garden, watching.

Movement behind her made her look to see Reese Turner, one of the guards, the one with the scarred face.

"Are you hungry, Reese?" she asked. Whenever she saw him around the apartment block she would take him coffee or some food, talk with him for a few minutes.

"No. I've already eaten. Zara's pizzas are legendary. How are you holding up?"

"Fine. I guess. Do you know who Bracken is?" she asked.

"Even to this day his reputation precedes him.

What happened to him was awful, and I for one am glad I didn't participate. Look what they did to his face, not to mention his body."

She swallowed the lump in her throat, and nodded. "It is awful."

Raine found herself staring at Bracken, wondering if she could ever find it in her heart to forgive him. He was part of The Family. She saw that now more than ever. There was no way she could kill him, or even convince Luiz to do it. In the past couple of months, or over the past few years, she had realized the importance of The Family, and why it needed to change. Luiz, Donnie, Tonio, and Jake, they were four men that had grown up in this life. They knew no different, and they believed in being fair. She had to trust in that.

****

Jake grabbed a bottle of soda out of the fridge and opened it up.

"Hey, I don't suppose you could tell me where the toilet is, do you?"

He lowered the can to see Emily, Bracken's daughter, standing in the doorway.

"Yeah, first floor on the right. You can't miss it."

Emily smiled. "Thank you." She turned away, turned back, and hesitated.

"What?" he asked.

"You're not one for pleasantries I see."

"Don't really have time for them."

"And you don't want to waste them on a man's daughter?" she asked.

Jake shrugged. "What do you want?"

She folded her arms. "You're the children of the monsters who ordered that done to his face, right?"

Jake gripped his soda can until it squashed sending liquid all over his hand. "What's your point?"

"I don't think he should trust you. He got hurt by you guys before, and it's in your blood to betray."

"Look, little girl, you think you know what you're talking about? You're wrong. None of us ordered that attack on your father. You can believe me or not, but we've gone through fucking hell and back to make sure no one suffers like he did, or anyone within The Family. So watch your tongue. Those men out there, they're my family. My brothers. Don't you dare insult them."

Emily paled. "I'm sorry."

"You should be." He moved away from her, and as he got to the door, he looked back to find her staring right back at him.

*Interesting.*

## Chapter Twelve

*Three months later*

Raine had been able to avoid any more Bracken meet-ups. Xander's ashes were still in the urn, and now she was looking into her future. Christie had settled into her new school, and cleaning the apartment every single day wasn't what she wanted to be doing for the next fifty years, so she grabbed Luiz's laptop, and just went ahead, and started on researching what to do with her life.

College was out of the question. She doubted she had what it actually took to stick with college. She loved being at home, cooking and baking, helping Christie out. There was something more she wanted to do. Christmas was just around the corner, and to get herself out there, she decided to take a small evening class three times a week in culinary school.

The local college had several classes, and she was working her way through them until she found something that suited her.

Other than Bracken, and her inability to know what to do next with her life, everything was perfect. Luiz was … amazing. He was the perfect guy, minus the job where he carried a gun and killed people.

He opened up to her about absolutely everything, so she knew that he wasn't always happy with doing what he did. It was his job, nothing more.

One December night, it was snowing quite badly, and she didn't want to call Luiz to pick her up, so she walked the few miles home. Her teacher had let them all out early so there was less risk with half of the class driving home. The entire city was aglow for Christmas, looking breathtakingly beautiful.

Putting in her earbuds, she wrapped her jacket

around her, and speed walked all the way to the apartment block.

She rushed in, giving Reese a wave as she always did and ran to the elevator. "Hold it, please," she said, rushing on.

Her hands were numb, as were her cheeks. She turned to say thank you only to freeze. There, by her side, stood Bracken.

"Oh," she said.

She was about to get off the elevator when it started moving up.

"Hello, Raine," he said.

His voice was incredibly deep, and scary. She nodded, and it was hard for her not to look at him, as their reflections could be easily seen in the doors. Closing her eyes, she wondered if anyone was actually looking down on her. Her music had died, the device running out of batteries. Now she was on an elevator, which suddenly stopped.

She frowned, looking at the buttons to see them all flashing.

"That's not good." Bracken reached out, tapping the buttons.

When that didn't work, he hit the console, and again, nothing happened.

"Stop hitting it. You'll break it." She grabbed his arm, and pulled him away. Going to the emergency phone, she dialed the front desk. "Hi, Reese," she said.

"We've already put a call out to come and help you."

"Does Luiz know I'm here?"

"Yes, and he's pissed. I've got you on the camera, you and Bracken."

Not that it would do any good. If Bracken wanted to murder her, he could do it easily now.

"Do you want to talk to them?" she asked.

He took the phone from her, and she took a seat in the corner of the elevator, and decided to just relax and wait.

"It's not like we can do a great deal, is it?" Bracken asked. Seconds later he slammed the phone down. She opened one eye to see him take a seat in the opposite corner. "Well, it looks like you can't avoid me anymore."

She glared at him and didn't say anything.

"You're going to remain silent the entire time."

Again, she ignored him.

Seconds passed, and when she was able to feel her fingers, she removed the gloves, followed by the scarf.

"I didn't ask for this," Bracken said.

She opened her eyes, and looked at him. "What?"

He pointed at his face. "Working for The Family was a great honor to me. I enjoyed it. I knew I could get men to be better."

"The very men you helped to save, ruined you."

"They didn't ruin me. I had loyal men, and they helped me to escape. Even Xander helped me, but he wanted something from me."

"And yet you still killed him." She stared at him, seeing the monster that he was, and yet, his eyes, they held a pain she had never even seen before. "Did you want to kill him?"

"No. I taught Xander. We used to train everyone together. We were the top dogs. Expendable to a point, but we knew who a snitch was from a good, hard-working soldier. We both knew a change was coming, and that we'd have to be expelled, eliminated. We posed a threat for our beliefs."

"What do you mean?" she asked.

"There are two types of soldiers in my mind. There's the type that will shoot first, ask questions later. Then there is one who will reason, who will do everything before blood is spilt."

"Which one were you?"

"I was the latter. I didn't believe violence was always the key, but the boys' parents, they believed that fear was the answer. Once you are feared, you will remain in power, ruling over the few."

"You didn't agree with that?" she asked.

"No. I'm of the great belief that you can reason with nearly everyone. There's some blood that has to be spilt. It always does. I was starting to become a problem because I wouldn't just start shooting. I'd wait. Bide my time. See what else there was to be done."

"They didn't like it."

"No, they didn't."

"So what happened for Xander? Why did you target him if he was one of the men that helped you?" she asked.

"When I came to, he was there, and he told me. He told me that he was disgusted with himself, and he didn't know why he didn't just pull the trigger and end my misery rather than add to it. Xander was ... broken before the attack, but this just took him over the edge."

"Would you want him to end your misery?" she asked.

Bracken shook his head. "No matter what was done to my body, I couldn't do that to Tulip. She is the light of my life."

She smiled, thinking of Luiz. "I know what you mean."

"The memory of her. That kept me safe."

"Xander gave me the gun, and told me to kill him. He told me to end his life, and I refused. I wasn't going to help him like that. So, we had an agreement. Xander helped me, and in return, in years to come, he was going to ask me for a favor, and I would have no choice but to do as he asked. He knew even then that the only person capable of having him killed was me. Xander was damn good at hiding, but he also knew that I wasn't going to kill him myself, and he wasn't going to force me that day, after everything."

"I know. He taught me everything I know, but I also know that Xander was a man who struggled at times."

Bracken nodded. "I got a call a week before, and he told me it was time. I asked him why now? Why not just live? I didn't want to kill him, and I could hear the happiness in his voice. I was over what had happened, and he needed to do the same."

Tears filled her eyes. "What did he say?"

"He told me that no matter how happy he was, he couldn't stop the darkness. It was his time to go. He'd done what he needed and that was to bring two people together. I had no idea you were there, Raine. I didn't want to do it, but a deal's a deal. Xander and I, we had an agreement, and I don't care if others understand it. It's between the two of us."

"You've killed the other men who hurt you?" she asked.

"Yes. The men who helped me, I spared. Killing Xander went against everything that I believe. I hope in time that you can forgive me, but I understand why you don't. Why you won't even talk with my wife."

The moment Tulip arrived at Paige or Zara's house, Raine always found an excuse to leave.

"Tulip, she's everything that is good. She's pure in so many things, and all I ask is you don't blame her for my shame."

Raine wiped away the tears that were sliding down her cheeks. "You certainly have a way with words."

"I would do anything to make this easier for you, Raine. I accept that I've hurt you. Every time I look at you, and at Luiz, I know I took someone dear to you. I can handle that pain. Don't do it to my wife. We want to make this work for all of us. I believe I can help make The Family great again, just like your man does. We can work together as a team."

Tears slid down her cheeks, and she released a little breath.

"I know this is going to sound weird, but I don't suppose I can give you a hug right now?" she asked.

"Even with this face?" he asked.

"Xander had a lot of scars. They mean nothing to me." He opened his arms, and she moved toward him, and sank against him. She knew Xander, knew him better than he even realized. Everything that Bracken said was the truth.

"Does this mean I'm forgiven?" he asked.

"Yes. It's hard. I'm not going to lie. I wanted to kill you. I hated that they were going to partner with you, but ... he taught me better than to act with the gun first." He'd trained her to keep an open mind, and she wasn't going to dishonor Xander's memory by going against his most fundamental teachings.

"Thank you, Raine. It means a lot to me."

She nodded.

"I hate to say this to you, but, erm, I really hate tight, closed spaces, and I'm struggling to keep it together," he said.

Raine looked up at him, and saw his brow was covered in perspiration. "You're not joking?"

"Nope. It's one fear I was never able to conquer."

He was breathing deeply.

"I think you're incredibly brave," she said. "Tell me about Tulip, and your kids."

She distracted him, helping him, and the situation was entirely surreal to her. For the next hour she listened to the love he had for his family, and knew in her heart that Xander would be proud of her. This would be what he wanted from her.

After two hours, they finally got out of the elevator. Luiz was there with Christie, as was the rest of The Family.

Going into Luiz's waiting arms, she enjoyed his warmth.

"Do I have to be worried?" he asked.

"No. Were you?"

"A little. I know how damn hot you are. Why didn't you call me to come and pick you up?" he asked.

Christie was asleep against his chest. She stroked a hand down their girl's back, and smiled. "I didn't want her to get worse."

She took another deep breath, and turned toward Tulip. "I was wondering if you and your family would like to come to our place tomorrow for dinner."

Tulip looked so damn happy, and nodded. "I'd love that."

It was the start of the future, and that was what she wanted to do.

\*\*\*\*

"What if she says no?" Charlene asked.

Luiz glared at her. "Whose side are you on?"

"Well, I don't know. Raine's side. You're asking her to marry you. Shouldn't you know she's going to say yes?"

"I'm hoping she'll love me enough to say yes."

"Oh, so you don't know?" Charlene asked.

"Stopping being mean," Tulip said. She carried out the plates. They were having dinner in Donnie and Paige's house. The tree was in the corner surrounded by presents. This year was going to be pretty special for him. He didn't have to worry about splitting his Christmas down between his friends and his family. They could all be together.

"Reese is bringing her and Christie. They had to pick up a couple of gifts," Paige said, entering the kitchen. She had given birth two weeks ago to a little boy, called Donnie Junior.

Luiz was really happy for his friends.

His hands were shaking as he looked down at the engagement ring.

"She'll say yes," Bracken said.

"How do you know?"

"She loves you, doesn't she? She gave up her whole life for you and Christie. Raine's a strong woman, and she doesn't strike me as the kind to do something like that unless she loved them." Bracken patted his shoulder. "Are you ready to be married?"

Luiz was more than ready. He wanted to bind Raine to him so that he didn't have to worry about her hiding from him. He was aware of Xander's skill. His friend had taught Raine everything he knew, and now it was up to Luiz to keep her by his side. The more he thought about it, the more he was sure that Xander had done it on purpose. Luiz had never have been one that liked things to come to him easily. He had always appreciated something that he had to work for.

"Yeah, I am."

The front door opened, and Luiz made his way toward her, and toward his future.

"Wow, that is so damn cold." Raine removed her jacket, and she stood beside Reese. The moment she caught sight of Luiz, she smiled. "Do you want to feel how cold I am?" she asked.

She placed her hands on his cheeks, and Luiz knew this was the perfect time.

Sinking to one knee, he held out the black velvet box.

"That wasn't what you practiced," Donnie said.

"Marry me, Raine. Please?" He held the box open, and she smiled. Behind her back, she held out another box.

"I'll marry you, if you marry me? What do you say?" she asked, going to one knee before him.

"You bought me a ring?"

"I figured if I left it to you, I might not get married until my thirties, and then my early forties before kids. I wanted to speed it along. Of course I'd marry you." She took the ring out of the box, and they placed their rings on their fingers.

Raine flung herself at him, wrapping her arms around his neck.

With their family and friends around them, he kissed Raine's mouth, thankful that she had never given up on him. She had made him the happiest man in the world, and he didn't care how clichéd it was.

## Epilogue

"Are you ready for this?" Raine asked.

"Yes. It's what he would have wanted, and keeping him on our shelf wouldn't have been it," Luiz said. He held the urn as he looked out of the ocean. They had taken a journey on a small ferry. He'd paid so that he and Raine were the only two there.

Christie was at school.

She was too young, and he didn't want this to touch her.

"Do you want to say anything?" he asked.

"Xander, I hope you find the peace that you've been craving all your life. I'll always remember you, and I'll always think of you. You'll never be forgotten," she said.

"Old man, there were times I wanted to kill you myself. You would always challenge me, always question me. You were just trying to make me a better man, and for that, I'll always be grateful. You gave me everything I was searching for. I hope that in the time that I knew you, I gave you something you always wanted." Luiz finished, and he swallowed away his own tears. Upending the urn, he watched as the ashes fell to the water.

Holding Raine's hand, they watched his ashes until there was nothing more to see. Pulling Raine into his arms, he held her tightly as the ferry took them back to land.

"I hate goodbyes," she said.

"This is going to be our last one," he said.

"I know. Tulip was telling me something the other day, and I don't know if I should believe it or not."

"What was it?" he asked.

"Bracken wants to bind our families tighter?"

"Yes, he does. We've had some ... complications."

"What kind?"

"A couple of our offices have been attacked, and stolen from. Bracken believes that if we bind our names together, we'll unite, and show the world that our partnership is not just rumors."

"How are you going to do that?" she asked.

"Emily and Jake."

She gasped. "Seriously?"

"They're the only two where it would be work. It's not like Bracken can marry anyone, nor me, Tonio, and Donnie. It leaves Jake, and seeing as he's one of us, it would bind us all together."

"Is he happy to do that?" she asked.

Luiz kissed her lips, and he smiled down at her. "I don't know if he's happy."

"It's one way of him getting over Charlene."

"A drastic way. One girl for another."

"Do you think Emily will like it?"

Luiz shrugged. "I don't know. I want to focus on us, no one else right now. We'll handle any problems in the future."

"Okay, husband, what do you want to do for the next fifty years?" she asked.

"I don't know about fifty years, but I want us to go and try that new mattress I brought. What do you say?"

"Take me home," she said, snuggling back against him.

\*\*\*\*

"No. No. No. Absolutely not. No! I don't know how many different ways I can tell you no, but no!" Emily folded her arms, and Jake smirked.

"You think I want this, princess?" he asked.

"Think about this, Emily."

"I don't even like him."

"It's not about like. It's about need. Sacrifices need to be made."

"And your oldest daughter is that sacrifice?" she asked.

"It's a need, sweetie, and I need you to do this for me," Bracken said.

Jake didn't want to get married. He didn't want to settle for someone who wasn't Charlene. Everyone told him he'd get over Charlene if he gave another woman a chance. He didn't believe them, and he still didn't. It was a waste of time to him.

Emily folded her arms, and looked damn sad.

He didn't like how it struck him. The last thing he wanted to see was her sad. "Is there someone else I can marry?" she asked. "He always looks moody."

"I'm afraid not, princess," Jake said. "It's me, or no one."

"I'd take no one!"

"Then me it is," Jake said.

He grabbed the ring he had, and slid it on her finger.

Emily glared at him, and he clapped his hands. The priest was there ready. There was no time to wait.

He was about to have a bride who hated him.

His happy ending wasn't ever going to happen. At least he was taking someone with him to hell.

Glancing at Emily, he wondered if she'd take him to heaven. She glared at him.

He was going straight to hell.

## The End

# SAM CRESCENT

# DEDICATION

I want to say a big thank you to all of my readers for your patience. Writing this series has been a pleasure, and even though I didn't want it to end, I'm pleased I've been able to follow this journey through.

Thank you all so much,

Sam

# SAM CRESCENT

# OUR WAR

## *The Family, 4*

### Sam Crescent

### Copyright © 2017

### Prologue

"There is no way I'm marrying a stranger!" Emily Bracken folded her arms and glared at her father and her mother. The great Francis and Tulip Bracken were not going to marry her off to some Family member. *Hell no.*

"Honey—"

"No, Mom." She looked toward her father, the feared and trusted leader who had been taken down, destroyed, ruined almost. If it wasn't for her mother, she knew she wouldn't have been born. Her father Francis Bracken would have died a slow and painful death. Her mother, against all odds, had taken him in, saved him, protected him, loved him, and now they were one big happy family.

A family who also had their share of wealth, of loyalty, and owning the half of the city that The Family didn't have. People followed Bracken because they loved him. He was fair, and others were not.

Tears filled her eyes as she stared at her father. "You promised me that I would never be married off."

"Emily."

She shook her head. "You're marrying me to Jake. Part of The Family. He's a damn soldier."

"He's one of the heads of The Family now, princess."

"No, you don't get to call me princess. You're selling me like a fucking cow!"

"Don't be so dramatic," Tulip, her mother said. "This is going to be good for you."

"I thought you told me that you would never make girls feel any less than boys."

"Baby girl, I'm not selling you to anyone. We're bringing our families together so no war has to happen. Jake is a good looking young man. He will look after you. He will take care of you, and in time, I do believe he will love you."

Emily laughed. "He loves that other woman. The one that likes other women. This is … I'm going to be miserable."

She turned her back on her parents, and stared out of the window. All of her life she had been fascinated by love, of falling for someone who would like her bigger figure. She was a fuller woman, and dieting had never worked for her.

There had been many hours where she had daydreamed about a man walking into a room while loads of other slender beautiful woman stared at him. He would look at her, and he'd kiss her, and everything else would fade away.

Yes, she was used to being overlooked all the time. It sucked. She had even heard some of his guards refer to her as "the chubby Bracken". Mortification was her middle name, or it would be with the way her life was going.

Now she was being forced to marry a man who probably couldn't stand her, and was doing it because he'd been told to. No, not told to. He was the only free agent of the four Family members. The group of four men, boys really, who had taken their fathers' places, killing them, and leading a new age of mafia. That's what they were, mafia royalty, and she hated them.

Jake had already told her that he didn't want to marry her. This was her continuing this conversation with her parents in the privacy of their own home.

"I think you have a chance of making Jake very happy. You're a beautiful couple."

She closed her eyes, and knew in her heart that no matter what she said, nothing would change. Her fate was sealed by men, and she would be ruled by men.

Her dream of falling in love, of being with someone who would love her, had crumbled into nothingness. All the books she had read ceased to be anything more than fairy tales.

*Fine.* If they wanted her to marry Jake, then she would marry him. But he better be prepared for a very bitchy bride, because she wasn't going to make this easy on anyone, least of all Jake.

## Chapter One

"This cements a new future for everyone," Donnie, his friend, said.

Jake looked at his three best friends and smiled. "You think you're going to pep talk me on my wedding day?"

"It's the least we can do," Luiz said.

"This is not happening. Not today. I'm the girl in this arrangement. Being married off as if I'm nothing more than cattle. I thought we were over that?" Jake asked, running his hands down his tuxedo jacket.

He looked fantastic. Just staring in the mirror, he knew he looked good, but then, a tuxedo could make anyone look good, and today was his wedding day. He was marrying a woman he'd barely spoken to, and from the looks she had given him, she hated his guts.

Well that was more than fine for him. He didn't like her much either, and he had a lot of other things to look forward to, like controlling his element of The Family, which included the soldiers that worked for him, along with the drugs that they helped to distribute. He hated every single part of the drugs, but he was in control, which meant he could focus on where that shit went.

"This will be the only time that we use a marriage to join forces," Donnie said.

"You can't promise that. This is a sad day for all of us. We are going back on our word," Tonio said.

"This is for the good of The Family. Emily, you'll treat her right?" Luiz asked.

Jake stared at his three friends and frowned. "I'm not a monster. I'm not going to hurt this woman, not at all. I won't even touch her."

"You know this marriage needs to be real. It has

to be for this to work," Donnie said.

"I'm not going to force a woman to bed me. I'll wait, and in time, we'll fuck, but until then, you need to back off. I'm doing what I need to do for The Family."

Donnie sighed. "We are better than our fathers. They didn't put The Family first. They just sold women for their own purpose."

"Are we not doing the same with Emily Bracken? It would benefit us all to be united, I get that. It's a shame that we couldn't just have deals that we kept, promises made, and all that stuff," Jake said. He looked away from the mirror and at his friends. "It doesn't matter how much we pretty this up. We're fucked either way. We broke our own code, our own ethics with this. Let's make sure we don't break any more."

He wasn't going to be mean to his wife.

"Is this about Charlene?" Donnie asked.

Jake smiled. "I'm over Charlene. She's happy, Donnie. I've moved on." He wasn't lying either. There had been a time he'd wanted to have that woman as his own, but he wasn't prepared to fight other pussy for that pleasure.

She hated men, and they had remained friends. In the beginning, he'd been hurt by her decision to be with women, but he couldn't change it. It was strange, but as time had gone by, and he'd seen how happy she was, that hurt had changed into acceptance, and now he was happy for her. His friends believed he was hurting, and wanting a woman he couldn't have, which was no longer the case. He'd gotten over it. His issues the past few months had been because he saw the reality of what they were doing. They couldn't change the world that their fathers created. There was no way to do what they always wanted, to walk away. There was no way for that, but what they could do was adapt, and slowly change the way they lived from within the core themselves. They handled everything, and they stayed on top of it all. They stopped the abuse, the sex trafficking, and their businesses were slowly changing as well.

Their fathers had been like an infection that needed to be gotten rid of.

There was a knock on the door. Luiz went to answer it, and Jake took a sip of his scotch. His wedding day, and he was drinking.

"I'd like to speak to Jake, please." Emily's voice had him turning toward the door. He couldn't see her as his three friends had all covered the door.

"It's bad luck for the groom to see the bride before the wedding," Donnie said.

"I don't care. This is not a real marriage. Jake, I need to talk to you."

"Let her in," Jake said. His three friends looked at him. "What? She knows this marriage isn't really real." He shrugged. "Let her in." He had no intention of lying to her, or being someone different, not even for her.

She entered the room, and he was completely shocked. Emily had long, blonde hair, sparkling blue eyes, and a figure that was so much fucking temptation. The wedding dress she wore molded to every single one of her lush curves, and it tempted him. His cock thickened, even though he didn't want to be attracted to his blushing bride.

He saw she was breathing heavily, and her tits pressed against the top of her bodice threatening to spill over, flashing the entire room.

"I want to be alone with her," he said, looking at his friends.

Donnie gave him a look, which he returned. After a few seconds, the door closed and they were alone. He held up his glass of whiskey. "You want one?"

She shook her head. "No, I don't."

Her blonde hair had little purple flowers within the tresses. He couldn't stop looking at her, and his dick was refusing to do as it was told.

"I don't want to be married to you."

"I know. I don't want to get married to you, but it'll be good for our families."

"I don't care about our families."

"That's rather selfish. I didn't have you pegged as being that kind of woman," he said, taking a sip of his whiskey. "Let's face it, without our union, the chances of war are higher."

"I don't believe it. You're all grown men. There's a way for you to have what you want, and my father the same."

Jake tusked. "You're wrong about that. You see, we have a bunch of people working for us, and whenever they are thirsty for blood, they will conspire, and before long retaliation after retaliation, it's inevitable for bloodshed."

"And you think marrying will stop that?"

"No, it doesn't stop that, but what it does is create a unity. We know that Bracken wants peace, and he knows we want peace. Unity of marriage works, and it's also good business."

She stepped up close to him, and the floral scent coming from her was highly arousing. She took the glass from him and gulped down the remaining liquid. He was impressed as she didn't cough or react like a stupid girl drinking for the first time. He found that rather interesting.

"So I'm a business deal."

"Think about it, you're going to be part of making sure there is no bloodshed. It's a pretty decent deal."

Emily handed him back the glass. "I don't want you to touch me. I don't want to sleep with you."

"Babe, believe me when we get to a bed, sleeping is going to be the last thing on my mind."

"So you're not above rape, then?"

He frowned and handed her back another glass of whiskey. "I'm not going to rape you. When we fuck, and we will, you're going to love every single second of it."

"Your ego knows no bounds."

Jake took the glass from her. Capturing her hand, he held her close. Taking a long swig, he swallowed down the burning liquid and stared into her eyes. "Think about it, princess. We're going to be alone, together, for a very long time. Close in ways very few couples are. I'm going to be open and honest with you. It's only going to be a matter of time before you look at me and wonder exactly how good I'll feel sliding into your tight pussy."

There was a spark in her eyes. He saw it and knew she was feeling something by being this close to him.

"I hate you."

"Good. It's a good feeling to have. I heard that angry sex is better than loving sex. Hate me all you want. Us two fucking is inevitable."

\*\*\*\*

That was it. Emily was now bound to this man without any way of getting out of it. She hated him and his assumptions. What she hated even more, was her body had betrayed her. The moment Jake had gotten close to her, it was like everything else had faded away into nothingness.

The priest had pronounced them husband and wife. Jake had pulled her into his arms, and as he kissed her, she had only heard the ominous sound of drumbeats.

Her heart was pounding against her chest as she waited for the kiss to be over. Closing her eyes, she hated that a part of her heart melted at that kiss. Twenty-one years old and it was the first time she'd been kissed.

It was stupid being a virgin at this age, but that was exactly what she was and not for lack of trying either. Having Francis Bracken as a father showed her the kind of men who were interested in her. None of them stuck around once they saw her father and was handed the threat that most fathers give. The only difference between her father compared to every other was he *would* shoot a guy in the head.

*Jake didn't back down!*

After photographs where everything had been elaborate and boring, they had been pushed into a waiting limo where she had to travel with Jake. Neither of them said a word. The hotel where the reception was being held was beautiful, and everything looked like it should be out of a magazine it was that perfect.

Within thirty minutes everyone had arrived and wished her congratulations. The moment she could, she made her escape and stood off to the side, alone, like always. These kinds of functions she never fit in, always unable to pretend to the fake bastards that she liked them.

Glancing around the room, she saw that Jake was looking at her. For a split second she held his gaze, and then forced herself to look away. He was an interesting man, and to her that meant a deadly one. Unlike his other three friends, Jake had come from a soldier, or in common speak, a minion. Not that his title or anything like that mattered to her. She didn't care about a person's title, or where they were in their mafia food chain.

Emily was nice to everyone and was even on speaking terms with one of the family's bodyguards, Beau. He was a married man and loyal to her father.

While she was growing up Beau would often sneak her treats, and he was just kind. Kindness within their world was something to marvel at.

"Come, dance with me," Jake said, pulling her out of her thoughts. He took hold of her hands, and she saw everyone was staring at them.

"You're causing a scene."

"I'm not. You will be if you don't dance with me."

"I don't want to dance with you."

"It's our wedding day, Emily. Stop being a pain in the ass. This is all for you." They got into the center of the room, and he tugged her the final few inches. His hand landed on her back at the base.

"What do you mean this is all for me? I didn't plan any of this."

"You didn't?" he asked.

She shook her head. "I was ordered about how my future was going to play out. I had no say in the flowers, the location, the dress."

"What would you change?" he asked.

Emily frowned and knew she couldn't say anything, and he smirked.

"You wouldn't change a thing, would you? You're just being difficult on purpose."

"I'm not being difficult at all. Everything is beautiful. I guess I just wished I felt more than hate for my partner."

"Oh please, you and I both know you fancy me. You want to fuck me, and we are going to do that. Have lots of sex, make beautiful babies."

"We're not having kids." She was twenty-one, and there was no way a baby was leaving her body. "Also, I'm a virgin, so you can keep your disease-riddled cock to yourself."

"I have to say, Emily, I rather love that smart mouth of yours. It makes me think of doing other more sinful things with it."

"You're crass, rude, and I really don't want to be having this conversation with you." She went to pull away, but Jake was too strong. He held her firmly in place.

"This is our wedding dance, and you will have this dance."

She rolled her eyes. "There is nothing normal about our arrangement. I guess you're going to have a lot of mistresses, right? Cheat on me every chance you get."

He sighed. "Actually, no."

The frown was back. "No?"

"You can believe me or not, Emily. We have an attraction. We don't like each other, nor do we like our circumstances. However, we have both made those sacrifices for the greater good in the name of family." She wanted to snort. "I intend to honor my vows to you. I will be faithful to you, as I expect you be to me. The only dick you will know is mine. I intend to fuck you often and everywhere."

"Even though you don't like me."

"Our arrangement is not the best, but why spend the next fifty plus years wasting a chance here? Tell me you're not soaking wet for me? That you're not wondering what it would be like with the two of us?"

Her throat had gone completely dry. She had no words to say to him, and he knew it.

"I'm offering you everything."

"But love."

"Love is an overrated emotion. Now, if you would like we can go to hating each other and spending every single moment wishing we were elsewhere. Or we can form a truce."

"A truce?"

"One that gives us both pleasure and makes this situation easier."

"Do you think that is even possible?"

"Anything is possible. I don't want to lose you, and I refuse to spend the rest of my life hating it and you. Unless of course you're a bitch, but I've got a feeling you're not."

She gritted her teeth and refused to tell him a thing.

"You can hate me all you want. The truth is the truth, and I checked you out."

"You had me investigated?"

"Of course, I did. Why wouldn't I? I was about to marry a woman I knew nothing about, but I think I know enough now. You help the homeless even though your father hates you doing it. You also have a thing for abandoned pets, and you're always trying to save them. You don't work, but your charity work keeps you busy. I was surprised to find that you weren't some pampered princess."

"I do not need your approval."

"Fine by me. You're not getting it. I've got a shitload of work to get through. I don't want to think about my lonely wife waiting at home. You won't be fucking anyone else but me, just so you know."

She rolled her eyes. "This is messed up. You have to admit this is messed up. I didn't want to get married."

"I didn't want to be part of The Family that sold its women to the highest bidder. I watched that happen, and I know it nearly destroyed my friend. I have no intention of letting our children be auctioned off. This is a business deal, and even though neither of us like it, we can make this work," Jake said.

The music came to a stop, and he took her hand,

pressing a kiss to her knuckles. Part of her wanted to tear her hand away and glare at him. What use would that be? Besides the fact it would make a scene, he was offering her a chance to actually be happy.

She nodded at him and removed her hand, leaving the dancefloor. Smiling at their guests, she left the hotel's main room, and rushed out, going toward the street. Holding onto the wall at the side of the hotel, she pressed a hand to her stomach. She felt sick, scared, tired, and she didn't have the first clue what she was going to do.

The choices had been taken from her. This was all her father's instruction of what he wanted from her. It wasn't fair. She hated it and wished there was a way to fight back.

"Baby," her mother said, coming up behind her.

Tulip rubbed her arms, trying to offer her comfort. "I know you're not happy right now, and for that I'm sorry."

"Mom, don't. You married Dad because you loved him. I don't even like that man in there, and yet I'm married to him. Bound to this stupid relationship, and I'm scared." She would never admit her feelings to anyone else but her mother.

"Jake's a good man, Emily. Your father loves you, and he wouldn't have done this with just anyone. I promise you. We're going to keep an eye on you. Nothing bad will happen. You never know, maybe you will fall in love with Jake."

"Yeah, and hell will freeze over."

## Chapter Two

"Stop looking at me as if I'm going to pounce on you. It's not going to happen. I don't believe in rape, and I'm getting tired of telling you," Jake said, glancing over his cards to stare at her.

"This is not exactly how I imagined my wedding night."

"Me neither, but then we can't be too choosy about what we do. Neither of us has that power." He picked up the card, saw it was a jack instead of a king, and put it down. "Your father has told me that we're going to be honeymooning on his island."

"What?"

"Yes. It's a rare treat, or so I've been told. Something for us both to enjoy. We'll be in the middle of nowhere, surrounded by vast oceans, beautiful views, and a beach house where we can get to know each other."

"Yay."

"I was about as thrilled as you were. Still, everything is arranged so we can go tomorrow."

"Did my dad threaten you?"

"No. He merely told me that a man takes charge of his future and his happiness. We want this to work, so we are going to do just that, make it work." He looked at Emily as she bit the corner of her lip. The pins holding up her blonde tresses had been removed, and she looked every inch the beautiful bride. She looked more like she was the kind to run away. He was sure if Tulip hadn't gone outside when she had, there was a chance Emily would have run. No matter, he'd have followed her anyway. There were times when he had been trained by his father, and learned the stuff about The Family that he had wanted to run and hide.

Tonio, Donnie, and Luiz all kept him sane.

"We're going?"

"Yes, we're going. It'll be good. Your mother has already packed you a bag, and it would be totally rude not to go."

"You care about being rude to someone?" she asked.

He chuckled. "Not so much. Some people don't listen."

Emily won the game of cards, and he smiled, taking a sip of his whiskey. They had left the wedding party an hour ago. He'd carried her over the threshold, and rather than get naked to fuck, they were playing cards.

"Is that dress irritating?" he asked.

"It is, but I don't know how to get out of it. My mom, and your friends' wives helped me into it. I don't even have a clue where to start."

He started laughing. "Stand up, turn around."

"You're not taking my dress off."

"I'm going to help you. Stop being a worrywart, Mrs. Carter." It was the first time he called her by her new name. She was his wife, and instead of being repulsed, he liked it.

She turned so her back was to him. "This is really strange."

"How so?"

"I don't know. I didn't expect our wedding night to go like this. I don't know anything about you."

"Nothing is going to happen that you don't want. I can promise you that." He tugged on the strings that kept the bodice together. It was a beautiful white dress, and it had taken every single ounce of control that he possessed not to stare at her all day.

"Do you ever think of running away?" she asked.

"I did once. We all did. Luiz, Tonio, Donnie, and myself. That's all we ever wanted. A fresh start away from all the danger and the risks of war. To make sure our families were taken care of."

"Did you want children?"

"Someday. Do you dream of running away?" he asked, curious once more.

"Yes, I do. I love my parents and my family. There's a time that my father talks about, and it makes me wish that we could go back there."

"What time?"

"After he was disposed of. When he became a no one. He told me that no one knew but a few that he was alive. For several years, he lived with that freedom, and then slowly, he began to build his own army."

Jake chuckled. "Is that how you see us, two armies?"

"Is it not the case?"

"I guess it is."

"What about you? What about your family? I didn't see anyone there, your father, your mother?"

"I have no one."

"You're an orphan? Is that why you're close to the others?"

Jake paused. "I'm not an orphan. I had a family. I don't anymore. My father was a traitor, and he tried to reject the four of us. We had a plan for The Family, and we intended to see it through. My father betrayed us, and I killed him."

Silence fell as he spoke.

"Do you miss him?" she asked a few seconds later.

"No."

"Surely you must miss him. Even though my father decided to sell me for peace in the name of marriage, I wouldn't want to see anything bad happen to him. He is my father, and regardless of what your dad did, you must love him."

Jake paused. The main bodice opened up revealing a pale, unblemished back. She had full hips and a generous curve to her ass. Emily was a fuller figured woman, with nice tits and ass. He'd noticed that about her the first time he met her. He'd also noticed her kind eyes, even as she was trying to put on a cold bitch show. She was a beautiful woman.

"I didn't love my parents, Emily. From a young age, I was taught that my life was expendable. Our parents were always trying to keep us apart. I was simply a guard to take the bullet meant for my friends. We found a bond in our hatred of our lifestyle. *They* are my family, and that is why I will never run. They will not leave, and I will not leave them. They need me." He ran his fingers down her back, and he heard her sigh.

"You're touching me."

"You're not telling me to stop." But he pulled away, giving himself space.

Emily turned, holding her bodice against her chest. "You really don't miss them."

"Where you love your father, and he spent Christmas and your birthday with you, loving you, handing you toys and stuff, my father gave me a beating. He taught me how to be hurt, and how to take the pain without saying a word. I would be cut and bleeding badly in a cold, darkened room, and he would leave me for days without any food or water. That was my memory. Every single birthday was a step closer to that fated day that I would take my place within The Family. He was a good dad I guess. He didn't disown me."

"Is that the kind of life you're wanting to keep?"

Jake shook his head. "You can think what you

want. We wanted a different way of life. All four of us wanted to leave The Family behind. Start afresh."

"Why didn't you?"

She was so naive.

"Someone is always willing to take our place, Emily. Monsters that hurt women and children. We decided that together we're the lesser of two evils." He ran fingers through his hair. "I need a drink."

He made to pass her, but she caught his arm, halting him. The angle that he stood gave him a clear view of her cleavage. There was only so much a man could take, and he was hanging on by a thread.

"What part do you play?"

Jake stared at her, waiting for her to flinch away. "You really want to know?"

"I don't want to be in the dark. I'm a big girl. I can handle this."

He smiled and reached out to touch her chin. Running his thumb across her lips, he wondered how much he could push her. *Just be honest.* "I handle the soldiers. Seeing as I was always supposed to be one, it makes perfect sense. I deal with the drugs as well. I handle distribution, and I make sure none of that shit hits back at us."

Her lip trembled.

"I'm not a good person, Emily. Don't even think for a second that you married someone good. I'm not. I've killed people and laughed while I did. I'm never going to be perfect, and you know what? I don't care. I'm going to be a good man to you, a good husband. Go and get showered. If you want to play more games, then I'll see you back here in twenty minutes."

With that, he left their hotel room. He needed to clear his head.

Being a married man wasn't how he imagined.

Emily was proving to be different from what he expected.

He liked her.

**\*\*\*\***

Emily didn't linger as she changed into a pair of jeans and a long shirt. They were comfortable, and right now that was exactly what she was after. She removed each of the flowers that had been placed in her hair, and wiped the makeup from her face.

As she changed each little part of her, it was like she was removing the fake, and allowing for the real her to shine through, which she liked. She had never been one to wear makeup, not liking the feel of it on her skin.

Leaving her hair down, she put some slippers onto her feet, and made her way out to find Jake already there.

"Are you ready to play?" he asked.

The innuendo was clear even as he shuffled the cards.

"Yes, I am, and I've been thinking about what you said, and I'm sorry about your dad and about your childhood."

"No need to be sorry. It's what helped me become the man I am today."

"A man determined to do everything it takes for his friends?"

"You got it." He started to deal out the cards. "Please don't be worried. I'm happy with the way I am. I won't keep any secrets from you. That I can promise you."

She nodded. "I was wondering what you thought about ground rules?"

"Ground rules?"

"Yeah, to make this marriage work. We didn't want to be part of it, but I have to say as much as I hate to admit it, I do in fact, see the benefits of it."

"This should be good. What rules do you have?"

"I know my parents had them, and it helped keep them together for over twenty years and they're happy."

"I can see that they are happy. I never thought I'd be the kind of guy to follow rules."

She chuckled. It was strange to actually be having fun with him. It wasn't something she ever imagined when she thought of him. He was even smiling at her, which was a step up from the constant growl he seemed to keep.

"I don't want you to keep anything from me. I'm your wife, and I made a vow today. I intend to keep that vow. I will never tell another living soul what we discuss, not even my father."

"What if he asks?"

"I'll tell him I'm a married woman, and he wouldn't want Mom spilling his secrets, so don't expect me to."

Jake sat back, taking another swig of his whiskey. "I underestimated you."

"And so did my father. If for a second he thought he could use me against you, he's mistaken. Not that I think that. My dad is an honorable man. It's what got him hurt in the first place from your parents."

"I'm aware of that now. Donnie, Luiz, Tonio, and I, we want to make this work. For the longest time people have thought we're just a bunch of kids that don't know what they're doing. They're wrong. We're strong, we know what we're doing, and we're determined."

"I saw the respect my father had for you. He won't underestimate you. You mentioned that you dealt with the drugs."

"I do."

"I don't want you to ever take them. I've seen

what can happen to people who become addicted I do not want that for you."

"You're worrying about me, Emily?"

She sighed and took his whiskey from him, taking a sip herself. "I'm in a marriage I didn't want. I don't know how many times you want me to tell you that, but I am. I'm trying to make the most of this the best way I can. Is that so hard to believe?"

"You're very passionate."

"Life has taught me that I have to be to get what I want."

"What is it you want?"

"I want to be happy. That's what I want. I don't want to live my life feeling utterly miserable."

Silence met her answer, and Jake took back his whiskey.

"I can understand what you want, and I will agree to it." She watched as his throat gulped down his whiskey, draining the glass. "I won't be taking the product that I sell. I promise you I don't need that shit to make me happy."

"Good. Thank you."

"Another rule?" he asked.

"I want you to be home at a reasonable time every single night. We want to make this work, I've got to find some way to like you, and you need to find some way to like me."

The smile on his lips turned him into a rather handsome man. No, she refused to think about what it did to his looks.

Jake was a sexy man. He knew it, and so did she.

"You know that could get me some stick from the other guys."

"I'm not married to the other guys. I don't care what they say."

"Deal. I'll do it."

"Good."

"Anything else?" Jake asked.

"I've got lots more."

"I want to hear them then," he said, pouring them both another glass of whiskey. He handed her one, and she thanked him, draining the glass.

"You must put the toilet seat up. If you're drunk, don't stand up to take a piss. I don't want to have to deal with that mess. I don't care if we have a housekeeper or whatever. I know what I like, and pissy toilets isn't one of them. Next, don't drink out of the milk cartoon. It's gross,and rude. Only ever use your own toothbrush. Don't cheat on me. I like to help with the crossword puzzle—"

Jake held his hand up. "I told you I wouldn't cheat."

"You were in love with someone else," she said.

"I'm not in love with her. Besides the fact she loves pussy, I realized a long time ago that I simply cared for her. I mistook that caring for actual love. It's not. She's gone, and I don't miss her."

"Oh," she said. "Are you sure?"

"Yes, I'm sure. I don't miss her. I don't wait for her call or anything. I don't even call her anymore. She calls me. I won't cheat on you."

"Okay."

"So now that you have made your demands, I think it's only fair that I make mine." Jake moved from his chair to sit next to her.

She bit her lip as he sat close. He'd removed his jacket and was only in a crisp white shirt, and his pants. The top buttons of his shirt were already undone, and she was finding it difficult to concentrate on anything else but him.

"What do you want?" she asked.

"I like your demands. I know neither of us wanted this, but we're here now, and I intend to make the most of it. I will be home in time for dinner. Can you cook?"

"Yeah, I can."

"That's good. I love good food. If not the other guys' wives will show you what I like."

She found that particularly funny. "You'd make them teach me?"

"Yes. How else would you learn?"

Holding her hands up, she nodded. "Fine. What is it you would like?" she asked.

"I want you to be happy, and one day I want kids. I know you're not wanting sex tonight, but one day soon, I'm going to want it. I'm a man, I have needs, and I don't believe in taking what I want."

She swallowed past the lump in her throat. This wasn't supposed to be happening. They shouldn't be talking right now. She'd imagined their wedding night to be one big fight, and yet they were talking, negotiating.

"I'm a virgin," she said.

"And that's why I'm giving you space. My demands are simple. You share our bed. You belong to me. You're mine. I want you to be happy. I have needs that when we eventually have sex, I'm going to want from you. I won't judge. Whatever you want, we will explore together."

"Are you sure you want to have sex with me?" she asked.

"Why wouldn't I want to have sex with you?"

"I'm not ... you know ... small. Slim."

"You have a nice pair of tits, juicy thighs, and a luscious ass. I want to sink my teeth into that ass and hold onto your tits as I fuck you, Emily. I have got no problems when it comes to your body."

"Oh." His words sent a little thrill through her. "I guess we won't have a problem then."

"No, we won't."

"When you mean share a bed?"

"I mean we will sleep together every single night. I will hold you in my arms. Do you have a problem with that?"

She shook her head. "No."

"Good." Jake leaned forward and pressed a kiss to her head. "Let's play."

## Chapter Three

Jake had made one fatal mistake. Staring across the bed at Emily's very sexy, sensual back, his cock throbbed to life. He hadn't been attracted to her the few times he'd met her. They hadn't really talked either, and yet, he wanted her. This was impossible. He shouldn't want a wife. He had thought she would be a total bitch and make his life a living hell.

His own mother had been the same with his father. They'd had a toxic relationship. When she died, Jake hadn't cared about that either. His father dying had been essential to what he and his friends were doing.

Yes, all he had wanted to do all of his life was to run away and never return. That was what a coward did, and he was no coward. He would stay and fight no matter what. Marrying Bracken's daughter had guaranteed both families to be safe, and now they were working side by side for a better, brighter, future. One he hoped that meant he could walk down the street and maybe relax.

It was a dream they had all had, during one of their many sleepovers. Their own personal vision of how they wanted their lives to become. The legacy their fathers had wasn't what they wanted for each other.

Rubbing at his eyes, he tensed up as she rolled over, and he saw she wasn't asleep.

"What's wrong?" she asked.

"Nothing."

"I've never shared a bed with anyone before. This is a little weird."

He laughed. "You think this is weird?"

"You can laugh all you want. To me, this is a little weird. Every time you move or make a sound, I hear and feel you. It makes falling to sleep next to impossible. What's wrong?" she asked.

"You want me to share my thoughts."

"Consider it a ground rule."

"Fine. I thought you would be a bitch. A mafia princess who would make my life hard, and I didn't expect to like you."

"You like me." She pushed some of her hair off her face and smiled at him. "Should I call the media, let them know that you could actually like me? If you know I help out at homeless shelters, and work at animal ones as well, didn't that clue you in to the kind of woman that you were marrying?"

"I didn't know if you were trying to piss your father off. I don't imagine he's too happy with how you put your life in danger."

"He's not, but I don't do it for him. I do it because I want to do it. I like helping. I'm never in danger, not really. There's always guards around, protecting, watching. That's never going to stop, is it?"

"It's not." He couldn't resist reaching out and touching her. "You're actually a really beautiful woman."

She giggled. "How much did you drink?"

"Not enough to send me to sleep." He stroked her cheek. "I don't want you to ever be afraid of me, Emily."

"Right now, there's no chance of that happening."

"I've done bad things. Things that would make a lot of people sick. I've killed, I've hunted, and I'm not a good person."

"So? You don't think I know that my father has killed people? I've seen it, Jake. I've seen him take a gun, place it against a man's head who was begging for his life, and pull the trigger."

Jake frowned. "How?"

Emily sighed. "It was a long time ago. I was about eleven years old. We had gone out to the country.

My mom owned a house there. We were having a family vacation. Dad decided that he didn't want anyone interrupting his time with us, so he made sure we went alone. It started out fantastic. Lots of fun, and stuff."

"It didn't last?"

"No. By the third night something went wrong. Dad got a call, and within three hours our guards were there. It started thundering and lightning, and I woke to yells, to shouts, to curses. The front door slammed open, and I rushed toward my window. Rain was pounding down, and there was a small light that showed me everything." She stopped, nibbling her lip. "I watched as the two guards held onto this man. He was bleeding, and I heard everything. The man was pleading for his life, and my father said it would be the last words he ever spoke. He'd put his family in danger and was trying to kill him. He couldn't let that stand. He took out his gun, pressed it against his temple, then moved it right between the eyes, and I heard the bang. I screamed, and my mom ran into my room."

"You must have been so scared.

"Even when I was eleven, I knew my father wasn't like other girls' dads. There were too many questions, and how I didn't know exactly what he did. I was scared, but it made me realize that nothing was as it seemed. There were people out there who would rather see us die. What I'm telling you, Jake, is you don't scare me. I don't think anyone can live in this life and be completely clean, do you?"

"I want to be, Emily. That's the point. I wanted to be. I can't be anymore."

She reached out and cupped his face. Covering her hand with her own, he stared into her blue eyes. "It'll be okay. I'm not going to run away from you, Jake."

"I've never slept with anyone either," he said.

"You're not a virgin."

"Of course not. I've never *slept* with a woman. That doesn't mean I haven't fucked one before. This is the first time I've had a woman close to me."

"And we're not even having sex."

"Can you even say the word fuck?" he asked.

"Of course I can. What makes you think I can't?"

"I've never heard you say it."

"I don't need to be crude."

"Let me hear you say it."

"Really? How old are you?" she asked.

He loved her smile. It was so sweet, and yet so rarely there. In all the times that he had seen her, he'd never seen her smile so brightly before.

"I'm old enough to know that I want to hear my woman tell me she wants to be fucked."

The smile vanished, and she stared into his eyes. He saw the way her pupils dilated, and her breathing deepened. She was aroused by him. *Good.* He wanted her to be aroused, to be desperate for him.

This time, he stroked his hand across her arm, up to cup her face. "Say it for me, Emily."

"Fuck," she said, whispering the word. Her cheeks were a deep shade of red.

"Say you want me to fuck you. I know you don't, but I'd just like to hear the words from you."

"I want you to fuck me, Jake," she said.

She sighed.

"Do you like that? Do you like the thought of me fucking you?"

"Yes."

"Good, because one day I will. Not because we have to either, baby. No, I'm going to fuck you because I can, and you're going to want it as well." He stroked her cheek and stared at her full lips. "You're so beautiful."

She sucked that lip into her mouth, and he just wanted to bite it himself. "Jake?"

"It's fine. We're not going to do anything. I want to kiss you. Will that be okay? Do you want me to leave you alone?"

She didn't answer for several seconds, and then she nodded. "Yes, you can kiss me. I'd like for you to kiss me."

He pressed his lips against hers. At first it was just the slightest touch, her soft lips crushed beneath his firm ones. That was all he wanted, but then it wasn't enough. He needed more, wanted more, craved it.

Sinking his fingers into her hair, he pulled her close, and explored her mouth, running his tongue across her full lips. She gasped, and he couldn't resist plundering inside, taking what he wanted more than anything. Taking hold of her hand, he locked their fingers together, pressing it against the bed.

Jake pulled her beneath him so that only his head was above her.

He pulled away. "You know we're going to have a good time."

"This doesn't mean I like you or anything." She smiled, biting her lip. "But I really like your kiss."

"Why do I feel that you're lying, baby? I think you like me a lot more than you're making out. That's okay. I can handle that." He pressed another kiss to her lips and pulled away, smiling. "How about we try to get to sleep?"

"I'd like that."

This time, instead of them being far apart, he pulled her against his chest and pressed a kiss to her shoulder.

"Have you ever killed anyone?" he asked.

She shook her head. "No. I haven't."

"Do you think less of me?" He waited for her answer.

"No, I don't."

\*\*\*\*

"You really think this is a good idea?" Paige asked, handing Donnie his beer.

Luiz, Tonio, and their women were sitting in his hotel room. Their kids were already put down for a nap. He rubbed at the back of his nape, tugging Paige down into his lap.

"I don't know if it's a good idea or not. Bracken has always been a man of his word. Marriage was inevitable," Donnie said.

"Even though we promised that marriage wouldn't be a means of furthering The Family when we were in power," Luiz said.

"You're worried," Tonio said.

"Of course I am. Wouldn't you be?" Luiz asked. "We all vowed that we wouldn't be like our fathers."

"You're not," Bracken said, entering the hotel room. He took a seat, and Donnie stared at the man whom he actually had respect for. "Sorry for the intrusion, but I figured I should be invited considering my daughter is now involved in this. We will always have enemies. That is a given. I do not see why you should be worried about future marriage proposals. I believe together we can form a future together, and I meant that."

"Are you not worried about your men feeling you're weak by aligning yourself with a bunch of schoolboys?" Donnie asked. He was aware of the whispered insults that took place behind their back.

"You're aware of those words, and yet you don't do anything about it?" Bracken asked.

"You would do something? I thought you didn't

agree in violence unless necessary," Luiz said.

Bracken looked at each of them, clearly assessing. Donnie recognized the look well. He'd seen it enough times on the men who had sworn their loyalty toward him. "Violence for the sake of violence is not necessary. Making sure that people know to respect you, and at times even fear you is just as important. The people that claim you to be nothing more than schoolboys have no respect for you at all. In fact, I would put every dollar I own that they are planning to kill you. Now, you don't want to be like your fathers, and I respect that. I would never have allowed my baby girl to be married to The Family. I know firsthand what happens when it goes to shit for people who hold too much power. There's a lot more than merely being a monster. Just looking in on the outside, it looks to me like you're afraid to do what is right for fear of turning into your fathers."

Donnie didn't like how close Bracken had gotten.

"You're all too damn smart to turn into those fuckers. If you want my advice, don't show any weakness. Your enemies accuse you of being exactly like your fathers, embrace it, and know the truth. You're better than they were. You can't run from this life, nor can you hide. There will always be someone to take over. You want to protect our families, then you will have to do what you never thought you had to do."

"Have you ever done shit you wished you hadn't?" Donnie asked.

"Every single day. This life is not for the fainthearted, but then, I've got a feeling you know that." Bracken looked at each of them. "I'm proud to see all three of you sitting here, and for my daughter to be married to Jake. I know you won't let me down."

With that, he turned and left.

Paige gripped his shoulder, and he turned to look at her. "He's right."

"We're all in or not at all," Luiz said. "There's no way we can have this life, and pretend we're not part of it."

Donnie had already figured that out while watching Jake get married to Emily. He couldn't believe that he had done this to his best friend, but the needs of The Family were important.

"When he gets back from his honeymoon, we'll be ready," Donnie said. "I'm going to go and talk to him now."

"Wait, he's on his wedding night," Tonio said.

"Don't care. He needs to know what's important."

Leaving his hotel room, Donnie made his way toward Jake's honeymoon suite. Knocking on the door he waited for Jake to answer.

Seconds passed, and finally Jake stood there, wearing no shirt and a pair of sweatpants.

"Why?" Jake asked.

"I'm sorry to interrupt your wedding night. We've been talking, and when you get back, we've got a lot of work to do."

Jake looked past him and shook his head. "Get in. We can talk inside."

Once Jake closed the door, Donnie brought him up to speed.

"All or nothing?" Jake asked.

"It's the only way."

"Nothing would mean certain death though, right? We both know it's not going to be easy to walk away." Jake paced the length of the floor. "I'm in. We may not have wanted this, but you find out where our weakest spots are, and when I get back, we'll work together. All four of us."

"You're going to go ahead with the honeymoon then?" Donnie asked.

"Of course I am. I intend to make this marriage work."

"Good, I'm glad."

"I'm not doing it for you."

"I didn't figure you were." Donnie took his hand and gave it a shake. "I love you like a brother. Thank you for always sticking by my side."

"You know I was only ever supposed to be a guard to you. Someone else to put a bullet inside."

"I know, and again, I'm pleased that we're friends." Donnie pulled him close for a hug. He really did see Jake, Luiz, and Tonio as the brothers he never had. They were as close as brothers, even if they had their secrets. Even family had secrets that no one else would know.

"Go, keep me updated."

"Tonio is taking over your duties while you're away. Have fun."

\*\*\*\*

Emily stood at the doorway watching as Donnie left. Jake hadn't seen her yet, and she saw how tired he was. He stared at the door, and there was a firmness to his face. He didn't like what Donnie had said, but he also believed in it as well.

"I know you're there," he said, turning toward her.

His gaze traveled up and down her negligee. It was pastel pink, sexy, and she loved the way it made her feel.

"I heard everything."

"Again, I figured as much." He went straight to the bottle of whiskey. "Want a drink?"

"Yeah, I do."

"Do you want me to put you somewhere far away from this mess? I can have guards with you and give you a very protected life."

She shook her head. "No." It was the cowardly way out. In a matter of hours, Jake had broken down all of her notions of what he was like. He was nothing like she first thought. Cold, callous, a monster—he was none of those things. There was something deep and beautiful inside him, and she wanted to be the one to bring it out.

"You know that means I've got to do things you're not going to like."

"I don't care. I'll find some way to pay you back." She took the glass of whiskey he offered. "Don't you think it was a little rude that he invaded our privacy?" She leaned in close. "We could have been fucking tonight."

He burst out laughing. "Now you say it without me asking you to."

"I want to keep you on your toes."

"We were falling to sleep. I don't think he had anything to worry about."

Drinking a large swallow of her drink, she moved over to the small stereo she had seen. Clicking it on, she turned the volume up.

"What the hell are you doing?" he asked.

"Why should we be old, playing card games, and snuggling in bed? We're going to be doing that in fifty years' time." She started to sing and pointed at him, while swaying her hips. She didn't even care that the pink negligee showed off her body. He was pretty much naked.

"This is crazy."

"Crazy? We're two strangers who just got married. You kill people, and I help homeless people and pets without homes. Come on, nothing could be more crazy." She finished her whiskey, placing the glass on the table. "We're not paying for the room. My dad is. Let's go crazy on our wedding night." She threw her hands in the air and started to jump around, letting out great whoops.

Jake walked toward her and shook his head. "Have you ever been to a party or a nightclub?"

"Nope. I'm making this up as I go along." She grabbed her glass. "Fill her up." The song changed to another, that had her hips swinging from side to side and singing right along. When she spun around, she started laughing as Jake was rolling his hips and dancing like a girl to the song.

"Here you go, Mrs. Carter." He handed her the whiskey, taking a drink of his own.

"Well, thank you, Mr. Carter."

Jake held his hand out for her to take, and together, in a completely uncoordinated mess, they danced to the song, trying to copy the moves they had clearly seen in the music video.

"You've got moves, Mrs. Carter."

"Thank you, Mr. Carter. You're not so bad."

He gave her a twirl so that her back was to his, and his cock was nestled against her ass. Her body came to life at his touch.

"You're really not a stuck-up bitch, are you?"

"Nope. No stuck-up bitch from me." She turned her head, and her gaze landed on hips. She licked her own lips, wanting his kiss. Together, they dropped their glasses. Jake turned her, and then slammed his lips against hers.

Sinking her fingers into his hair, she pressed her body against his, needing his touch. His hands moved down her back, grabbing her ass. One song changed into another, and Jake pulled away from that kiss.

"I bet you're wet for me, aren't you?" he asked.

They didn't stop dancing, and she saw he wasn't trying to be mean with his words. "We made a mess."

"I can think of many other things to do that can make a mess."

Emily pulled out of his hands, and rushed toward the sofa. "I'm so not allowed to do this at home. It's completely immature, right?"

"We can be exactly that. We can always tell your dad that we were fucking like animals."

She started bouncing on the sofa as Jake ran across the chairs.

It was stupid of them, really immature, but she couldn't help it. Just once, she wanted to act out, and on her wedding night, it seemed the most appropriate place to do it.

Jake grabbed the bottle and started drinking straight from it. She knew she was going to hung over tomorrow, and she didn't care. This was a much better way of spending her honeymoon than being scared of her husband's touch.

She loved his kisses. Just from his naked chest, she knew she loved his body as well. For the first time, she didn't feel overly aware of her fuller, size eighteen figure.

There was a chance that she could be friends with him, and that to her, meant more than anything else.

She had never had a friend before, and she really did look forward to a future with him.

Jake handed her the bottle, and he stood behind her, holding onto her hips. They swayed, and she drank deeply, not caring that her father was going to be disappointed in her. Jumping off the sofa, Jake misjudged and knocked something into the coffee table that was there, breaking the glass. They both jumped back, and then started giggling.

"You're not hurt, are you?" he asked.

"No, are you?" She assessed their hands and feet. They were both clear, and neither of them had been hurt by the broken glass.

"Whoops," he said.

"We've been a little bad." She giggled, swigging the whiskey.

"That we have. Nice tits," he said.

She glanced down and saw her breasts had popped out over the edge. "Ass."

"I'm not complaining. They're damn good, and they're all mine." He winked at her, and she just couldn't be mad at him.

## Chapter Four

The following day Jake and Emily arrived on her father's private island, and he still had a headache. They'd spent the entire night drinking whiskey, doing shots, dancing, and had passed out on the bedroom floor, curled up together.

When they hadn't answered the door, Bracken and Donnie had gotten the management to open it, and they had found them hung over. Jake was sure Bracken held both him and Emily over the toilet as they both vomited.

He rubbed at his temple and moaned. "I'm never giving you whiskey again."

"Tell me about it. It officially sucks." She groaned. "Dad didn't need to yell at us." They entered the house that was near the beach. It was so romantic, and really quiet.

Jake dropped his bags down and went to the bed. Emily was right there beside him, and together, they dropped to the bed.

Pulling her against him, they fell asleep. Being yelled at for having a party on his wedding night, and completely trashing the place hadn't been how he wanted to spend the morning.

Several hours later, Jake woke up to find Emily still in his arms, and the headache he'd been sporting during the journey on his honeymoon had gone. He was able to think straight, and as he looked around the large, decadent room, he liked it.

Leaving Emily to sleep, he made his way out of the bedroom and finally got a good look around the luxury room. This was the island that Blacken had paid for so that his family could spend time away with no one getting to them. It was dark outside. Force of habit had

Jake closing and locking the doors. He also pulled the curtains closed so they would have privacy.

Heading into the kitchen, he turned on the lights and went straight to the fridge. His pocket vibrated, and he took it out to see Bracken calling.

"We're not even gone all that long and you're calling?"

"I've been calling you for a few hours. What took you so long?"

"I got completely drunk with my wife last night, woke up way too early this morning. Moment we got here, we passed out. The last thing I thought to do was call. I'm surprised you didn't know when we landed, and just put two and two together." The fridge was fully stocked. He removed a bottle of water, twisted the cap, and took a healthy gulp.

"Where is Emily?"

"She's still sleeping. I'm not going to wake her up." He was going to attempt to make food instead. "You know we're going to be fine, right?"

"From the state of the room, I doubt it."

Jake laughed. "Would you believe me if I actually said to you we had fun?" It had been too long since he had been bent over laughing at being a complete goofball. Dancing, drinking, singing, it was another life for someone else.

Emily made him feel free, and that was fucking strange, considering they were both tied to each other.

Speaking of the devil, Emily walked into the kitchen. He handed her the bottle of water, which she took.

"She's now alive and awake to the world." He pulled the phone away from his ear. "Your dad."

Emily took the phone and placed it on speaker. "Hey, Dad."

"Hey, baby. Is he treating you okay?"

"Of course he is. You wouldn't expect anything less, would you?" she asked. "Or are you going to admit that you made a mistake?"

She finished the water, and Jake pulled out another one, along with the makings of a stir-fry. He held the ingredients up for her, and she nodded, giving him thumbs up.

"No, I don't think I made a mistake," Bracken said. She rolled her eyes. "I want you to be happy."

"Dad, we're on our honeymoon. Are you going to call every single day to check in and see how we're doing?"

"I worry."

"Let us have some fun. Now, what do we do if stocks start to run low?" she asked, finding several spices and dried herbs in the cupboard.

"I have arranged for delivery on Thursday. There should be enough for the two of you. I love you, baby girl."

"Love you, too, Dad."

Jake took the cell phone and clicked it off. "Why did you put it on speaker?"

"Anything he had to say to me, he could say to you. I've got nothing to hide."

He watched as she grabbed some chili, five spice, and other Chinese ingredients.

"Stir-fry is what you're thinking, right?" she asked.

"Yep. It's the only thing I know how to cook. It's a step up from noodles."

She laughed. "You do know that this has noodles in it?"

"Yep, but you can also put in as much veg as you like. I think of everything."

She rolled her eyes, and he found it cute.

Emily grabbed a wok and a saucepan, placing them on top of the stove. She wore a white shirt, a pair of jeans, some slip-on sandals, and no makeup at all. She looked utterly beautiful. He was finding it harder to look away from her as she smiled at him.

"Do you want to chop the peppers, onion, and garlic, or would you like the chicken?" she asked.

"I'm a meat man. I'll handle the chicken. I do know what I'm doing."

"Okay, big man. I think if we marinate the chicken first, it will give us some gutsy flavor."

He watched as she grabbed a bowl and started sprinkling out spices. He wasn't going to worry. She seemed to know what she was doing, so he began to thinly slice the chicken.

"This seems to be a very ... domestic thing to be doing. I wonder how many couples are doing this right now?"

"I don't think a lot are. I've only got my friends to compare it to. Paige loves cooking for Donnie and the gang. Donnie wouldn't be seen dead in a kitchen. He's takeout if Paige is sick. He tried to cook her soup once. On top of her illness, she got food poisoning. She was lucky to come out of it alive. Donnie has since banned himself from cooking. Zara makes one hell of a pizza. That's what her family used to do. They owned a pizzeria. Fantastic food, I love her pizza. Then there's Raine, and again, she's a good cook. You're up against a great deal of competition."

"I'm not worried. My mom loved to cook, and I've always been in the kitchen with her." She took the chicken from him, added it to the bowl with some minced garlic, soy, and other ingredients. "Will you mix that all together?"

He took the bowl, got his fingers in, and mixed it all together as she chopped up vegetables.

"I trust you and your father. You don't need to tell me everything that he tells you," he said.

She shrugged. "I don't mind. Did he moan about the state of the room?"

"Not really. I think he did his moaning this morning."

Emily giggled. "It's the first time he has ever told me that he's disappointed in me. I didn't care though. Does that mean I'm growing up?"

"I have no idea. I just wanted him to shut the fuck up. His moaning was giving me a headache."

"I know, right? Mom told him to calm down." She sighed and filled up a pan with water. "It was nice to be reckless. Don't get me wrong, I won't be doing it often. The headache alone was going to kill me. It's gone now though. I just have this need to eat, and to eat lots."

"I know what you mean." For the next twenty minutes, he stood back and watched as Emily got to work, heating up a wok and cooking the chicken, followed by the vegetables. She was humming as she did.

He liked listening to her as he got the stock she wanted from the fridge, and began to pour it into the stir-fry. She drizzled in more sauces, and it was a turn-on watching how confident she was. Next, she drained the noodles, added them to the pot, gave it a flip thing with her hand, and then decanted the food into two large bowls.

"Dinner is served."

"Woman, if we weren't already married, I would beg you to marry me," he said, grabbing a fork.

That first bite, and he was in love, totally besotted with his new bride.

"This is heaven."

"I'm pleased you like it."

They took their bowls to the sitting room, and he saw there was no television. "Why don't we have any television?" he asked.

"Whenever Dad came here, he always wanted us to be a family. Devices were not allowed, apart from cell phones."

"That sucks. We could have been watching porn, got you in the mood and all that."

She rolled her eyes. "You're an ass."

"Will I be getting sex?" he asked.

"Not with the way you're going."

"Sucks being me." He nudged her and winked.

****

Jake loved her food, and Emily was so proud of the hours she spent by her mother's side watching her cook. She enjoyed being in the kitchen, and one of her first memories was baking cookies in the kitchen with her mother.

Taking the bowl from Jake, she went to do the dishes, and once again hummed to herself.

"You're always doing that, you know," he said.

"What am I always doing?" she asked, cleaning away the mess.

Jake grabbed a towel and began to dry. She was shocked that he seemed happy to do most chores. It was nice, and it was something she enjoyed seeing.

"You're humming."

"Sorry. I do that when I'm happy."

The smile on his face made her pause.

"Wow, you smile."

"Sorry, I'll remember to be stern. You're happy, and that makes me so as well."

Pushing some hair out of her face, she stepped back and saw the kitchen was already clean. There was no television, no books. Only a few games, some cards, and each other to keep company. He put the towel down on the counter and stared at her.

"What to do now?" he asked.

"I think I've got a good idea what is going on in your head."

"Really? So you want to go swimming as well?"

"Swimming?"

"There's a pool out back. I saw it, and I bet you and your family spent a lot of time in the water."

"Of course we did." She had forgotten about the pool. It had been a long time since she had been here, a few years. Between school and commitments back in the city, coming away to the island had been something her parents did, together.

"You weren't thinking about the pool, were you?" he asked, taking a step toward her.

She didn't move back and waited for him to get close.

"No, I wasn't thinking about the pool."

"Tell me, Emily Carter, exactly what were you thinking about?"

She tilted her head back to look at him and smiled. "That is for me to know, and you to never find out."

"Now you're just teasing me." He winked at her, and then pulled away.

"I didn't pack a costume."

"I'm going in the pool naked. We're newlyweds, and I'm going to see you completely naked soon."

"But not yet."

"You're not coming for a swim then?" he asked, already heading out the door. "Tell me you're not a bit curious about all of this. You, me, what we're doing here?"

She kept her mouth closed.

"Cat got your tongue?" He took a step toward her and cupped her hips, drawing her close. "Were you thinking about me touching you?"

"Go and have your swim, Jake."

"Come and join me. I've got nothing to hide."

Before she could stop him, he had her hand in his and was walking toward the pool. They left the house, and the back yard had several lights outside, which showed off the pool.

Jake released her, and she watched as he began to remove his clothes.

When he was naked last night, she had seen the ink down his arm and on his back were the names of his friends. The four of them were written on the inside of a heart. She figured the symbol was his love of family.

He unbuttoned his jeans and slid them off. Next, his boxer briefs, which gave him extra points as they were black, not white.

"You've not looked away yet. You little perv," he said, winking at her.

She covered her face with her hands and shook her head. "You're horrible."

"Emily, look at me please."

Dropping her hands, she looked at him, to find him completely naked. His cock was rock hard as it pointed at her.

"I've got nothing to hide from you. This is me, this is who I am."

"Doesn't that hurt?" she asked."

"It aches. You're safe with me. I know how to control myself." He jumped in the pool. "Your turn. I got naked first."

She hesitated and looked around the garden. It was secluded, and not only that, it was a damn island.

Removing her shirt, she didn't look at him as she wriggled out of her jeans, toeing out of her sandals as she did. She stood in her underwear that was lacy and white.

"Now that is pretty," he said. "I like that color on you. Soon, that color will not match your status."

"Status?"

"Married, and well fucked. You won't be a virgin for long."

"You just can't help yourself, can you?"

"Why try to pretend? We both know it's going to happen. You couldn't even look away from me. I bet you're soaking wet right now."

She removed her bra, and with her breasts naked, that seemed to silence him, and for now, she wanted him quiet.

He whistled. "They are perfect."

Her cheeks heated under his assessment.

"You like them?"

She wiggled out of her panties and went to the steps leading toward the pool.

*Think confidence, Emily.*

Jake walked toward the steps and took her hand, tugging her close. She hit his chest with a thump, making her gasp. He was rock hard compared to her.

"They feel amazing," he said. "Yes, I like them, and one day soon, you're going to hold them closed while I fuck you between your tits." His hand went to her back, holding her close. "I love the color of your eyes. They remind me of the ocean."

"You're fanciful."

He shook his head. "No, I know what I like, and I like looking into your eyes." The hand on her back moved, and both of his hands cupped her face, and she felt raw, open, exposed to his touch. "Your lips are always begging to be touched, to be kissed."

One of his thumbs ran across her lips, and she couldn't look away from him. It was like he cast a spell, and that held her against him, making it impossible for her to move.

"What are you thinking?" she asked.

"Would she be offended if I kissed her tonight and touched her?"

"Touched me?"

"I won't touch you unless you want it. I want to make you feel good, and to show you how good it could be between us." He leaned in close and pressed his lips against her ear. "Even before we had sex, I could make it amazing for you. Make you come with my hands or my mouth. You could touch me, hold me."

"And if I don't want to?" she asked.

"Then I would stop, and we would have a nice swim."

She knew he wouldn't be upset with her. This was them entering new territory.

"I want to touch you as well," she said. "I don't want you to laugh at me when I do."

He smiled. "I've got no problem with that." In the next second, his lips were back on hers, and she moaned, holding onto his shoulders, needing him. His cock pressed against her stomach, and she didn't try to push him away.

Out of everything, she trusted him more than anyone else.

When his tongue traced over her lips, she opened up to him and ran her hands down his arms, going past his stomach, to wrap her fingers around his hard cock. He jerked away from the kiss and released a hiss.

"What is it?" she asked. "You said I could touch you."

"I know, and it feels so good."

She had released his cock, and she pulled away from him. "Maybe we should take this slow," she said.

"Yeah, I think we need to."

"When did you last have sex with someone?" she asked.

"A year ago." He stalked toward her, and she rather liked the way he looked at her body. Ducking under the water, she broke the surface, tucking hair behind her ears. "Do you know what happens when two people fuck?"

"Yes, I do. I'm not that young that I don't know that babies come out women's bellies from men's kisses." At his pause, she chuckled. "I'm kidding. Wow, you're easy to tease."

"Some fathers keep their daughters away from any influence and make them so damn innocent that their husbands scare them."

"My father had the dreaded talk with me. We were both grossed out, and I want to keep that memory out of my head."

"My first time was with a whore that my dad told me I had to screw."

"Oh, wow, really?"

"Yep. It was. I think half of the boys have that where we come from."

"Dad's never done that to Gabe." Gabe was her younger brother.

"I don't think about it anymore," he said. His gaze traveled down her body, and she couldn't help the shiver that he created. She wanted him; there was no denying that. This attraction between them scared her a little.

She was supposed to hate the man she had been ordered to marry, wasn't she?

## Chapter Five

Jake had her naked in the pool, and his cock was rock hard, and yet he didn't want to fuck her. Correction, he wanted to fuck her, but first, he just wanted to talk to her, to get to know her a little more. She was very different from how he imagined she would be. There was a fire, a passion burning in her eyes that he found so damn attractive.

"You don't think about sex anymore?" Emily asked, a wicked smile on her face.

"I think about sex a hell of a lot but not about when it started. I'm a grown ass man, and I don't need to think about it."

"You have a lot of sex?"

"You're my wife, and you're curious about my sex life?"

"I've not had one. Of course I'm curious." She turned her back to him and sank beneath the water. He found that a shame seeing as he liked looking at her. She faced him once again with a smile on her face.

"I could show you."

"Show me?"

"I could make you feel good. No sex, promise. My cock will stay away from your very pretty pussy."

Her cheeks were a glorious shade of pink.

"You don't know if I've got a pretty one."

"Oh, I know for a fact that you've got one, baby. There's no way you don't have it." He moved toward her, and she didn't move back. Touching her shoulder, he stroked across her pulse. Moving her blonde hair aside, he pressed a kiss to her neck, loving the way she seemed to move toward him.

"Jake?"

"Don't worry. I won't do anything to you that

you don't like. I'm not a monster. I want to give you something, to help make you feel good."

She chuckled. "Is that what you say to all the women?"

He shook his head. "No. I don't spend time making small talk. It has been a long time for me, Emily. I won't break our marriage vows." He pulled away to look into her eyes.

"Why are you being so nice to me?" she asked.

"You're my wife, and you've never given me a reason to not be nice to you."

"What would make you hate me?"

He laughed. "I'm thinking about fucking you, about sliding my fingers between your pussy, and making you so wet that you come, and you're wanting to find out what makes me angry."

"I think now is the best time to ask you. You're distracted, and I need to know in case I ever do something you hate."

Jake saw the spark of fear in her eyes, and he cupped her face. "No, don't ever be afraid of me. I'm many things, Emily, but I will never harm or hurt you." He didn't want her to be afraid of him. "I need you to believe me."

For several seconds neither of them spoke, nor said a word.

She kept her gaze on him, and then held his face in exactly the same way he held hers. "I believe you, Jake. I know you wouldn't hurt me. I just … I was curious about you and everything. I shouldn't have asked."

He smiled. "It's fine. Nothing makes me angry that would ever affect you. I love my family. Luiz, Donnie, Tonio, they are all like brothers. Their families are just an extension of mine. I'm not going to lie to you.

I don't know what Bracken's deal is. I don't trust him."

"Then trust me, Jake. Know that loyalty means a great deal to all of us. My father, he wants to make life better. He doesn't want men with families to be shooting people on the front lawn. You guys could work together."

"Even though you and I are married."

She smiled, and the wicked glint in her eye wasn't hard to see. "I think you and I are perfectly capable of handling each other."

"You think so?"

"I know so." She ran her hand from his cheek to his neck. "Now, I think we need to add to our ground rules. You need to stop being worried about me and about if I'm afraid of you. There are going to be times that I am afraid, but I know you'd never hurt me. My mom told me that you need to be strong, that you need a strong woman by your side to face the enemies you've got. I'm going to be strong for you. I was going to be a total bitch, but I've decided to give you the benefit of the doubt."

He moved his hand from her face to stroke down her back. Her eyes closed, and she moved a little closer so that the tips of her breasts were stroking across his chest.

"How about I show you a little something you could be looking forward to."

She licked her lips, and he wanted to kiss those lips, to show her exactly what she was missing out on.

"What do you want to show me?"

Sinking his fingers into her hair, he held onto her head. His cock was rock hard, pressing against her stomach. He wanted inside her so damn much, but he wanted to wait. He wanted them both to be craving each other with equal measure. Slamming his lips against hers, he plundered her mouth with his tongue, wanting her to think of nothing else but him. Biting her lip, he released her to find her eyes closed. "Can I touch you?" he asked.

He made sure that he asked first. There was nothing wrong with being a gentleman to his wife.

*You want her to like you.*

This was a total change for him. He'd not cared when he first agreed. He didn't give a shit if she liked him or not. All he wanted to do was get married, to get it out of the way, and maybe place her somewhere far away from him.

Being with her for their honeymoon, and now like this, he didn't want to lose her. He enjoyed her company. She wasn't the spoilt little brat that he had first thought she was. She was something so much more, and he wanted that.

"Jake?" she asked.

"What is it?"

"I need your hands on me, touching me."

Moving his hands from her head and face, he glided them down, spinning her so that her back was to him. The curve of her ass nestled against his cock, and he groaned, sucking on her neck right over her pulse.

She cried out, and he loved her sounds. They only served to drive him wild and want her even more.

Cupping her tits, he pinched her nipples, giving them light tugs to create a small spark a pain but not enough to scare her. She was a virgin, and he wanted to test her limits and to see how far they could both go.

He continued to lick and stroke her neck as he caressed her body going down to cup her between her thighs. He found her clit and stroked it.

She gasped and shook within his arms from that one touch.

"I can make you feel so good, baby. You'll never

know anything else but what I can give you." He nibbled her neck, stroking in small circles over her nub. She pressed her thighs together, and then opened them again, pushing against his hand.

"I don't want you to stop. It feels so good when you do that."

"I know it does, babe. It's going to get a hell of a lot better."

"How?"

"You're going to have to trust me." He stroked her clit, and her hands moved up, cupping her tits. Her movements seemed completely inexperienced, but he liked that. She belonged to him, and only him.

They had a fucked-up marriage, but he was going to make sure she didn't go without.

"Do you want to touch my cock?" he asked.

She tensed up.

"I said touch not fuck."

"I know. Can I?" she asked.

He took one of her hands in his and placed it behind her to wrap around his length. He groaned as her fingers covered his length and started to stroke his cock. He closed his eyes, loving the feel of her moving up and down.

"A-am I doing this right?"

"So right, baby. So right." He kissed her neck, groaning as her touch created so much pleasure he struggled to focus on her.

Caressing her clit, he felt her wetness, the way she responded to his touch. He wanted her so damn bad. It was like the start of an addiction, and he just couldn't help it.

"I'm not supposed to like you," he said.

She chuckled. "We've agreed, we hate each other."

It felt so good to hate her then.

"Oh, Jake," she said, moaning his name as her body grew tighter. He wished he was inside her right now and felt every ripple of her pussy around his dick.

"That's it, baby, come for me. Come all over my cock."

She cried out, and he couldn't hold back any longer. They both came, his cum erupting in the water as she did as well, pressing against her fingers.

"I love hating you," he said. In his heart, he knew he didn't hate her.

****

A couple of days later Emily walked the beach alone, watching the ocean as it seemed to be completely calm. She wore a long blue dress and crossed her arms beneath her breasts. Being a married woman was somewhat surreal to her. Jake wasn't like anything she had ever imagined. He was actually fun to be around, and they had a lot of fun.

Glancing over her shoulder she saw Jake standing at the edge of the house staring at her. There had been a call come through from one of his friends, she didn't know who. He held his hand up, giving her a wave, and she did the same, smiling. It was the little things she liked. He left the toilet seat down, and he put the cap on the toothpaste. Every morning there was always freshly brewed coffee. He couldn't cook, which she'd found out last night, but that didn't matter. She loved to cook.

He had a beautiful reading voice. Last night they had lain in the sitting room, and she had her head in his lap while he read a book. It had been … weird. Turning her back to him, she looked out toward the ocean wondering what the hell was going on. Nothing made any sense to her anymore.

Biting her lip, she closed her eyes and allowed

the peace and quiet to settle all around her. There was nothing to be afraid of here. She was safe, and her parents were back at home taking care of everything This was what her father, their family wanted.

Her cell phone began to ring invading her space and peace. Pulling her cell phone out of her pocket she saw it was her mother, Tulip, calling.

"Hey, Mom," she said.

"Honey, I thought I would give you a little time to get settled in. How is everything?"

She stared back at the house to find Jake still in the same place. "It's fine."

"And how is Jake?"

Emily giggled. "Is this to find out how I am doing, or to see how he's doing as a husband?"

"I wanted to make sure you're okay. Believe it or not, honey, I do love you."

"Enough to force me into a marriage with a man I don't know."

Tulip sighed over the line.

"Mom, I don't want to fight with you. I'm sorry. Everything is fine, great even."

"Why are you making that sound bad?"

"I don't know. I didn't know what to expect."

"Your father and I would have found another way if we could. None of us wanted you to have to go through this. It's tough times right now, more so than I've ever known it."

"I get it, Mom, I do—"

"No, you don't understand, honey. There have been ... attacks."

"Attacks?"

"Yes. Families that have shown loyalty to your father and to The Family, some soldiers have died, and they are targeting women and children as well."

Fear gripped Emily as she looked toward Jake. He was pacing now, walking backward and forward, completely lost in his own little world. "Jake runs the soldiers for The Family."

"We know. We know exactly what they do."

"Do you need us to come home?"

"No. What we need is for you to make this work. This is for the greater good."

Emily laughed, even though it sounded more on the verge of hysteria than actual laughter. "This is crazy."

"I know you just want to think that we're all a bunch of criminals and we don't know what to do without killing people, but I can promise you, honey, it's not like that. There is a huge responsibility with being who we are. Even as women we have the same weight on our shoulders."

"Have you been attacked?"

"No. We just have a few death threats at the moment. We're trying to figure out who they are so we can deal with it."

Emily closed her eyes. Deal was such a negative word, at least in their world it was. Deal meant kill, death, the end. Opening her eyes, she knew there was no way to hide from it.

"I just wanted to call to make sure you're okay."

"Yeah, I'm fine. I wish we had the means of watching television or doing something else."

"Something that didn't allow you to be together."

"It's confusing me when we're together all the time."

There was some commotion in the background, and Emily frowned.

"I've got to, honey. Love you."

Before she said anything else, her mother hung up the phone. Gritting her teeth, she stared out at the ocean, which no longer held any appeal to look at. Heading back up toward Jake, she saw he had also finished his call.

"What's wrong?" he asked.

"Nothing. My mother ... I don't know. It's probably nothing."

"That was Donnie on the phone. He's kind of like our leader seeing as he took over from his dad. There have been attacks on my soldiers. Men I trust."

"You know the men who have been attacked?"

"Yes, a couple of them have been killed. Their families have been taken to keep them safe. A couple of wives are in the hospital, and some of my men are missing."

She saw the worry on his face. "We need to go back home."

Jake shook his head. "Donnie said they are handling it."

"We're the ones that are in control of our marriage. They want this union to work more than anything, and I get it, I do. I don't think we'll work well if another of your men dies while you get to know me. I won't have that on my head. I can't. I refuse to."

"You want to go back home?"

She nodded. "Yes. Something is clearly happening. I'm not stupid, and as much as they don't think they need you, clearly they're wrong."

"I don't know about that. They told me there was no way of knowing."

Emily shrugged. "They don't know that. You're gone. What if they felt something and they would have told you but not anyone else. I know I would have told my mom before I told my dad. There are people we work for who we trust more than others."

Jake looked torn. "You're sure about this."

"I'm not petty. Men are dying, and they're your

221

men." She held her arms out in surrender. "My parents and your friends wanted this to work, right? Then let's make it work by being a team. We can do that, right? Scare the absolute crap out of them, by getting this entirely right."

He started to laugh. "You know, I may start to like you."

She pressed her hands to her heart and gasped. "No, that is not possible. You cannot like me no matter what you say. Remember, we hate each other." Emily would have loved to have stayed another few days, maybe even a few more weeks, but this was more important than her, and even him. "Make the call, Jake. It's time for us to head home."

She made to move past him, but Jake caught her arm, stopping her from leaving. Staring at where he held her, she finally looked up into his eyes. "What's wrong?"

"Thank you, Emily. I mean that."

She smiled. "Don't worry, mister, I will make you pay."

He cupped her cheek and slammed his lips down on hers silencing any protest or … anything from her. His kiss was firm and yet tender, which was totally not happening. Her body began to melt, and before she could stop herself she sank her fingers into his hair and held him close.

Jake broke the kiss and pressed his head against hers. "Thank you so much, Emily. I will never forget this moment."

She didn't like the way her heart was racing, or the feelings it was inspiring. She needed to nip this in the bud right now. "It'll cost you a diamond necklace." She pulled away, heading toward the bedroom, knowing she didn't want anything from him. The kiss was enough for her.

## Chapter Six

"You didn't need to come home," Luiz said.

Jake shook his head. "No offense but our family is more important than a honeymoon. Emily understands that, and she was the one who suggested we come home. I need to find out who is killing our men, and I want to kill them." He looked around the table at Donnie and Tonio. Neither of them had spoken just yet, but that was fine for him. They had all told him he should have stayed on his honeymoon. "So, what do we know so far?"

Donnie sighed. "Bracken was right. There is a lot of disrespect right now. It would appear having four *boys* isn't what some of our enemies or even our people wanted. There are a lot of rumors that we're going to be taken out, picked off one by one."

"There are attacks planned?" Jake asked.

"Yes. Our wives are all heavily guarded, and so are our families," Donnie said. "We have three men, Rufus Conwell, Ryan Charles, and Damon Seagus." One by one, Donnie handed over the files. Jake picked them up looking through the details.

"Crime lords?"

"Yep, they deal in guns, drugs, women, and they've been spreading out their territory as well. They've been looking for supporters," Luiz said. "According to Bracken's sources, Damon's the one that we need to be looking at. He is wider spread, taking up more territory."

"Usually they're too busy with their own conflict to bother us, and when it's on the small scale it doesn't usually affect us," Tonio said.

"When we overthrew our fathers, we opened up their interest. We're four boys. Our fathers had a lot of support when they were in power, and that didn't transfer. So they've branched out, moved on," Donnie said.

"We killed a lot of their supporters," Jake said. "The big party. We took them out."

"We took out the ones we knew. There are some that bided their time. They waited for the right moment, and while we were focusing on our internal problem, externally, they were building up a big problem," Donnie said. "We took our eye off the ball, and because of it, we now got it fix it."

"No, we didn't take our eye off the ball. We were all hoping for a different future. We've changed our path, and now we have to keep on going." Jake ran a hand down his face, and then released a sigh. "Where do we start?"

"Damon's gone into hiding. We've got alerts out to let us know when he shows up. We did a trace on all of our guys' activities, and several of our men have shown up to have taken some suspicious payment," Tonio said.

"Suspicious payment?"

"They're being paid to give out information. Our information." Tonio held up the details of the men he was talking about.

Jake took the letter and glanced through the names. "I know these men. They're our soldiers."

"We knew you'd say that, which is why we also have this," Luiz said, taking out another file.

"Wow, I've been gone a handful of days, and already you're filed up. You know they still chop down trees. Whole forests have probably been demolished for this use of paper," Jake said, opening up the file.

"Very funny. I take it the honeymoon didn't go according to plan. I was expecting you to be accused of murder," Donnie said.

"The honeymoon went fine. Murder? What the fuck for?" Jake asked, looking up.

"You didn't look happy about being married to her, and you said yourself she's a bitch."

Jake shook his head. "I was wrong about her." He glanced over the files, which were the men's bank transfers, and he didn't like what he was seeing. *Fucking traitors*. He couldn't stand them.

Looking up, he saw his three friends staring at him.

"What?"

"You like her?" Luiz asked.

He frowned.

"You know, like *like, like* her?" Tonio asked.

"Planning a happy future together?" Donnie asked.

"You guys need to get a life and to stop thinking about mine. Next time I see your woman, I'm telling them you need to all get laid."

"Come on, give us the juicy details," Tonio said. "You're the only one of us that isn't married, and then you're with a woman you don't know. It's Bracken's daughter for crying out loud."

"Emily is just fine. You don't have to worry about me killing her any time soon. I actually like her. She's a nice woman, charming, sweet," he said.

"Wait, we're all talking about the same woman here?" Donnie asked. "Bracken's daughter."

Jake sighed. "Fine? What do you want to know? That we're both pissed about being married to each other. Check, we are. But guess what? We're dealing with it. Neither of us wants to spend the rest of our lives hating each other. We are going to do the best we can. We're going to make this marriage work. If we somehow fall in love for it, then great. If we're good friends, then great. Is that what you want to know?"

"Falling in love?" Tonio asked. "That's a big step for you."

Jake held up his finger and thumb. "I'm this close to putting a bullet in all of you. I'll be friendless, and I'll have an opening. Don't tempt me."

Silence fell in the room, and he watched as his friends sat back with a sigh.

"Told you he'd figure something out," Donnie said.

Jake rolled his eyes and went back through the files. When he saw the transaction that was the largest, he knew who he wanted to go and see first. "This one here, Matt Veno. He had a transaction of fifty thousand go into his account."

"You're changing the subject," Luiz said.

"No, I'm getting down to business. We all what this marriage merger to work, right? I'm making it work. Now we've got business. We can sit around and talk like girls, or we can move on, and then talk when everything is over, and we prove once again we're not boys." He was getting tired of having to prove himself. All of his life, he'd done nothing but have to do the same thing. Fighting to prove that he had a right to be here.

"The only language these men know is that of violence," Luiz said.

"It's a good job we all know how to respond in kind then," Tonio said. "If violence is what they know, then they are all going to regret the day that they awakened us. We are all monsters. Our women, they keep us at bay, but I'm growing tired of fighting this. Once and for all we make our final stand. We kill anyone who stands in our way, agreed?"

"We do not allow for excuses either," Donnie said.

Jake stood up. "Let's go."

They left the apartment building, which was heavily guarded with their closest friends. Bracken and his family had also taken up residence, and had included his closest security team.

His wife was in that building, and as Jake waited to climb into the car beside Tonio, he glanced up at the building. For a couple of days, he had been able to forget and had been given the pleasure of simply being a man with Emily. Having her lay her head on his lap as he read to her had been one of the greatest pleasures of his life.

He wanted to do that again, and soon.

The car ride to Matt Veno's place didn't take very long. Jake had his final transaction at a casino place that they owned.

The manager, Greg, was a friend of Jake's and had called him ahead to let him know that Matt was gambling away a lot of money, and had also brought dope into the establishment.

Jake asked for Greg to meet him at the back entrance, and to make sure no one alerted Matt to their presence.

Greg was smoking a cigarette as they arrived.

"Hello, Greg. Good to see you," Jake said, climbing out of the car and shaking the man's hand. He was a few years older than the four friends, close to thirty. He had three kids, one with asthma that ran up in medical bills, which Jake took care of.

"I'm so sorry, Mr. Carter. I want to promise you men that I'm a full and loyal Family supporter."

"We know," Jake said.

"Matt is saying that shit is going to change, and that he'll own the casino, and he said to just put a bullet in my boy's head because I will be gone. He doesn't want trash like me working his zone, Mr. Carter."

"I've told you many times to call me Jake."

"I'm sorry, Jake. I really am. There's so much talk, and we're all scared," Greg said.

"You have nothing to be afraid of," Donnie said. "We're in this together, and we're going to fight for it, I promise."

Jake didn't like the fear in Greg's eyes, and he was going to make sure that his men didn't feel this way again. Being part of The Family, they were his men, and he would protect them.

Greg led the way, taking up the back entrance that also provided access to every single part of the casino.

"He brought women and drugs here?" Jake asked.

"Yes. Told me that I was a dog and needed to learn to respect my masters, and that he was one of them." Greg touched his face, and Jake had noticed the shiner there. "This is what you get for disobeying orders."

Greg was not a violent man. This casino was a legit business, and they made sure that none of their illegal shit touched this place. It was a diversion for the Feds.

"He has guards, two of them," Greg said once they were outside the floor.

"Bring them out here," Jake said.

He, Luiz, Tonio, and Donnie grabbed their guns and waited. The moment the door opened, Jake grabbed one guy, slamming his head into the wall, and then the other. Years of training made him tackle the danger first.

His life didn't mean anything. His father had taught him that, so he handled the threat always. Luiz and Tonio, grabbed the first man, silencing him. Jake just went to him, pressing the silencer on his gun against the man's head, and shot.

They only needed one man, and they didn't really *need* that. With the next, he held him against the wall and shot again.

"Jake, what the fuck?" Luiz asked.

"They're working for Matt. We only need Matt alive." Jake went to the two men, grabbing out their identification and tossing it over to Donnie. "We put a search on their names when we get back, and see what we get."

Leaving the staircase, he nodded at Greg, who knew what to do next. This wasn't Greg's first time handling dead bodies.

With his three friends at his back, Jake put his hand on the door.

"Jake, you don't have to go first," Donnie said.

Luiz and Tonio agreed.

"We can talk about this another time. Right now, we've got to get to the bottom of this. You want to kiss my ass some more?" Jake asked, smirking at them.

"Get your ass shot off then," Donnie said.

"Emily will kiss it all better," Tonio said, to which Luiz started making kissing noises.

Jake rolled his eyes and entered the hotel room.

At first Matt didn't even seen them. He was too busy fucking one woman as another woman watched.

This wasn't a sight he'd not seen before.

The woman watching looked toward them, and her eyes grew wide. Clearly, this wasn't new to her either. He pressed a finger to his lips and moved closer to Matt.

"Your fucking pussy is so fucking good. I could fuck it all day long. So fucking good." Matt kept on slamming inside the woman, who was moaning like the guy was the best lover in the world.

They were paid to do that, though.

"Yeah, take my big, rock, hard dick, baby."

This was just getting worse, and Jake was now bored. Pressing the gun against Matt's neck, Jake tutted. "You know, you really shouldn't brag about how big your dick is. Poor woman probably doesn't even know if you're fucking her.

"Jake, what are you doing here?" Matt asked.

"I thought you and I would have a little chat. I'm sorry to say this, ladies, party time is over."

The woman who had Matt's dick inside her, moved away. She didn't look at Matt. She just grabbed her bags and clothing, and left without a word. The two women were talking about groceries even before they left the room.

Luiz pulled out a chair and forced Matt into a seat.

"It would appear, Matt, that our generosity is not good enough for you." Jake began walking around the chair.

"Whatever that fucking bastard has said, he's lying."

"Oh, Greg's lying, is he?" Donnie asked. "So you didn't tell him that you were going to own this casino, and he'd be out on his ass."

Matt shook his head.

Jake crouched down and stared into the man's eyes. "Or that he should put a bullet in his kid's head." The man went pale. "You should be afraid right now." Jake put his gun on the bed, and bent down, pulling out his knife. He had gotten it on his eighteenth birthday. "I was given this by my father who believed that I had more than earned my loyalty to him. He told me that this very blade had cut more than a hundred men's throats open." The blade was clean, shiny. The handle showed the age. "It was passed down from father to son, for several generations. The moment a son proved himself, this was handed to him as if it was a pot of gold. He also told me that not only did this slit men's throats. It also gutted them. Simply opened them up like butter."

Matt whimpered.

Donnie, Luiz, and Tonio stood back, giving him the stage. Greg was his friend, his ally, and it was up to Jake to protect, no one else.

"Who do you work for?"

Matt shook his head. "He'll kill me."

Jake burst out laughing. "He'll kill you. There's four men right now who would love nothing more than to see your pasty ass dead. Who are you working for?"

Matt continued to be silent, shaking his head.

Growing bored, Jake held the knife and pierced Matt's leg.

Screams filled the room and echoed off the walls. Jake was completely numb to it. He didn't give a shit at all. He didn't pull the blade out, and as Matt fought, Luiz, Tonio, and Donnie held him down.

Jake didn't pull the knife out of the man's leg. He continued to move it down, cutting through muscle, and wiggling it a little just to add a little more pain. He made sure not to nick any major arteries. He didn't want his fun ending just yet.

"Do you need me to stop?" Jake asked. Matt was panting and looking pale. The pain had to be excruciating. "Fine, I'll stop." He removed the blade and grabbed the shirt on the floor. Wiping the blade, he hummed to himself.

"Who are you working for?" Donnie asked.

Matt began to cry then. He had already pissed and shit himself. The scent tainted the air, and Jake waited.

"Damon Seagus. He's reaching out, and has taken land from Rufus Conwell and Ryan Charles. He's planning a takeover. Said that you are just a bunch of fucking babies that haven't been off your mother's tits long enough to rule this city," Matt said. "Please don't kill me."

"What is his plan?"

Matt sobbed and panted. "I'm losing too much blood."

"What is his plan?"

"He has men everywhere, okay? He wants you gone, and The Family will be his to control. This was supposed to be mine."

"Where is he going to start?" Jake asked.

Matt looked at Jake, and he saw the evil lurking beneath the surface. Matt was a monster to the core.

"You should already be dead," Matt said.

"And why is that?"

"Because he knows where your apartments are. He knows how you like to keep your women close. There's an attack on the hotel tonight. He's going to take your women, and sell them. Make sure they're fucked up real good, and keep you guys alive long enough to watch, and then he was going to take you down, one by one."

Fear gripped Jake, and he hid it, as did all of his friends. Their families were at the apartment, and right now, they couldn't do anything.

Jake got up from the bed, and slid the blade cleanly into Matt's throat. None of them spoke as they left the room.

"Come on, Paige, pick up," Donnie said, already on his cell phone.

Jake got his cell phone, and even though he wanted to call Emily, he put a call through to Bracken.

The call kept ringing. Cursing, he tried again until he was told the call was not available. This was just one fucked up moment after another.

They climbed into the car, and Donnie was already pulling out of the casino as Jake closed the door.

"Fuck, fuck, fuck, fuck, fuck!" Donnie yelled each word getting louder as they drove their way back to their apartment building.

"Bracken knows what to do," Jake said. In that moment, he had to have faith in his father-in-law. He just had to. There was no way that Emily could die. Not when he had turned his back for just a moment.

## Chapter Seven

Emily stared at Jake's space and was shocked by how bland and boring he was. The furniture was all black, and the walls a pristine white. In the far corner, next to the sitting room, was a punching bag. The windows were huge, and looking out over the city seemed to be a big deal to The Family.

She wondered if he was compensating for something, but then didn't want to think about it.

Running fingers through her hair, she spun in a full circle. There was no way she could live here for a long time. It was like a bad omen waiting to happen. This was the kind of apartment that filled scary horror movies with phantoms and ghosts. Running her hands up and down her arms, she scrunched up her nose.

The apartment screamed coldness.

Jake wasn't a cold person.

She had noticed that he was a very charming kind of guy. A bit different but then, no one was perfect.

Blowing out a breath, she took a seat on one of the large, overbearing black seats. She sat down and sank into it, only it wasn't comfortable.

He had furniture that was so uncomfortable it wasn't even funny. Falling into the seat, she stared up at the ceiling just as a knocking came at Jake's door. Climbing out of the chair, she made her way toward the door and opened it up.

Paige, Donnie's wife, stood on the other side as did Zara and Raine.

"Hey," she said, looking at the three women.

"Hi, we thought we would interest you in a bit of a girly day. Your mom decided to take the kids and asked if we'd come around to meet you."

Each woman held a platter of some kind. She

looked at the woman with the pizza, and her mouth watered. Moving out of the way, Emily gave them a chance to enter. Closing the door, she secured the lock and followed them in.

"I'm Emily," she said.

"We all know," Zara said. "I'm Tonio's woman."

"I belong to Luiz," Raine said.

"Well, I don't belong to Jake, but I'm his wife." She held up her hand. "We've all met, and all done the introductions so you don't need to redo them." Around other women, she was awkward. It had always been this way.

Jake being the first person who didn't seem to mind that she was a little different.

The three women looked at her with smiles on their faces.

This was making life a little uncomfortable for her.

"Erm, why are you here?" she asked.

"Oh, well, we wanted to get to know you. You're Jake's wife, and seeing as we're all wives, it's kind of a secret club."

"Right," Emily said, looking at each of them and frowning. "You brought pizza."

"Yes, I cook pizza. I'm good at it." Zara opened the wrapping and offered one.

Unable to resist pizza, which was what got the women in the apartment in the first place, Emily took a piece followed by a bite.

Emily fell in love. "Wow," she said in between chews.

"You like it?"

"Can you marry me? In like all seriousness. I know it's cold, but that is the best pizza ever."

"You should try it hot," Paige said.

Emily finished her pizza and went for another slice.

Somehow, they all ended up in the sitting room. Emily didn't take one of the chairs, and instead took the floor, which was more comfortable.

"How is Jake?" Paige asked.

Emily took another bite of her second pizza and stared at Paige. She was beautiful, and she had heard a lot about Paige. The stepdaughter who was forced to marry her stepbrother. From the pictures that Emily had seen, there was no fear. Paige was in love with Donnie.

"He's fine I guess. He's with you guys' husbands, right now." They were all watching her, and Emily hated being the center of attention. "I'm really not used to this, like at all. It's kind of scary. Could you just tell me what you want? I really don't know what this is?" She pointed between them all.

"We told you. We want to get to know you. You're Jake's woman, and we're all a family in our own way. Isn't that okay?" Paige asked.

Emily winced. "I'm sorry. I'm really not good with this, and I'm not really part of the friendship—"

"We didn't all know each other," Zara said. "We all became friends, and it helps. It keeps the guys on their toes."

"Oh, okay."

"Have you ever been friends with anyone?" Raine asked.

"Yeah, sure, totally, lots of time. I have friends all over the globe," she said, lying.

"Really?" Raine asked.

"Being Bracken's daughter doesn't come with an all you can eat buffet of friends, if that makes sense? That's kind of weird, isn't it? All you can eat buffet?" Emily ran her fingers through her hair. "In case you hadn't noticed, I am really, really bad at all of this."

"You totally couldn't tell. You seemed to be a total natural," Paige said, laughing.

Smiling, Emily looked at her pizza.

"Don't worry. You now have the three of us, and we'll get you in total BFF shape," Raine said.

"You forgot Charlene. She's a sweetie as well," Zara said.

Paige coughed and looked at her. Emily saw they were all doing that silent communicating thing that friends seem to do.

"Don't be nervous about Jake's feelings for her."

"You know?"

"It's not secret news. Jake told me, and he also told me that he didn't have feelings for her anymore, so no need to worry. I look forward to getting to know Charlene."

"She's a lesbian as well. She won't be stealing your guy," Zara said.

Emily chuckled. "I know. Jake's many things, but I know he won't cheat on me."

"He's told you that?" Paige asked.

"Yep. We've got an agreement, and we're both going to work to make sure we're happy and safe. No big deal." She was happy with their arrangement, more than happy. There were no complaints coming from her. The three women stared at her a little confused. She was about to say something when she heard her cell phone ringing from the kitchen. "Excuse me, I've got to get that."

She got to her feet and left the room, pleased to have a small break. It was sweet of the three women to try to make her feel welcome and part of their group, but it was kind of weird to her. She was used to being on her own. When she went away to high school, a lot of people were afraid of her because of who her father was. Humming to herself, she glanced down to see that it was Jake calling her. Accepting the call, she couldn't help smile. "Hey, Jake, gu—"

"Babe, there's guys coming to the building. I can't get in touch with your father, but I need you to go to my room and grab my gun in the drawer beside my bed."

Emily started moving straight away. She didn't freeze up, even as her heart started to pound.

"Do you have it?"

"I've got it. Jake, Paige and the other are here."

He cursed. "Keep them there, baby. We're close. You've got to protect yourselves."

She nodded, and then frowned. "Don't worry. Dad taught us all how to shoot." She held the phone against her ear and walked back into the sitting room. Zara and Raine were dancing. Turning off the music, the three women looked toward her. "Can I tell them?"

"Do it. They'll help you, and I don't want anything bad happening to you."

Emily didn't have time to think about his words. "Men are coming," she said. "They may already be in the building." The sounds of shots and screams rang out. She didn't know what floor they were on. Turning off the lights, the music, she made sure the other three hid after they grabbed something to hurt whoever was coming toward them.

"Did you hear that, Jake?"

"I heard it. We'll be right there," he said. "Don't hang up."

She was petrified, but she moved so that she was covered behind the wall near the kitchen, and was able to look down the long hallway toward the main door.

"Are you okay?" Jake asked.

"I'm fine."

"You're scared?"

"Of course I am. My dad trained me for this. He's got your friends' kids, Jake. If something has happened to him—"

"Don't think about it right now. Focus on those men. They're coming, and it's between you and me to stop them."

"Why does it always have to be you?" she asked.

"We'll talk about that another time."

She closed her eyes as the someone shimmied the doorbell. "Someone's here," she said.

"We've just arrived, baby. I'll be there as soon as I can."

She heard the car doors opening, and then the sound of him running. There was a loud crash outside her door. They were trying to break the locks, and with a few short jabs, they were inside the apartment.

Her heart was racing. She had never been so scared in all of her life.

*Help Jake.*

*Save them.*

*Save yourself.*

*When it's over, kiss him.*

It was probably stupid, but she was really looking forward to kissing him.

They were inside the apartment. The gun was locked and loaded. She had already checked that back in the bedroom.

"What do we do?" one of the men asked.

"Our orders are to take no prisoners. Anyone we see in this building will die tonight."

The moment she saw the ankles of one of the men, she had slid down the wall to be on her ass, lower down than where they were looking. That's what her father always told her to do. She pointed the gun, aimed, and fired. The first man went down, screaming.

Emily had given away her location, and the second man aimed his gun at her. She thought she was a goner until Raine slammed a metal lamp over the back of his head with so much force she knocked him clean out.

Before the other man could reach for a weapon, Emily moved quickly, kicking it out of his way. She pointed the gun at his face, staring down at him. She didn't recognize him.

"Who do you work for?" she asked.

"I don't talk to little girls."

Raine came over and smirked. "Little girls? You're down on your ass, and we're alive."

Paige and Zara held their weapons over the falling man. Emily kept her focus on the one that could do damage. "I won't ask again," she said.

She held the gun straight at his chest, near his neck.

"I'm not telling you anything. You won't shoot me."

His arms were spread out.

"I hate cocky men." She pointed at his arm and shot. He immediately jerked, holding onto his arm. Bending down, she pressed her knee against his chest. She wasn't a small woman, never had been. For the first time, she didn't give a shit if she made a guy uncomfortable with her weight bearing down. This man had come to kill them. "Answer my question."

****

Jake rushed the building. His friend behind him. He fired off his gun, taking down three men who were waiting at the ground floor. The time for answering questions was not now. He had to get to his floor, to Emily. He didn't know if she would be able to protect his friends' wives.

Moving to the main stairs, he began the ascent to his floor. There were another three men in the stairwell, on his way up. After slamming them into the wall, he shot them, and threw them over the rail so they landed with a sickening crunch at the bottom.

Whoever thought for a second they were dealing with little children, were sadly mistaken, and he was bored.

That's right, he was fucking bored with this shit. Once and for all they were making a stand, and as far as Jake was concerned, war had been declared. Damon thought he could take The Family easily and without a fight. That bastard didn't realize what he'd woken up.

Breaking off onto Bracken's floor, Jake saw Emily's father was guarding one door. There was blood seeping from Bracken's shoulder, and several dead bodies lined the floor.

"I've got your kids. Go and save my daughter, Jake. Now!" the man yelled, but Jake was already running the last few feet up toward his room.

He needed to get there to protect her. They had only just found each other and already he couldn't lose her. There was no way he would be able to live with himself.

The moment the entered the floor, he saw that his door was wide open, when he entered his apartment, he paused.

Emily was kneeling on the man's chest, putting a great deal of force behind it. Raine stood over her, holding a metal lamp.

Paige and Zara were staring down at another man, who was unconscious.

"Who sent you?" Emily asked.

"Fuck you!"

"You want me to do the other arm?"

Jake turned on the lights, and all four women turned toward him. Emily still had the gun trained at the man's throat.

"Didn't your father ever teach you that you shouldn't ask, baby?"

"He's being stubborn and won't tell me, Jake."

Jake tutted. He moved forward and helped Emily off the man. "Are you done asking nicely?" he asked.

"Yes."

"Good, now, ladies, I suggest you leave if another man being punished is not really your thing." He didn't wait for the women to leave as he grabbed the man and slammed him against the wall. "Who sent you?"

"Fuck you."

"Nah, thanks. I'm already married." He slammed his fist against the guy's face. Instead of asking a question, though, he just kept pounding him.

The man tried to fight him, but Jake saw red. He was so fucking angry that this bastard had come into his home, and had made Emily hold a gun at him, and even shoot him.

"Jake, we need him to talk," Donnie said.

He looked behind him to find Emily still there, but Donnie, Tonio, and Luiz were also there.

"You should go," he said, talking to Emily.

"I'm not leaving. I want to know who sent him as well."

His friends had already tied up the other man, and there was a chair ready for this guy he pummeled.

Handing him to his three friends, he went toward his wife. Cupping her face, he stared into her eyes. "Are you okay, baby?"

She covered his hands on her face. "I'm not leaving. He didn't get the chance to hurt any of us."

"Where's your dad?" he asked.

"Dealing with the clean-up. Several of your soldiers are down, Jake. It was an ambush of twenty men. They did everything they could."

"Two men still got here. They still got close to you, and we can't have that. Not at all. I need you to go so that I can do this."

She shook her head. "Whatever you need to do doesn't scare me. You think I can't handle this? I can, and I will." She pressed a kiss to his inner palm. "I'm not leaving you."

He didn't want her to leave, but he also didn't want her staring at him like the monster that he was.

Pulling her in close, he pressed a kiss to her head. "We'll have our honeymoon."

"We will. First you need to get rid of this threat. No turning back, Jake."

When he went to turn away, she grabbed his arm, turned him back, and held onto his head. She pressed her lips to his. The kiss was hard, firm, and exactly what he needed.

In those few moments on his cell phone he had feared that he wouldn't see her again.

"Do you want a coffee?" she asked.

"We could all do with one," he said.

"Then that's what I'll do."

She left the sitting room, going straight to the kitchen, which provided him with visibly privacy.

"The Family are training women now. That's a first," said the man Emily shot.

Jake laughed. "That's Bracken's daughter."

Even with blood dripping from the man's face, Jake saw him pale. "Bracken?"

"You guys didn't know?"

The man who had been unconscious spoke. "No,

we didn't know. This was a kill mission. The whole of The Family would be here. They are four young boys who a little cocky. Kill them, and everyone within the building. We had no idea that Bracken was here."

"But you've heard of him?" Donnie asked.

"Of course we've heard of him. Anyone in this life has heard of him. Man's a living legend. He survived The Family, to then start his own organization." The man was very talkative.

"And you just threatened his eldest daughter, my wife," Jake said.

"We're as good as dead."

"I liked Bracken," the one bleeding said. "He … he saved my father." The man looked toward him, and there was a steely determination in his eyes. "Damon has been working for years to infiltrate The Family. Your fathers' greed allowed this to happen. He's making a move. Ryan and Rufus are already in his pocket. He has their men, including his own."

"Why the sudden change?" Jake asked, to the man bleeding.

"Bracken. He … he's a man that deserves loyalty. There was talk that you four could also hold that same loyalty, but you guys were too limp wristed. You were busy wanting to lead your own lives, and pretend that this was not happening. The world, the city is always at war. You choose what you want to do, otherwise we're all dead."

This had been a change from what Jake anticipated.

"I'll go and get Bracken," Jake said.

He didn't wait around, and left to go and get Emily's father.

## Chapter Eight

*Several hours later*

Emily closed her eyes as she pressed her back against the wall trying to ignore the sounds of bodies being taken away. Her father was talking with her husband and his friends. The man who had attacked them, the one she had shot, had known Bracken. From what she heard the name of the man whom she had shot was Craig. He'd worked for The Family since he was a kid and had been loyal until they killed his father.

Donnie, Luiz, Tonio, and Jake had killed his father, and he'd sworn his allegiance to Damon Seagus.

"Craig was a good man," Bracken said. "His father, he was stuck in the old ways. Even when I saved him from your fathers several years back, he was still determined to follow their orders. Man was loyal to the very end."

"He was loyal to a cause that was all but dead," Donnie said.

"Not to him. You need to understand that when fresh blood takes over, there are always a lot of the old timers who struggle. They remember the old ways. They remember being protected, and a lot of mess happens in the process. At least they're still alive, as are most of their family and friends, Donnie. This shit, it's not a game, and you four have been playing this as if it's a game you can just restart."

"This isn't a game to us," Jake said.

"It's not? Then why have I heard more whining about how you four want to completely annihilate The Family?" Bracken asked.

Emily had heard her father talking many times over the past couple of years about those four men. He admired them for having the courage to take out their own fathers. What he always said was he hoped they had the wisdom to know what they had really done. They had simply sped up the process of them taking over, and with it, put their own lives at risk.

Silence met her father's question.

"You all thought you had the choice to walk away. There is no walking away. Now you should see that more than ever before. I was fucking dead to The Family, but I couldn't just walk away. The moment you become part of this world, there is no backing the fuck down. You make your place, and you work like hell to get your fucking loyalty worth something. Those men I have, they would die for me, and they would die for my family before they saw anyone else take my place. All four of you have that capacity. I see it inside all of you. If I didn't, we wouldn't be having this conversation right now. Get your heads out of your fucking asses, and fix this problem."

Bracken moved away, and when Emily opened her eyes, she saw her father standing in front of her.

"Hey, Dad," she said.

"You made me proud tonight, baby girl." He pulled her in for a hug and kissed the top of her head. "Thank you for protecting those women. I taught you well."

"Are Mom and the others okay?"

"I've got everything covered. You need me, call."

She watched her dad leave, and then one by one Jake's friends left with the promise they would be meeting early the next morning at Donnie's house.

When they were alone, Jake looked toward her. "Are you okay?" he asked.

"I'm fine. Peachy."

"What you heard, and what you witnessed, I never wanted you to go through that."

"It's fine." She was a little shaken, but there really was nothing to say or do. "The threat was very real and very scary." She blew out a breath. "I'm just pleased those women were here with me rather than at home."

"Paige is pregnant for the fourth time. She's only just showing, but she wears large clothes to hide it," Jake said. "She already has four kids. Donnie wants to keep her barefoot and pregnant. They've been together a long time now."

"Oh." Emily frowned. "I think I recall someone saying that. She has a set of twins, right? I'm so sorry." Her parents had been looking after Paige, Zara, and Raine's children.

"Don't worry about it. You did everything you could, and Paige was fine. She's a fighter, and she has been through a lot more. She's married to Donnie."

"This isn't a joke. Those men were sent to kill everyone in this apartment block. Is that what you guys are doing? Playing a game? Wanting out of this life?" She knew that Jake had wanted a life outside of The Family. Wanting it and having it were two different things. She knew there was no way out for her. She had been born into this life, and being Bracken's daughter always made her life that little bit more interesting.

There was no getting away from this, not for either of them, unless they killed each other.

"We, erm, were hoping that it would bring the end of The Family. It was our end game. We'd get to live separate lives, divide the legal businesses among the four of us, work together, that kind of thing."

Emily laughed. "I can now see why some people believe you're just boys." She saw him clench his jaw. "That's a fantasy, Jake."

"We all know that. We have known it for a long time, but we've been half-asses with it. We got fucking tired of fighting. Donnie was with his woman, and so were Tonio and Luiz. We never asked for this. Our original plan was to take over and to change shit. It's hard to change a poison that is on the inside."

She ran fingers through her hair and looked down at the red spots of blood, like little ponds on their floor. Just looking at it made her sick to her stomach. "This isn't a game."

"We know it's not. We've known for a long time, but clearly we took our eyes off the ball, and now it's coming to bite us in the ass." Jake moved toward her, holding onto her shoulders and staring into her eyes. "I'm sorry I failed you, and I failed the beginning of our marriage. I won't do it again. I'll fight for us, for our Family. I need to know you're on my side."

"I proved that I'm on your side tonight. I don't shoot anyone for the hell of it, Jake. Never have. I need a good reason."

"You're a good shot."

"Thank you." She released a breath. "We can't stay here."

"No, and the next few months are going to be tough. We can't have anyone thinking we're weak, not anymore. I'm going to have to do things you're not going to like. Will you be able to handle that?"

"I can handle anything," she said. Her mother had taught her how to be, what to do, to be strong.

Jake needed a strong woman by his side. He needed someone who wouldn't turn her back on him and would continue to be there for him no matter what.

"We're going to declare war, and it's going to get ugly."

"Make sure I have a gun, and I can help you."

He cupped her neck, his thumb stroking across her cheek. "I'm going to do everything I can to protect you."

"I know. I trust you, and I believe you." She cupped his face. "You need to stop feeling guilty, Jake This is who you are, and you can't keep fighting that, no matter how much you want to. We got handed the shitty bargain of lie. That doesn't mean we can't make the most of it." She pressed her lips to his. "I'm going to go and start packing for the two of us."

There was no way they would settle in this apartment, and she wouldn't sleep well here either.

There was no doubt in her mind that war was coming. Jake, Tonio, Luiz, and Donnie had often been judged as children, boys. Someone now intended to take their place, and by doing so, cast doubt on their leadership, on their own struggles as young men.

She grabbed a large suitcase, and began to fill it. Jake surprised her as he stood by her side, helping.

"We're in this together, right?" he asked.

"Yes."

"You're a strange woman, Emily."

"I guess I'm nothing like Charlene then." She was aware of the woman he'd thought he was in love with.

"I didn't love her. Talk about a reality check," he said.

"What do you think you felt for her then?" She threw in several pairs of sneakers, and no heels. She made sure to pack jeans and long shirts. There was no way she was going to be caught in dresses and heels, at least not yet.

"I helped save her from Donnie's father. She's the mother of Donnie's half-sister. She had been captured with the intent of selling her, but Anthony Martinez, Donnie's dead old daddy, decided he wanted her for himself. I helped to save her, and I spent a lot of time with her. In our line of work, you don't meet a lot of good woman. My friends found their soul mates, and they had nothing to do with this life. Apart from Paige, whose dad was a soldier, but she didn't know it at the time. You're a good woman as well."

"Thank you. I will take that as a compliment."

"You should. You're a fighter, I like that. Charlene was never a fighter. She was more the damsel that needed to be rescued. Over time, I stopped feeling anything for her. I think I was in love with the idea of being the savior."

Emily smiled and touched his arm. "That's not a bad thing. You're not a bad guy."

"Thank you." He took her hand and kissed it. "So you'll forgive me for thinking you would be a mega bitch?" he asked.

"Totally not. We're so not being friends."

"You can't resist me. Admit it." He winked at her, and she liked the change inside him. There was a part of Jake that she was sure he kept hidden from the rest of the world. She was determined to find out his every secret, and to prove to him, the world was not all bad.

****

The following morning Jake sat with his friends and Bracken around Donnie's table. Before they left the apartment building last night, all of The Family had decided to go to Donnie's safe house. There were enough bedrooms, and security to house all of them, including their kids. Bracken and his family were also in residence. Emily had woken early, helping out the women to take care of the kids and breakfast.

"It's Damon Seagus. He's taken all of Conwell's and Charles's territories," Donnie said. "I got a call from our informant on the inside. Their bodies have just washed up to shore. Their throats slits, and their cocks shoved inside them. Nasty business but totally Damon's signature."

"Classy," Tonio said, wrinkling his nose. "Would you hold the cock, and then sever?" Tonio made the hand actions, grabbing a cock, and then drawing the blade down.

All of the men winced, and shook their heads.

"Nasty way to go," Bracken said.

"Did they do it first?" Tonio asked.

"For fuck's sake, Tonio? What does it matter?" Donnie asked.

"I'm just curious. This guy is coming after us, we should know everything. If I lose my dick, I lose my will to live."

Jake sat back, and he couldn't help laughing. Donnie was getting angrier with every passing second. It probably shouldn't have been a big deal, but even Jake knew he wouldn't want to live without his cock.

"Moving on," Bracken said.

"He's heavily guarded, and he thought he was in a position to take us out, and last night, we wouldn't have seen it coming," Donnie said.

"What we need to do is begin to reclaim what was ours. We need to find the people who betrayed us, starting with the soldiers," Jake said. "I know how to do that. According to Matt's records, whenever Damon wanted to meet, he would send out a key text with a location where to meet."

"What do you suggest? Sending out a mass text and see who turns up?" Luiz asked. "We do that, and all of our guys will respond."

"It was a burner phone. One word, Loyalty, text, and it would hand out coordinates of where to meet," Jake said. "It's lame, and kind of tacky, but it worked, and it kept them low key. None of our men questioned their messages."

Bracken sat back, laughing. "You guys don't see it." Jake smiled as he saw that Bracken understood.

"Well enlighten me?" Donnie asked.

"We gave them their phones," Jake said, putting Matt's cell phone on the table. "We pay for them as part of The Family. We have access to every single phone who is given that location." Jake then put another file down. "Last night while you guys were sleeping, I did a little computer work, and cross-referenced the same number, and I have found out every single man that has betrayed us, and you're not going to like it."

"I knew there was a reason I wanted you to marry my girl," Bracken said.

"It's not good news though. There are a lot of our men who have betrayed us, Donnie."

He waited as his friends looked through the file. Some of them they had thought were their allies.

"We've got to do a mass purge," Luiz said. "These men, some of them control our stocks. They're businessmen, Donnie."

Jake knew there was going to be some trouble. He'd spent all night doing his research, and Emily had been helping him as well. She was hot when it came to a computer, and they had worked side by side.

"The trafficking of girls has also restarted up. Three women have gone missing, all of them last seen leaving one of our nightclubs," Jake said. "I checked in at the docks as well. My guy Reese, he's the one that lets me know if something has been going shifty. Told me that he was given papers signed by me to allow a shipment to be received of women, Donnie. My signature."

Donnie cursed, stood up, and paced.

"We fucked up. People think they can take from

us. That we are too young to rule, and that's not the case. We have to make our stand and show everyone that when they fuck with, they won't like what they're dealing with."

"We can't split apart and handle this shit ourselves. We've got to fight this together, the four of us," Jake said. "Starting with the soldiers."

"You want to take out that mass scale?" Luiz asked.

"Got no choice, do I? They betrayed us, and you know what? I think it's time those who fuck with us get to see how well our fathers trained us. I am tired of being considered a boy. I'm not a fucking boy. I'm a man, and they are going to show us the respect that we are due. That's fucking final. We take no prisoners. We don't allow anyone to escape this. They made their decision, and I'm not going to allow them to make the same mistake twice." Jake looked toward Bracken. "Are you going to have a problem with that?"

"No, I'm not. You've been betrayed by those who pledged their life to you. They walked away, and now they must suffer the consequences. This is good what you're all doing. My men will be there to help you," Bracken said.

"Why are you helping us?" Luiz asked. "Why not partner with Damon Seagus?"

"First, do you see Emily accepting the Seagus name?" Jake started to laugh just thinking about it as Bracken went on. "Sorry, poor joke. It's in bad taste. Damon is not a man of honor. I'm a killer. I've taken lives without asking questions, and I'm a monster. I know this, I accept it. My daughter, she's a strong woman, a good woman, and I knew that Damon would hurt her because he could never hurt me. You," he looked at Jake, "are a good man. You're all men of honor. No matter what your parents did, you have come out ten times better than they would ever be. That's why I help you. That is why I wanted my daughter to be with you. You're loyal, you're strong, and you will care for her. Do not let me regret my decision."

Silence fell around the table.

"We need to eat, and then we need to send a mass text to these men and get them at the warehouse. Can we get this done by lunchtime?" Donnie asked.

"Already on it. I've got men from our side, and yours. They know the drill and what to do," Jake said. "We'll be there to see it through."

"Are you sure you can handle that?" Tonio asked. "Some of these men, you were close to a lot of them."

"And a lot of them screwed up. They made the wrong choice, and they're going to have to live with that. Our family comes first. It always will. Let's go eat. I'm starving." Jake stood up, and headed toward the door. Not only was he starving but he wanted to go and check on Emily.

She had stayed with him, helping him cross-reference, and even handling the text on the computer that would go out. It was like an alert that had been registered to the phones. He was disappointed, gutted that so many of his soldiers had turned their backs on him.

*"I don't want to be a solider, Daddy."*

*"You will be, son. It's in your blood. It's what you do, and you will have to look those men that you control in the eye, and see if they are lying or not."*

*"What if they're lying?"*

*"Then you will kill them."*

*"I don't want to be a murderer."*

*"If you love your family. If you love Tonio, Luiz, and Donnie as your brothers, then you will do it. You*

*have no choice but to kill or be killed."*

Jake pulled out the memory. They had been in the basement, and what he'd not known was his father held a traitor. At the age of eight years old, he had watched his father kill a man, a soldier, for daring to defy The Family laws by escaping. No one escaped. They wanted to leave, fine, they left The Family six feet under, never to be seen or heard from again.

Entering the kitchen, he saw Emily standing at the stove. She was the only one in the kitchen, and the scent of bacon and sausage was heavy in the air. He heard the kids in another room, laughing, and shouting. It was like something out of his own fantasies. Only, he didn't have any children to his name. One day, he wanted to have loads of them.

He moved up behind Emily, wrapping his arms around her, and pressing his face against her neck.

"What's the matter?" she asked, running her hand up his arm. She was turning bacon, and he liked how natural this felt between them.

"Nothing. I just wanted to hold you. I couldn't resist."

She sighed, leaning against him. "You're done with your meeting?"

"Yeah, after breakfast I've got a lot to do. I won't be able to linger. How are you feeling? Tired?"

"I'm fine. It's not the first all-nighter I've pulled. It won't be my last, so please don't worry about me."

"You're going to be safe here."

"I know."

"I have a place out in the country. It's about an hour from this place. I don't go there often because my business always keeps me in the city. When this all blows over, I'll take you there."

"For now we're just here, with your friends?" she

asked.

"I know it's not ideal. It's all I've got. What I want you to do though is to take your time, and plan our honeymoon."

"We've just gotten back from our first."

"No, we didn't have a honeymoon, we had a mini-vacation. I want to take you back to that island, and I want us to play board games, read to each other, take long walks." Jake nibbled her neck. "What do you think?"

"I think it sounds like a very good idea." She turned her head, and he couldn't resist kissing her lip. Pressing his body against hers, her ass nestled against his cock, all Jake wanted to do was take her to bed.

"I want to hold you tonight," he said.

"Then be home in time, and I'll stay awake for you."

Paige entered the kitchen. "Crap, I'm so sorry. I didn't think. The kids are wanting breakfast, and so are the guys."

Jake laughed, kissing Emily's neck. "No worries."

He was looking forward to tonight.

## Chapter Nine

Emily sat on the edge of the bed holding the photo album that she had found there twenty minutes ago. The moment breakfast had ended, Jake, his friends, her father, and several of the men had left. She'd helped clean away breakfast and put the kids down for a nap. Her mother was out in the garden with her own siblings giving them a lesson that the school had sent to her via e-mail.

When they had missed days at school, her mother always made sure they were able to catch up. None of her kids were ever going to be thick or stupid, that's what her mother would always say.

Holding the book close to her chest, Emily knew Jake had left it out, and for some strange reason, she hadn't been able to open it.

When a knock sounded at the door, she yelled for whoever it was to enter. She was surprised to see it was Zara, Tonio's wife, entering.

"Hey," she said. "I just put Suzie down for a nap. I think all this excitement has her tired."

"Excitement?" Emily asked, frowning.

"I wouldn't tell my little girl that we're under threat, and people are trying to murder us. The aim is to have our kids who are not afraid to go to sleep."

"Right, right, sorry. Ignore me, I'm just a little lost right now." Emily rubbed at her temple as Zara took a seat beside her.

"It's fine. This life is really hard to get used to. I know. Tonio, when I first met him, he was so lost. Such a broken soul, and he helped me, and together we help each other."

"You know Jake?" Emily asked.

"I don't know if anyone ever really knows Jake.

He's one of those guys that you think you can tag a label to, but something tells me, he's the kind of guy that always surprises you."

"He's always surprising me," Emily said. "I wanted to hate him. In fact, I did hate him. From the moment my father told me I was going to be marrying him, I hated him."

"You don't anymore?" Zara asked.

"How can you hate someone who is always so determined to take care of everyone else?"

"From what Tonio told me, Jake is always the first one into the room. He was supposed to only be a soldier. His life was expendable," Zara said. "It's sad really."

"Yeah, it's sad. I think Jake has lived all of his life believing he can be overlooked." Emily shook her head. "How can you hate someone who is prepared at every single moment to protect those around him at the cost of his own life?"

"You do care about him?" Zara asked.

"I think I do. I don't know. I'm confused."

Zara chuckled. "It's okay to be confused. There are times that I don't like Tonio. He can be a hard ass, and that's marriage. It's life. You can never be one hundred percent happy every single time. You can just be content, and know that you'll want to kill each other, but deep down you love each other."

Emily ran her hand over the album. "Do you think it's possible for two strangers to love each other?"

"I think anything is possible if you want it badly enough. Do you want your marriage to Jake to work? Can you handle this life?"

"You do know there's no way out of this life, right?" Emily asked. "I've known that for a long time. My father, he's my link here. Tonio's father's his link.

The only way out is death."

"I know. I think the guys wanted to leave for a short time. Who wouldn't?" Zara asked. "There was a time I thought it would be possible for us to live a normal life, but Tonio, this is in his blood, and what the hell is wrong with living with how we are, you know?"

"I know. I think from when I was about fourteen, I knew there was no way I'd have the white picket fence, and the four kids, with a man who had a nine to five job. My dad was once part of the mafia known as The Family. I was warned, and trained to use a gun, and how to protect myself. You did good with the lamp, by the way."

"If I had a gun, I would do better, believe me. Tonio taught me how to shoot. He knew there was no getting out of this. He wants to protect his family to the very end."

"It's what everyone wants to do." Emily looked back down at the album. "I think Jake left this out for me."

"Probably. Tonio has one similar. It's got the guys' memories. They were like a brotherhood." Zara sighed. "I think you're good for Jake."

"You don't even know me."

"No, but I've seen Jake smile. He's usually very sad like all the time, and he's not the best when it comes to family get-togethers. Today at breakfast, I saw a change. He couldn't take his eyes away from you."

Emily liked that.

"I am going to go and help. Suzie is easy to put to sleep, but George, my oldest, he's a nightmare. Him and Petal together, not a good combo."

Zara left her alone with her thoughts.

Opening up the book, Emily ran her hand over the first photograph. It was of Jake, she knew it without a doubt. He had a dimple in the corner of his mouth, and he looked totally out of place, and the smile was so wide, so pure. He couldn't have been older than six. She found herself smiling just by looking at it.

The next photograph was a complete contrast. A nightmare. The smile was gone, and looking into his dark eyes, she knew the boy in the picture had seen stuff that no child should ever have to see. Running her fingers across the page, she felt a wave of sadness wash over her.

Jake deserved so much. Turning the page, she started to see Jake with each of his friends, with his parents, and then as she went along, more of him growing up. Each time she looked at him, it was like a new layer of pain had been added to him, and it saddened her to see.

Sniffling, she found herself crying just as Jake entered the room. Looking toward the clock, she saw it was a little after four in the afternoon.

"Jake," she said.

"Why are you crying? I thought you would like to see," he said.

She put the photograph album down and moved toward him, wrapping her arms around his neck and holding him close. "There is another way."

"Another way?"

"For our family to have a life that was stolen from you. My father, I knew what he was, and I saw it firsthand, but I know we can have that life with our kids. They don't have to grow up with fear, with no value." She cupped his face and stared into his eyes. "From now on, you will value your life. Your life is just as sacred as theirs and became so the moment you married me."

"Emily, this is what I've known. I'm an old dog."

"I care about you, Jake."

"You don't know me."

"And you don't know me, but would you like me to not care about my life?" she asked. She saw the frown on his brow. "You and I have been pushed together, and I'm telling you, Jake, your life means a great deal to me. Promise me you'll take care of it."

"I promise."

"Good." She couldn't resist putting her lips to his and holding him close. He ran his hands up her back, and she liked the way he gripped her, as if he didn't want to let her go.

"I wasn't supposed to like you."

"Me neither," she said, opening her eyes. She pulled away and began wiping underneath them. "I'm sorry. I don't usually get emotional." When she was more herself, she looked at him and saw that he was stressed. "Did it go well?"

"Yes. Over a hundred of our men arrived at the warehouse, and there are now a hundred bodies burning."

"Can the warehouse be traced back to you?" she asked.

"Nope. That warehouse is registered to Damon, and believe me, we've sent a message. Tomorrow, we go to the docks and handle business there." He walked toward the bathroom, and she followed him.

Emily plugged the bath in and began to run water, adding bubbles as she did.

Jake held onto the bathroom sink and stared at his reflection. "Every time I look in this mirror, I swear I see a bigger monster there every single time."

"You're not a monster, Jake."

"I told them not to take any prisoners, not to listen to anyone. We couldn't afford to take traitors back, and I didn't." He ran a hand down his face. "Today I killed fathers, sons, brothers, husbands, you name it, they were there."

She didn't say a word, knowing that even as he knew he had to kill them, death still weighed heavy on his soul.

Once the bath was ready, she helped him out of his clothes. She had seen her husband naked a few times now, and she was still a virgin. His body aroused her, and she knew hers aroused him. When he was completely naked, she led him to the bath, and helped him inside. When she turned to grab some soap, he caught her wrist. "Please don't leave me."

"I'm getting the soap, Jake."

"That's not what I meant."

She looked at his hand on her wrist, and then into his tortured eyes. "I'm not going anywhere. I promised you that."

"I want a family."

"I know."

"With you," he said.

Emily smiled. "I wouldn't expect anything less."

"That means we have to have sex."

"We won't be getting a family overnight. I know that, and I also know we're going to have to have sex." She took his hand and held it tightly. "When we're ready, we'll get started."

For some strange reason, heat flooded her pussy as he held her hand and pressed a kiss to it. "I'll make it good for you."

"I don't expect anything less."

He released her long enough for her to grab the soap and come back to him. Sinking down to her knees, she took the sponge and began to wash his body. He wasn't dirty, but she knew he needed to feel clean right now. She hummed as she worked, hoping she was helping to soothe him.

"I like it when you hum. You have a nice voice."

"You're full of compliments tonight." She liked listening to him talk. "I think you've got a really nice reading voice."

He chuckled.

"Are you okay, Jake?"

"I will, baby, I will be." He took her arm and pressed a kiss to the inside. She loved it when he touched her like that.

\*\*\*\*

Later that night, Jake watched as Emily walked around the room, brushing her hair as she did. The negligee she wore was so sheer that as she moved it only served to tantalize him. She was humming to herself again, and he wondered what made her do that. He found it really calming to listen to.

Dinner had been a tense affair. They were all under one roof, including Emily's family. Not far from his bedroom, her parents were sleeping.

This was the only way he believed they could all be safe.

"What's wrong?" she asked.

"Nothing. It's just weird knowing your parents are not that far. I wonder if they're listening to us." He raised his brow, and she laughed.

"Nah, they've got more important things to do.

"Are you talking about your parents fucking?"

"They're human as well. I'm not under any illusions when it comes to my parents. I know they have sex. They love each other so much. Watching them over the years, it's like they have their own language. It's what I've always wanted. Whenever I was asked what I wanted when I grew up, it was to have a relationship like my parents'."

Jake patted the bed, and she lowered herself in front of him. He took the brush from her hand and helped her to turn so her back was to him.

"You're going to brush my hair?"

"Yes, that is what I'm going to do, and you're going to love it."

She giggled. "Okay, fine. My mom hasn't brushed my hair in years."

He began small slow strokes, teasing out the ends. The blonde locks were so fine, so beautiful, and so soft.

Neither of them spoke for a long time. He was the first to break the silence. "I love brushing your hair."

"Thank you," she said.

"No problem, baby." He handed her back the brush and kissed her shoulder. He heard her slight gasp, and she turned to face him.

She reached out, cupping his cheek. "I want you, Jake."

"Emily, we've not been married that long."

"I know, and it's strange. We haven't been together that long, and yet for me, it feels like we've never been apart."

He felt that way, too. He'd never been so consumed with another person before, or felt that connected. Emily, she was part of him, even when he didn't want her to be. Running the tips of his fingers up her arm, he stared into her deep blue eyes.

Unable to resist, he pulled her close, and pressed a kiss to her lips. She gasped, and he glided his tongue over, before plunging inside.

He caught her hands as she held onto his shoulder. "No, I don't want you to regret this."

"I'm not going to regret this, Jake. I will if I don't get this chance with you again." She turned completely so that she straddled his lap. Sinking her fingers into his hair, she held onto him, and he loved it. He loved the way she wasn't afraid to hold him, to take what she wanted.

Emily pressed her lips to his, and he kissed her back with the same fever that she did him. Gripping her ass, he moved her against his cock. The only material separating them were his boxer briefs. She wasn't even wearing panties.

The negligee hid nothing from his view. Moving beneath it, he began to stroke her pussy, which was already soaking wet. She pulled away from the kiss and gave out a little moan.

"You want me?" he asked.

"Yes, do you want me, Jake?"

"Yes, fuck yes, I do. I want you to want it, baby."

She held onto his face and stared into his eyes.

He'd never been so captured, so out of control.

"Then fuck me, Jake. Make me yours. I want you so much, and I know I'm not going to regret this. I need you." She released his face, her hand going to his cock and gripping him tightly.

This was insane. His life was crazy, and yet he'd been able to find a woman that he wanted more than anything. "Don't you want your first time to be in our own bed? When we're not at risk?"

"We're going to be at risk every single day. It's never going to change, Jake. I don't care about a new bed, or waiting." She took his hand and glided it down her chest to her breast. "This is what I want. I want you, more than anything. I don't want to wait another day. Anything could happen. Stop hesitating. Stop being the good guy. I want you. Take me. I'm offering myself to you."

He palmed her breast, feeling the beaded nipple press against him. Moving his other hand to her free breast, he pinched the nipple as she squirmed with excitement down on his crotch.

"Tell me again what you want?" he asked.

"I want you to fuck me, Jake. I want you to take me, and make me yours."

Jake loved every single word that was coming from her lips. Sliding his hand up into her hair, he gathered it in his fist and pulled her close, slamming his lips onto hers. He plundered her mouth, wanting her kiss, needing it more than anything.

Her nails sank into his shoulders, holding onto him, gripping him hard as she ground her pussy against his cock.

In one quick move, he pressed her against the bed as he climbed above her.

"What are you doing?" she asked.

"I'm the one in charge. Not you, baby." He leaned down kiss her neck and took the tiny straps of her negligee, pulling them down her arms. "You're a little inexperienced in all of this, but don't worry. I'll take complete care of you." He pressed his lips against her shoulder, and then down to her chest where the sheer negligee covered her breasts. Licking a path along that edge he felt her shake, and glancing up, he saw she was looking right at him. He wanted her eyes on him and to never look away. While his gaze was still on hers, he began to move the straps down the rest of the way. The material slid across her breasts and moved down. Still, he didn't release her eyes as he went to her sides, moving as he took the negligee off her. Now, he could have just torn it from her body, but he wanted to keep the negligee. It was fucking sexy. He also wanted another excuse to touch her, to heighten her arousal and need for him.

Once she was naked beneath him, he climbed off the bed and removed his pants, ignoring his rock-hard cock. He wasn't some boy that couldn't control himself.

Tonight was all about her and her pleasure. There would be many nights that he would get to play, to tease her.

Climbing back on the bed at her feet, he took one of her ankles and pressed a kiss to the side, and then to the base of her foot. She giggled and tried to pull her foot away. Her laughter made him smile, and he held her foot a little tighter. He continued to press kisses, making her laugh and wriggle on the bed.

"Stop, stop, it's too much," she said, covering her face.

"This is supposed to be sensual, baby." He flicked his tongue, and they both just started laughing.

"Don't ever do that. It's not sensual. It's funny. That is what it is. So funny."

He placed her ankle against his chest and began to stroke down her thigh getting nearer to her pussy. He stopped when he was right there, making her gasp and squirm as she tried to get his fingers near to where she wanted them.

"Jake, please," she said, biting her lip.

"You want me to touch that pretty, virgin pussy."

She nodded. "Yes."

He stroked her thigh, and this time he didn't stop, nor did he pull away. Putting his fingers against her pussy, stroking over her clit. She gasped, arching up, thrusting herself against his fingers, needing him inside her.

"It feels so good."

"I can make it feel even better." Jake moved so that he was above her pussy. Emily spread her thighs, and he flicked his tongue against her clit, and she screamed his name. He couldn't resist smiling against her pussy.

Being with Emily, it lightened his entire world, and it made him hungry for so much more. He knew only she had that power over him, and he welcomed her control, needed it more than anything else. Teasing her clit, he sucked, nipped, and flicked, wanting to make her come. At the same time, he didn't want this to be over.

Her flesh was not tainted by any other man. She was fresh, new, and he wanted to completely consume her for himself. No other man would have what belonged to him. They were bound together in ways that couldn't tear them apart.

She screamed his name as he bit just a little too harshly.

"Come for me, Emily. Come for me, and I will fill your pussy with my cock." He wouldn't be wearing a rubber either. He wanted to feel her warm, slick heat around his cock, to claim her, to make her his.

She wriggled beneath him, her hands sinking into his hair, smashing his face against her cunt, and then releasing him to fist the blanket.

Using his fingers and his tongue, he began the stroke that he knew would send her over the edge into a release that would totally take her to new heights. He wanted her completely at his mercy, desperate, begging, so that she wanted him to fuck her again and again.

The moment she hurtled over the edge, he licked her release, swallowing her down, tasting her, filling every one of his senses with his need for her. Throughout it all, she shouted for him.

Jake wanted to beat his chest like a damn ape he was so fucking thrilled. There was no one else for this woman but him. She was his completely.

## Chapter Ten

Emily's body was on fire. She was on cloud nine, and didn't want to come down, not for anything. Jake moved between her thighs, and he fisted his rock-hard cock in his hand. The tip leaked pre-cum as he slid the head up and down her slit, bumping her clit. With each stroke over her nub, she moaned, finding it impossible to focus on anything but the pleasure of his touch.

"This is going to hurt the first time, baby," he said.

"I know. I don't care. I want you, Jake. Make me yours."

She saw the flare in his eyes and knew that she had surprised him. This thing between them, it wasn't going away. Her feelings for him were getting stronger with every single hour. She didn't want this to stop, to end. Knowing he was putting his life at risk terrified her. She only hoped that he would fight for her, for them, for what they could have together. Emily sensed something within him. She didn't understand it, but knew deep down in her soul that he was a good man, a kind man, someone that she had the potential to love. That scared her a little. What if she *already* loved him?

Cutting off that thought right now, she stared at where his cock was sliding between her slit, covered in her cream.

"Don't stop. I want you, Jake. Please, make me yours."

She stared into his eyes and refused to look away. His cock moved from her clit and slid down her body, going to her entrance. She tried not to tense but knew she had failed. This was something she hadn't even realized that he wanted.

Jake stroked her clit and melted away her tension

until she was lying on the bed, desperate for him. His hand moved from her pussy, going to her hips, where he held her. In one quick thrust, he filled her pussy, breaking through her barrier and claiming her completely as his.

Emily cried out, and then covered her mouth. The last thing she wanted was someone knocking on the door when she had asked for this, when she had begged.

Jake took her hands, locking their fingers together as tears leaked from her eyes. "I'm so sorry, baby. I'm really sorry. I didn't want you to hurt."

"It's fine." She sank her teeth into her lip, and he caressed her cheek. The tender way he touched her made her ache for so much more.

"It's not fine. I knew it would hurt, I was hoping to get you off so that you didn't feel any pain."

She nodded, and then glanced down. They were chest to chest. His cock was like a burning brand inside her, scalding every inch within.

"Will it ease?" she asked.

"I sure hope so. I don't want to hurt you anymore, and I'm not moving until you're ready."

"Don't you just want to get it over with?"

"I'm not a monster, Emily. I won't just fuck you to get it over with." He released one of her hands and teased several strands of her hair. "I can feel every time your pussy clenches around me. You're so tight."

"We can't get our marriage annulled now."

"There was no way I was ever going to let you get away from me. No way at all."

"And if I was a bitch like you first thought?" she asked, smiling. The pain had started to lessen, and she was no longer hurting. It was tight and strange, but that was turning into something more.

"You're not a bitch at all. In fact, I think you're a

total softie. You've not got a single bad bone in your body." He pressed a kiss to her lips. "You're a beautiful woman, you know."

"I didn't know." Her cheeks heated under his perusal.

He chuckled. "Then you're going to get tired of me constantly telling you. I think you are." The backs of his fingers caressed her cheek.

She wriggled, wanting to know if she was okay for him to move. He groaned, and she stopped.

"You're so tight," he said. "I can feel every single pulse, every wave, all of it." He pressed his lips against her cheek. His breath fanned near her ear, and she closed her eyes, loving the feel of him.

"Do you want me to fuck you?" he asked.

"Yes."

She didn't know if the pain would still be there, but she wanted him to move. An ache had started deep within, and she couldn't take it anymore. She needed to know the truth.

"Oh, fuck, baby," he said and began to slide out.

Emily couldn't help the gasp that escaped. She was totally unprepared for the pleasure that rushed over her, and it made her release his hands to grip his ass. "Don't stop." It felt so good.

"I'm not going to stop." He continued his withdrawal until only the tip was inside him, and then he slammed back inside, going to the hilt, drawing a cry of pleasure from her lips. "But I need to be able to move if you want that kind of pleasure to continue."

He kissed her neck, flicking his tongue over her pulse. He pulled all of the way out of her once again and then thrust back inside her. She cried out, looking down at where they were connected with that one piece of flesh. His cock appeared, and it was covered in her cream, glistening.

"Oh, Jake, it feels so good." She arched up, her nails sinking into his ass where she still held him.

He began to rock inside her, going in and out, making her want more. She wanted him to fuck her, to drive his cock within her.

She felt possessed as need completely swamped her, stopping all kind of rational thought. She didn't understand it, and in that moment, she didn't care either. All that mattered was the pleasure that was consuming the two of them.

He rode her hard, and she held onto him, needing him to be so deep inside her that she didn't know where she ended and he began.

"Oh fuck, Emily, you feel so good, so fucking good." He growled the words against her skin as he nibbled on her neck. She held onto his ass, forcing him inside her. "I'm not going to last. Oh, fuck!"

Jake let go completely, and fucked her harder, driving into her with a force that had the headboard slamming against the wall. Neither of them stopped, and finally, he filled her, thrusting every single inch of his rock-hard cock inside her.

She felt every pulse, every ripple as his cock filled her with his cum. Seconds passed, minutes even, until he collapsed over her, panting.

"I'm so sorry," he said.

Emily frowned. "Why?"

"I wanted you to come again. I couldn't wait."

She released his ass. Her fingers were numb from holding him so tightly. "Don't worry. That was amazing."

He eased back to look at her, and she cupped his face, pushing some of his hair that fell on his brow. "You've bewitched me."

Laughter filled her. "You're crazy."

"Yeah, I am. I'm crazy for thinking this thing between us wouldn't work. I was mistaken, and for that I'm sorry."

"You don't need to be sorry, Jake. I accept all gifts." She pressed a kiss to his lips.

"I wish we were back on your father's island. I could do all kinds of wicked things to you."

"We can go back there when all of this is over." The lightness in his eyes slowly ebbed away. "What is it?"

"This thing, Em, it's dangerous. I may not—"

"Do not for a second finish that, Jake. You're strong. You survived the abuse of your father. You can handle everything. I have every single faith in you." She pressed another kiss to his lips. "Don't for a second try to say good-bye. I won't accept it. Not now, not ever. We've got each other, and that is more than enough for me." Tears filled her eyes, and he shushed her.

"Fine. I will."

"You can't go, Jake. Not now. We've got so much to fight for. I'm going to stay by your side and help you."

She loved his touch, and he stroked her cheek once again. Every night she would wait for the moment that he would join her in their bed, and they would make love, or fuck. She didn't care which one, only that he made her feel, and she didn't want to lose that.

With every second that passed, she felt herself losing her heart to him. Jake was not a cocky bastard. He wasn't an asshole.

He was a kind man, a caring one, the kind of man she had prayed for a long time ago. She had believed that her prayers would never be answered, and yet here he was, her husband. She would fight for him in ways that no one else could.

\*\*\*\*

Jake pulled out of her tight pussy and glanced down to find small dots of blood on the bedsheet. Leaving the bed, he made his way into the bathroom. There was an ache in his heart, and he didn't like the direction his thoughts were taking.

Emily saw something inside him. He knew it without a doubt with the way she looked at him. To Emily he was more than Jake the solider. He had meaning to her, and fuck him, he relished it. He wanted to be something special to her.

It was like a drug in his veins. He couldn't hold back, and he was constantly staring into her eyes because he loved more than anything what he saw in them. She was falling for him. There was no mistaking it or her feelings. He felt the same way.

When he first saw her, he'd thought she was a mega-bitch who would do anything to get what she wanted.

There was nothing bitchy about her. She had felt exactly like him, trapped in a life neither of them could escape. Only now, neither of them wanted to. This was their life, and there was no getting away from that.

He had accepted it and had finally broken away the claws of regret. There was no way in hell he was going to live hoping for an out. Living like that had caused this mess. This was his family, his home, his job, his very existence, and he'd fought it because of his father. He would be everything his father had said he'd be, only he'd be better. The Family would be worth ten times more than their own fathers. Their Family would become more, mean more, so much that people would swear their loyalty rather than kill them. He had a new mission now, a new surge of feeling.

The time for hating what he once was had passed. Now he could grab hold of his own destiny, and instead of being embarrassed by it, he'd embrace it, take it, love it, and show it everything he could.

Once the bath was filled up, he made his way into the bedroom to find Emily stripping the bed.

"I was going to do that."

"It's embarrassing." She turned to him with a pout.

"I think it's damn sexy." He moved up behind her, wrapping his arms around her, and tugging her close. She giggled and held onto him. "It shows that I am the only man you'll ever have, and you know what? It makes you all mine. I think I should keep the sheets as a token of our first time."

"Ew, gross."

He laughed and kissed her neck. Picking her up in his arms, he carried her back through to the bathroom and eased her into the water. Unlike the last time when she washed him, he eased in behind her, wrapping his arms around her.

"You seem different. Full of life. Do I have a magic pussy?" she asked.

Cupping her tits, Jake held onto her. "You have the best pussy in the world. Nice, warm, tight. I can't wait to be inside you again."

"I'm a little sore, but I'd like to feel you again."

"You're a woman after my heart," he said. "Yes, I'm happy, and you've helped me to see that just because I'm my father's son, doesn't mean I can't be better than him. Tonio, Luiz, Donnie, and I, we've all been looking at this completely wrong. They are not in control of us We're in control of us, and no one can take that away, and I refuse to let them." He kissed her cheek. "It's all thanks to you that I can see that now."

"My magic pussy. Don't be telling everyone. They'll be wanting a taste."

He growled against her skin. "They will all die. No one will ever take what is mine. You're mine, Emily. Don't ever forget that." He gripped her chin and tilted her head so that she had no choice but to look at him.

"There's no one else that I could ever want, Jake. I only want you. You're the first man that I've been with, and you're going to be the only man." She stroked his fingers.

He didn't like the strike of jealousy that hit him, but he also knew she was only teasing.

"So the plan tomorrow?" she asked. "What do you have to do?"

"We're heading to the docks. There have been fake documents supplied by one of the soldiers. We're going to free the women, and whoever else they have."

She tensed. "You mean kids as well?"

"Kids, men, people desperate enough to offer themselves as payment to try and make a better life. It's not a good thing, not at all."

"It's not the first time The Family have dealt with it either."

"No, The Family has a history of buying and selling women."

"Yeah, you mentioned that Charlene was kept as some kind of trophy."

Jake hummed. "Yeah, she was. No one deserves that life, no one at all."

"I agree. What do you do after that?" she asked.

"The docks are a big deal. We've got a guy in the law. He's going to help the women, and make sure they're taken home, or at least taken to their families. You'd be surprised how many women are taken from their own towns and streets. They watch women for weeks, finding out if they would be missed or not. In most instances, they take strays. It's wrong. No one misses them, and when they wind up dead in some lake, no one questions how."

"It's bad that you know all of this, Jake. You had a horrible childhood."

"I didn't have a horrible one at all. Not compared to Tonio. Out of all four of his, he had the worst."

When she didn't question him, Jake grew worried.

"Tonio was—"

"I know about him, Jake. You don't need to tell me everything. It's horrible beyond words or thought the animals that raised him. The women, the boys, the children, it's all too much to bear. Zara is a good woman for him. She brings him back, and I can see that. I saw it at dinner. She was holding him, and it was like with every passing second, her Tonio came back to her. Their kids' father as well."

Jake had witnessed it. Killing people always took its toll on all of them. There was never a happy ending in death, only more fear and hurt. Zara had hugged Tonio tightly to her body, and his friend had held her. She had brought him back, and then his kids had pounced on him, and it was like all the evil had been wiped from his gaze. It was beautiful to witness.

Releasing her breasts, Jake grabbed the soap, and using his hands as a sponge, he began to wash her body. He paid careful attention to her tits making sure he cleaned all around and beneath them. Gliding his hands down her body, he cupped her pussy and washed traces of blood that were on her thighs. When the soap was gone from his hand, he teased a finger down her slit and loved the sound of her gasp.

"That feels so good."

"Are you sore?" he asked.

"A little but I don't care." She moved in the bath and spun around, pressing her lips against his. "I want you to fuck me, Jake, right here, right now."

He lifted her up, took his already hard cock in his hand, and pressed the tip to her entrance. Slowly, she eased over him, and he filled her soaking wet pussy. He was careful as he didn't want to hurt her, and he took his time filling her.

"Oh, Jake," she said. There was something else in her eyes, like she wanted to say something important.

Jake knew what he wished to hear, and he waited. But she didn't say anything else. Her teeth sank into her lip, and she held onto his shoulders instead, riding his cock. Water sloshed over the sides of the bath, soaking the floor, but he'd deal with that later. For now, he needed her lips. Sinking his fingers into her hair, she held him tightly as well, holding the back of his head as their teeth clashed with their need.

Her pussy was so tight, it felt like heaven wrapped around his cock.

"You're mine, Emily," he said, in between kisses.

"I know. You're mine, Jake. No other woman can have you. You're all mine."

"There's no one else that I want. You're the only woman I need." He let go of her hair and slid his hands down to her hips, holding her in place as he thrust up, fucking her. Not once did Emily let him go. She took his pounding and begged for more. By the time they were finished, and they had come together, there was barely any water in the bath. He'd released the plug.

"We're bad," she said.

"The worst."

And he was falling in love with his wife, something he never thought he'd do.

## Chapter Eleven

Out in the garden, Emily ran her hands across flowers that were growing up verandas, which gave her tunnels to walk down that were the most beautiful. Jake and his friends had left an hour ago, and she couldn't stay indoors listening to children having fun. It was great they were having fun, but she felt sick to her stomach.

Her man was out there, and he needed help. She felt so useless being cooped up while her was out there and she was just here, walking around a stupid, pretty garden.

Dropping her hand from the bright red rose, she closed her eyes and tried to get her emotions in check.

"It's hard, isn't it?" her father asked.

She turned to find him approaching. The sunlight caught the graying hair at his temples.

"Do you mean walking around while people you care about are in danger? Yeah, it's hard."

She averted her gaze and began walking, aware of Bracken stepping beside her. Whenever she had these moods her mother always sent him out to find her. This was not the first time she'd struggled like this, and she doubted it would be the last.

"You care about Jake?"

"Out of everything I just said that is all you can think about."

"It's a big step considering you hated me for agreeing to give your hand in marriage."

"Yeah, well guess what, it's everything you hoped for." She'd always had a love/ hate relationship when it came to her father. She loved him, there was no denying that. He was a good father, the best. She had been lucky. Of course, he made decisions that made her hate him for a short time, or even longer.

"It was actually. You think I just dumped you with the first available man, but I didn't. Do you really think I'd have risked you being miserable?" he asked, catching her arm and forcing her to stop to look at him.

Gritting her teeth, she stared at his hand and rolled her eyes. "Fine, I care about him, Dad. I think I may even be in love with him, and that is so scary." She blew out a breath as tears flooded her eyes. "This is hard, okay? You said I'd never have to marry anyone, and now I'm scared. This would be so much easier if he wasn't so nice."

"The Family boys, they have all had to go through a lot. Donnie, he had to hold his dead brother in his arms and deal with a lot more. He's the head of The Family. Luiz's father was a monster, and he had to hide the girl he loved for fear he'd kill Christie. Tonio, he was part of a fucking child porn ring that fucking sickens me. Jake, all of his life he's been told that his life means nothing. He's expendable, and not worth the time or effort."

The tears that had only been in her eyes fell down her cheeks, and she turned her back on her father, wiping them away.

"I knew the moment I met Jake, and everything I'd heard about him that you would be the best thing that ever happened to him. You want me to regret my decision? I can't. You're good for him. You care, and I know in time, if he's not already, he's going to fall in love with you." He hugged her close. "You're a strong woman, Emily. Never forget that. You have power yourself, and no one can stop you."

"I want to help him."

"You can't help him like that. You know this. He'll be too worried about you, and he'll slip up, get himself hurt or killed. You wouldn't be able to live with that."

He let her go, and she continued to walk to try to clear her head.

"I know what you say is true. It doesn't make any of this any easier for any of us."

He laughed. "I know. You've always been a strong person, Emily. Even when you were younger. You were so determined all the time. When you went to nursery," he stopped to smile, "if there was a bully in the playground, it didn't matter if they were bigger than you, you'd step up. You would always fight for that other person. Even if you got hurt, you never stopped. Day after day, we were called to the nursery, and every single time I was so angry with you, and yet so proud."

The tears didn't let up, and she openly cried.

"Tulip said that something would happen to break that spirit. I knew all those years ago that no one was going to break my baby's spirit. I was going to make sure she could handle herself."

Memories came to her, of him training her to defend herself, using a gun, the basic fighting moves. Everything he had taught her had helped in her mission to help those who needed it. From school through to high school. Even when she no longer went to school and passed something that she didn't like, she couldn't walk away.

"I've been very stubborn."

"You and Jake are a lot alike. Neither of you can walk away, and together you are going to make great things."

"Why are you telling me this?"

"I can't have my little girl looking at me with anger. I love you, Emily. You're my eldest child." This time she saw tears in his eyes, and it shocked her. She didn't recall a moment growing up when he ever cried.

Emily knew he suffered from nightmares from his past abuse that had brought him to where he was now. Never had he cried though. "I can live with you hating me for a little while, but I can't have you not come to me when you need help. Hate me all you want, but don't think badly of me. Know everything I have done, I have done it for you."

She couldn't resist anymore and walked into his arms. "Daddy, I'm so scared. I don't want him to die."

"I know, honey." He kissed the top of her head. "He has his friends. There is nothing more that you can do."

She nodded, even as she wanted to argue. It was next to impossible not to worry. The docks were known for having a lot of bad shit going on.

"You know you could come in and help," he said. "You know you're good with kids, and you'll be able to calm them down. Maybe tell them a story."

She rolled her eyes. "That's why you came out to find me."

"No, not at all." He kissed her head. "I came out here because I've never seen you look so lost before, and you're still my daughter. I can help you when you need it."

She took her father's hand, and they made their way back inside. "How come you didn't go with them?" she asked.

"I'm staying here. They told me that this was their mess, and I am more than happy for them to clean it up."

"Are we under threat?" she asked.

"Always, Emily. Has Jake shared everything with you?"

"Yes. I know what happened yesterday."

"Good. It won't be long before Damon gets

suspicious."

"Over a hundred men defied The Family," she said, shaking her head. "Is it really because they're so young?"

"It could be. Some men really don't like taking orders from people they consider nothing more than boys. Whatever Damon was offering it was better than what they had. Add to the fact that he could drum up doubt on your ability to rule. You killed your fathers, but you weren't in a position to lead. People who want to listen, will. Fear is also a great motivator. One day you guys will be taken out, and who better to lead than him? He's better than you, and he knows what he's doing. He's older, and shit like that. All of this can be used, and I'm just thinking of it off the top of my head. There are plenty of men ready to take their place and more than happy to kill for it. Damon was just one person who decided to stand up for it."

Entering the kitchen, she went straight to the freezer and took out a carton of chocolate ice cream. Milkshakes always calmed kids, or at least it had her siblings.

"You're a target, Emily," he said.

"I know."

"You do?"

"The moment I became Jake's wife, I knew I was a target. I'm careful. I promise. I won't put anyone else in danger."

She made her way over to the food blender, but her father hadn't left. When she looked at him, she saw he was still struggling. "What's up, Dad?"

"You know how I told you when you were younger you had a history of being stubborn and doing whatever the hell you wanted."

"Protecting others?"

"Yes. I want you to think twice about that."

She paused in scooping out the ice cream. "What do you mean?"

"Damon is a sly bastard. He will take you out. He knows you're my daughter, and that you're married to Jake Carter. He could reach out to you. Don't fall for any of his tricks, and don't put yourself in a situation that could get you hurt."

She nodded. "I won't."

"Good."

It was the first time that she had seen her father really nervous. It didn't settle well in the pit of her stomach.

\*\*\*\*

"I was walking past your bedroom last night, and I heard moaning," Luiz said. "I take it your marriage is in full effect?"

Jake didn't take his eyes off the road and shook his head. "You need to think about your own relationship rather than mine. Wow, I can't even believe you stayed to listen. Did you get your rocks off?"

"I didn't stay to listen. I was ... curious."

Donnie and Tonio were chuckling in the back.

"You're a perv."

"I couldn't resist, okay? You sounded happy. It's not normal, and with how chipper you are right now, clearly, it was a good night."

"I'm not talking about my sex life with you. It's never going to happen, so get you head out of your ass."

"I hear anal sex is fun. You've got to tell your woman you've got a small dick, and all that."

Jake held his hand up. "Luiz, shut the fuck up."

"What's the plan?" Donnie asked. "We go in guns blazing?"

"I think we have a nice little chat at reception. I

want to see my signature."

"Why? You think you'll figure out who signed it from a simple signature?" Tonio asked.

"I don't know what. They also have security footage, right? We can see who they're meeting up with."

"I've got Brian on the ready for when we crack open the crates," Donnie said. "Can you believe they're actually storing women, children, and men at the docks? They have sales late at night, and the guards are paid handsomely to look the other way."

"It's fucking sick. Is it like an auction?" Tonio asked.

"According to our new information," Donnie said.

"I just can't believe for a fucking second that our men would think we sign off on this." Jake was so fucking angered that someone had used his signature. It had been a soldier who was already dead, and he had a feeling he was going to wish that fucker was still alive just so he could kill him again.

Gripping the steering wheel tightly, Jake pulled into the dock's parking lot. It was nearly deserted, but in a few hours, it would be humming with activity. None of them intended to do much killing. Jake had learned from the dead soldiers that there were only a few guards during the day. The noise and exhaustion kept their victims quiet. Also the threat of being hunted down and killed if they made a noise kept them good little puppets.

Jake had seen some sick shit in his time, and he just knew it was about to get worse.

There was no time to back down or to pace, or to prepare. They just needed to get in and get the job done.

"Are you going to have kids?" Donnie asked while they were at the trunk of the car. Jake put the relevant guns in their holders beneath his jacket.

"Kids? You want to talk about them right now?"

Donnie shrugged. "I don't know. I think I want to do anything but go and find out what exactly we've let happen right under our noses." He shook his head. "These fuckers need to be taught a lesson."

Jake couldn't argue with his friend. Damon had made a big fucking error in thinking he could take The Family from them. They were young, but they had lived, breathed, and been completely devoted to The Family ever since they were kids. Gripping the back of Donnie's neck, he pressed his forehead against his. "Don't let it get to you. We'll fix it, and that's all we need to do, brother. That's all we're doing. No more half assed shit. This is our Family. It's time for us to prove that we're better than our fathers. Come on, let's go and handle this shit." Slamming the trunk closed, they spent ten minutes in the office, and Jake scrunched up the letter, pocketing it.

They gave a strict order that next time, they put a call through to one of them. The Family belonged to them, and they did not handle human trafficking of any kind.

Leaving the office, they had the guard take them to the crates that were right in the back, far away from any activity. There was no one guarding the three of them, which pissed Jake off. Damon was so sure they wouldn't figure this shit out, or that they would have been dead. One by one, the three crates opened up, and Jake held his gun up ready. The door cranked open, and the scent of piss, shit, and death was heavy in the air. In one crate, there were about fifty women, three of them were dead on the floor. The others looked filthy. Three men were in another, and again, they looked close to death. What broke Jake's heart was the third and final crate. Five children, all of them pale, and all of them looked terrified. One was on the ground. It was a little girl with blonde hair, and vomit was coming out of her mouth. He pocketed his gun and went to her. She was hot to the touch.

"Jake?"

"She needs a hospital." Something inside him was telling him that he couldn't leave her. "Call our guy. I'm not waiting around. I need to get her to the hospital." He picked her up and rushed out of the crate. He was going to find Damon and kill him with his bare hands. He was going to make that fucker rot, fester, and pray for death long before he gave it.

He got to the car and found Tonio had followed him. "I'll drive."

Climbing into the back of the car, he held the girl and tried to rub her back. She had so many bruises.

"We have to kill those fuckers," Jake said.

"We will, Jake. You can guarantee it."

"They were doing this shit right under our noses. We're going to find every single person they have taken and sold. We're going to bring them back."

"You got it."

His rage was so fucking strong that he could taste it. His thirst for blood was right there. If Damon had any sense, the bastard would run.

Jake would find him, of that there was a guarantee.

The girl coughed and began to throw up. She was all skin and bones, nothing to her.

Entering the hospital, he barked orders, getting nurses and doctors to help.

Jake made sure they focused on the girl, and when she was taken, he followed. They tried to hold him back, but he wouldn't have it.

"I found her. I will make sure she is fucking

protected."

He followed, watching as the doctors worked. Tonio said he would handle everything. With their contacts in the police force Jake didn't anticipate any problem on that front. Time passed, he didn't know how much until he had no choice but to leave to take a piss.

After taking his bathroom break, he went in search of Tonio and found Emily sitting next to him with Bracken. His father-in-law nodded at him, and Emily went to him. He held his arms open, and she stepped right into them. "Tonio told us what happened."

"Who is taking care of everyone else?" he asked.

"Donnie and Luiz are back at home," Tonio said.

Jake nodded. "Thank you."

Emily pressed her head to his and kissed his lips. It was a relief having her with him.

"I'm fine," he said.

"I know, but I'm here if you need me. You know that."

He held her tightly, breathing in her sweet scent. "She's so young."

"Take me to her," Emily said.

Jake took her hand, and they made their way back to where he had left the young girl. She was hooked up to tubes, and per his request, there was a nurse providing twenty-four-hour care.

"She looks a little like you," Jake said. "I just saw her, and I had to help."

"You don't have to explain anything to me, Jake. I'm here with you, remember? You did the right thing."

She took his hand, and he felt her strength.

"I'm going to kill the bastard, Emily."

"I know. I hope I can be there to watch."

He glanced toward her. "I'm not so sweet throughout, Jake. Even I want to see the end to this monster. Men, women, children, nothing is sacred anymore, and it needs to be. That young girl shouldn't be in hospital, beaten, hurting. She should be at home enjoying a warm meal, her family's love around her. Whatever you need, all you have to do is ask."

Jake squeezed her hand. "You're doing everything that I need. You give me strength."

"Good. I'm glad."

Silence fell between them.

"Your men in the force have taken care of the people they've found. From what I heard they are being sent back to their families."

"They weren't even strays?" he asked.

"No. They just disappeared, and there are searches out for them."

Jake shook his head. His temper growing. "I hate these monsters."

"You're helping to stop it though."

Emily squeezed his hand, and he was thankful for it.

Never would he turn his back again.

## Chapter Twelve

The days that followed were tough. Jake spent a great deal of time at the hospital, and Emily stayed with him. Her father or one of his friends were there. The girl had been taken from the streets, and her family had been alerted.

Jake, Donnie, Luiz, and Tonio fought left, right, and center. They took back what was rightfully theirs, and showed their enemies that they were not boys to be toyed with. All four of them set an example, being sure that their voice was heard.

Many men lost their lives, and those that betrayed them begged for death, but they made sure their threat was shown. Damon had no strength against the true force of the four boys. Jake could finally laugh at how easy it was to take back their city, to control those who had turned their backs on them.

What helped to put his life into focus was saving that girl. In a strange kind of way, the girl was a sign of hope for him. He had been able to save her, and in doing so, he was able to save what he was fighting for. Jake didn't keep any secrets from Emily, and every evening he told her of the progress they were making, how he was going to make sure they were safe.

A week after Jake brought the girl to the hospital they learned that her name was Michelle, and her family had been searching for her. He'd not wanted to let her family know that she was alive. He wanted to adopt her, but one look at her family, and he knew he couldn't keep her from her family. On the day they came to collect her, it was hard. They were a nice couple, and Emily knew that Jake was feeling much better when they had taken her.

The main threat from Damon had been destroyed

as The Family had taken away his followers, and broken down his power, so they were able to leave Donnie's safe house. Jake took her to his home, the one in the country he had told her about. They were going to spend the weekend together, but then he was taking her back to the city so that he could be where he needed to be for all of his commitments.

Within two weeks, between his hospital visits and dealing with the threat, she had only gotten him to herself at night. She missed him and wasn't afraid to say that she was looking forward to having him all to herself.

His home was set back, and the gates were obscured by several trees.

"How long have you lived here?"

"I bought this when we took over The Family. I wanted somewhere that was safe and that I could call my own."

"Have you brought anyone else here?"

"No. I've not even brought Charlene here in case you asked."

She held her hands up in surrender, laughing. "That was not what I was thinking about."

"You're a little liar, but that's okay." He took her hand, pressing a kiss to her hand. "I'm pleased you're here."

"How is Michelle?" she asked.

She knew he'd asked if he could keep in touch. He wanted to make sure that she was fine, and her parents were more than happy with that. They had told him they were indebted to him, and anything he wanted, they would give him.

Jake just wanted to know that she was fine.

"She's back at home. I've got a guy there keeping an eye. I don't want anyone to think for a second they can take her. He will let me know if any of Damon's guys are there."

"How is it looking with Damon?"

"He's proving to be a man of many talents. We've closed down three of his massage parlors. They were fronts for brothels. The women that were working there were starved. They were working for food. The bastard is a fucking pig." He pulled up at the front of the house.

Emily stared at it and fell in love. It wasn't overly large or garish. It looked like a beautiful home, not a mansion either.

She climbed out of the car and stared. "Jake, it's beautiful."

"I had to do a lot of redecoration inside. I like it here." He took her hand and led her into the main door. He took out a key and opened it up. "I have a housekeeper, and she came earlier, opening it up for me. There should also be food."

"Are you sure we can take this weekend? I know things are moving forward with The Family."

"I'm sure. Damon thought he could take us on, and that's not the case. The guys know we're going to kill him. We've taken out his brothels and several of his drug loops." He bent down, lifting her up. "We have taken care of a lot of trouble in the past couple of weeks. The men who would betray us are gone, and they're not going to rise from the dead. I deserve one weekend with my wife, and I'm going to get it."

"My dad."

"I know what he said that Damon was unstable. Guess what? Let him be. It will draw him out, and then I'm going to spend the next year torturing him before I kill him. Michelle is safe, our friends and their families are safe. I should be on some little island right now with my very beautiful wife." He spun her around, and he didn't stop. "Now, I want to get reacquainted with her body. I don't remember if you have any freckles or blemishes. I just remember pure beauty."

She started laughing even as heat flooded her pussy. "I'll stop putting a downer on our time together." Wrapping her arms and legs around his waist, she pressed kisses to his neck. "Is it wrong that I want you all to myself?"

"Nope. That is exactly what I want. I want you all to myself, and no one is going to interrupt up." He moved down a long hallway, kicking open a door.

"I feel like a virgin again. It has been too long since my husband showed me that I belonged to him."

"I can't have that. I've got to have my woman all ready to take my big cock." He dropped her onto the bed, making her laugh even more. "Oops, your husband doesn't have the energy to be very nice at the moment."

He tugged his jacket off and started to peel each layer of his clothing from his body. She couldn't help but watch. His body was a work of art, his skin covered with tattoos, and his devotion to The Family.

She stood up, removing her jacket, and then her shirt, followed by her jeans. When she was naked, Jake caught her up in his arms, and pressed kisses across her chest, up to her neck, and then over her pulse. Down he went, sucking on her nipples once again, only this time he continued his journey, going between her thighs where he opened her slit.

Going to her elbows, she watched as he ran his tongue between her pussy lips, circling her clit as he did. She dropped her head back and moaned. The pleasure was instant and totally insane.

"No, Emily, I want you to watch me. Watch as I lick this pretty little cunt that belongs to me, and only to me." He spread her pussy wide, and his tongue flicked over her clit. It was next to impossible not to close her eyes and just bask in the pleasure. "You taste so good, and what makes you even better is the fact I know you're all mine. This is all mine." He pressed his hand to her pussy. "Who does this belong to?"

"You, it belongs to you. I'm all yours, Jake. All yours." She kept on saying what he wanted to hear, loving the way he looked at her hungrily.

"You have no idea how much I fucking love hearing you say that."

It wasn't a declaration of love, but for Emily it meant something to her. She was falling for him. Jake was such a loving man. He gave so much of himself, and no one really knew how much he did.

"Hold your pussy open for me, baby. Show me how much you want my tongue on your cunt."

She groaned. Those words shouldn't arouse her. She shouldn't get excited by him, but she did. She wanted him so much.

"You want my tongue?"

"Yes, Jake, lick my pussy." She knew what he wanted to hear, and she gave it to him. Emily knew without a doubt that she would give him everything he ever wanted, without holding back.

His tongue danced across her clit before sliding down inside her. She closed her eyes, loving the feel of his touch. Opening her eyes, she watched as he pulled away. His hand went around his cock, the tip leaking pre-cum. She licked her lips, and suddenly, she wanted a taste of him.

"I want to suck you," she said.

"You never fail to surprise me."

"I know what I want."

"And I think it's damn sexy watching you go after it." He stroked his thumb across the tip and held it out. "Have a taste. See if you can handle more."

She took his wrist and flicked her tongue across the tip. Looking him in the eye, she sucked his thumb into her mouth, and released a little moan. The taste wasn't strong enough, but the way he watched her, that hungry need, made her want to do it all over again. Jake inspired her in ways she didn't think possible. Her body awakened beneath his touch. Bending forward so her ass was in the air, she circled his cock with her hand, and then flicked the tip.

He hissed out a breath, and she smiled against his cock. Following the path of the vein at the side, she ran her tongue down it, and then covered his entire cock, sucking him deep. He growled, and his hands sank into her hair, wrapping the length around his fist. She closed her eyes, loving the way he pumped his hips. Did he even realize that he was fucking her face? She didn't know, nor did she care.

This man, her husband, was making her want things in ways she never thought possible.

****

Emily's mouth was heaven. Jake just wanted to thrust to the back of her throat, close his eyes, and bask in the pleasure, but no matter what, he couldn't do that. He wanted to watch as she sucked his cock, as her tongue teased, tantalized, and pleasured him. Her caresses were not in any way skilled, and yet, he loved the feel of her mouth on him.

There was no other woman for him. He knew without a shadow of a doubt that she belonged to him. This wasn't just because she was his wife. No, their beginning hadn't been the best, but they were two souls. He really did believe that she was his soul mate, the one destined to be his.

Her blonde hair was so soft, and he stroked his

fingers through the length as she continued to suck him off. Everything about Emily drew him in. He was a sucker for her.

*You love her.*

It seemed too damn good to be real. His feelings for her, they had grown so much in the past couple of weeks. Even from their wedding night when they had spent it getting drunk, and dancing. She had been the first person in a long time to demand he have fun. Even with all the crap going on around them, he had her. Coming home was a pleasure, was a joy. When Bracken finally went to check on his own area, she had stayed behind. Jake didn't know why he expected her to go with her father, but he just did.

Emily was his. Plain and simple.

They belonged to each other.

He thrust into her mouth, and she sucked him deep. Her hand covered where her mouth couldn't, driving him wild.

When he couldn't take anymore, he tugged on her hair, and she released him. He let go of her blonde tresses, cupped her hips, and moved her so that she was on her knees before him. Running a hand down her back, he grabbed her ass cheeks, and spread them wide, eying her tight anus and wet cunt. His cock already pressed to her entrance, he slowly began to ease inside her. He was so fucking hard that he didn't even need to use his hands to guide himself inside her. With the tip at her entrance, she was so wet that he slid right on home.

They both moaned as he filled her up, her tight pussy squeezing him.

He held onto her hips as he slowly pulled out, watching his cock glisten in the light. She was so wet, and he was so hard.

Rocking in and out of her, Jake took his time,

drawing more cries from her. He let go of her hip, and slid one hand between them, stroking her clit. "I want you to come all over me, baby." He teased, stroked, and brought her off with his fingers. She screamed his name, and he vowed that it would be the only name she ever said in pleasure.

"Oh, Jake, it feels so good. Please don't stop. I don't want you to."

He didn't stop. He continued to stroke her soaking wet clit, even as she begged him not to. His cock drenched in her sweet cream, he brought to a second orgasm that her screaming and shaking in equal measure. Her whole body was his and belonged to him alone. Kissing her neck, her shoulder, he began to thrust deep inside her, making her take the whole length of his cock.

The pleasure was too much, and yet not enough. He needed her, wanted her, was completely consumed by everything that was Emily, his beautiful, sweet, sexy wife. The woman he didn't ever want, and yet the only one he could ever dream of being with. She was the light to his dark, his soul, everything.

He pounded inside her, feeling every ripple, every pulse, hoping that he filled her with his baby. It was the strangest feeling in the world, and not one he was used to. He wanted to bind Emily to him for fucking ever. No woman had ever made him feel this way, and he wanted to keep it, to cherish it, and to hold onto her.

"Please, Jake, it's so good."

"I know, baby. I know." He slammed to the hilt within her, finding the building of his own peak. The pleasure grew intense with every passing second. They were both screaming, crying, begging for more. It wasn't enough, and yet together it totally was. The entire world could have ended, and he wouldn't have cared.

They came together, calling each other's name.

Jake filled her pussy, loving every pulse and ripple as she squeezed his come from him.

When it was over, he didn't pull away. With his arms wrapped around her, he stayed deep inside her, never wanting to let her go.

Through the foggy pleasure haze, Jake knew without a doubt that he was in love with his wife. Not only was he in love, but it hadn't taken him long. She stroked his arm, and even from that touch, he felt an immense amount of pleasure.

"Jake," she said.

"Yeah, baby."

"I've got a confession to make."

He kissed her neck, waiting to hear whatever it was she was going to say.

"I don't hate you anymore."

"I don't hate you either," he said.

"Jake?"

"Yeah?" He couldn't help but smile against the flesh of her neck. She turned her head and looked at him.

"I'm in love with you."

He reached up, stroking her cheek. Pulling out of her pussy, he moved so that he was lying in front of her. Pressing his lips against hers, he smiled into her eyes. "I'm in love with you as well."

"You don't have to say that."

"Em, babe, I don't just say stuff to make you feel better. I know what I feel."

"Have you felt it before?" she asked.

In that moment, he saw how vulnerable she was.

"No. I've never felt like this before. You're the first woman that has made me feel like for the first time in my life, I have something that belongs to me, and me alone. This is not just as a possession. This is about a whole lot more."

"Jake?"

"I'm not a good man, Emily. I kill without blinking an eye. My life has been about protecting others. For the first time, all I want to do is protect you, to love you, to give you a life you deserve. I never wanted this. You're right. Me, Tonio, Donnie, and Luiz, in the beginning, we didn't have as big of a commitment as we should have. Damon played on everyone's fears, and in doing so, he made us look weak. Our enemies took advantage of that apparent weakness, and I will not, we will not let that happen again. I love you, Emily. I love you so much that it scares me. You're mine. I want you so much. Coming home is the best part of the day to me. Seeing your smile, that's what I want more than anything." Tears glistened in her eyes, and Jake knew he had to be honest with her. He had to tell her exactly how he felt. "I didn't want to be married. It's why we wanted to make changes, so no one was forced into any marriage. My friends, they got lucky. I didn't think there was anyone out there for me, but I was wrong, so totally wrong. I want to keep you for myself. You give me hope that the moment I walk through that door, I can forget what I do, and why I do it, and know that you care for me."

"I do, Jake. I care. I love you. I want a family. I know this is not what you wanted. You would probably do anything to be out of this life, but there is no out for us. We're born into this, just like there isn't an out for your friends. This is what it is." She pressed a kiss to his lips. "That's doesn't mean we can't make this the best damn life there is. Together, we can build a better future for our family, for our friends. I will be there by your side because I know it is possible."

He pressed kisses to her lips, knowing that together they could do anything.

"Truth or dare?" he asked.

"Dare."

"I dare you to love me for the rest of your life, even if you hate me."

She giggled. "Then you must complete the same dare. I'm not going anywhere, Jake. I'm all yours for the taking."

And he took her. All night, he showed Emily exactly what he wanted and how much he loved her, not giving her a moment to second guess his love for her.

## Chapter Thirteen

For the next three months, Jake and his friends worked tirelessly with her father, Bracken, to get rid of the threat to The Family. Every single day they took back businesses that had been infiltrated by Damon Seagus, and with each revelation, they left a trail of bodies piling all the way back to their enemy's door.

Emily was at their place every single night, waiting for Jake's return. He always made sure she was heavily guarded with no fewer than four soldiers at any one time. Each night he would come home and tell her everything they had done. This was all after dinner. She spent a great deal of time preparing them food, baking for him to take them into work to share with others. It was probably lame, but she loved doing it. Her father had once told her that it was the small details that helped to create loyalty. Remembering a person's name, the stuff that was going on in their lives. Jake, he remembered his men and the women that worked for him. He made sure to keep those details of their family close. In return, whenever he was going to one of his businesses, she made sure he took a batch of muffins, cookies, or tray bakes. She could imagine everyone laughing at her, but each night, Jake would come home with a smile on his face.

Food was the key to people's hearts, or so her mother had said growing up. She believed that you could win everyone's love through the power of baked goods. Emily had had her doubts, but so far, it seemed to be working.

"I'm shocked," Charlene said.

"About what?"

Jake was out of the house, but Emily had requested to meet Charlene. She didn't want there to be any animosity between her and Charlene.

"You inviting me here. You are aware of Jake once having feelings for me, right?"

"Yes, I am. It's why I wanted to see you, and for you to see that I don't mind. Jake told me that he thought himself in love with you. You never felt that way about him?"

"I've never been attracted to men. I've always loved women, and I'm very happy. I did tell Jake this, and I don't think he loved me. I think he loved the idea of being in love with me. We were never together like that."

Emily took a seat opposite the woman. They were sitting in the sitting room in Jake's large house. Over the past few months she had made changes, starting with putting his stamp along with hers on this place, which meant photographs. She made him pose for pictures, and then she made all of his friends pose with him to make a large one. Over the fireplace was one of her and Jake on their wedding day. They both looked nervous as hell, but for her, she wouldn't have had it any other way. Their wedding day defined them as a couple.

She picked up her cup and took a sip. "You're his friend, and he loves you like a friend. We don't know each other, but I would like to extend that friendship to you."

Charlene frowned, and Emily saw she'd unnerved the other woman.

"You're not what I expected."

"It would seem that being Bracken's daughter seems to come with an element of, erm, spoilt bitch rumors, right?"

The other woman chuckled.

"I'm not a spoilt bitch. Far from it in fact. I don't even like the sound of it." She put her cup down. "I'd like you and your partner, and your daughter to come and visit whenever you want. I don't want you to be a stranger."

Charlene smiled. "You're good for Jake. I can see it. You're going to show him that he is worth something. I even see what you've done with the place. Jake never brought me here. He only ever showed me pictures of it You've changed it. The pictures, the colors. Jake has been way too dark for way too long. He's been trapped in what his father said he should be. I hated that."

"Jake told you about his father?"

"No. He didn't. Donnie's father liked to brag about their sons, and how they had trained them well, to be nothing more than submissive minions. He clearly didn't keep a good enough eye on his son. His death was one I wish I could have seen."

Emily saw the darkness in her gaze, and she reached out, taking her hand.

Tears filled Charlene's eyes, and Emily sat listening to her.

"Thank you for making him see that there is no turning back. No matter how much he wanted it. I knew he couldn't ... Donnie's father..." She paused, and took a breath. "He would always brag about dragging down his son. Making it impossible for anyone to leave The Family."

"I have no intention of leaving, Charlene, and neither does Jake. We're going to fight this together, because this is our home, this is our family, and I would love for you to be part of it." She squeezed the woman's hand, trying to give her comfort. Her mother, Tulip, once said that being the wife of a man's who held so much responsibility was a tough place. She was part of a mafia family, and with it, she needed to learn to step up with her man, and make sure no one saw him as weak. Behind closed doors, he could drop the veil that hid the truth, and in her arms, he could be free. To everyone else, he was a strong wall, something that couldn't be broken. Emily had never seen her mother as weak, but sitting in her home right now, she felt that responsibility to her core. Jake needed her just as much as she needed him.

"I'm pleased that he has been able to find that love with you. I didn't for a second think he loved me. I did believe he was in love with the idea of being in love with me. I offered him something else at the time." Charlene gave her hand a reassuring squeeze. "You're a good woman, Emily."

"Thank you. I know Jake is helping to make life better for us." She had wanted to clear the air between her and Charlene. "In a couple of weeks, I'm hoping to host a barbeque, and you will come, right?"

"I'd love to."

Once she and Charlene had caught up, Emily made her way out toward the garden, basking in the summer's heat. She never liked the summer normally, but life just seemed to be that little brighter, and she loved it.

Jake had told her last night after they made love on a rug in front of the fireplace that Damon Seagus was on the run. They had chased him off, and had cut all ties that he'd been making. The Family was once again a force to be reckoned with.

Leaving the garden, she made her way toward the far back near the trees. She turned around, and looked up at the house, loving the beauty that Jake had created for her, for the two of them. Tucking some hair behind her ear, she couldn't help the smile that grew on her face.

Her mother always told her that a man she finally ended up with would be lucky. For Emily, she truly believed that she had been the lucky one. There was no way she would have married Jake, and yet for her, it was the best thing that had ever happened to her.

Suddenly, she was grabbed from behind, a rough hand grabbing her waist as another cupped her mouth.

"I suggest you relish that smile, slut, 'cause I'm about to make your life a fucking misery." He dragged her toward the house and released her mouth.

The moment her mouth was free, she screamed.

"Good girl, I couldn't have timed this better myself." He pressed a gun to her head, ready to shoot.

Her heart started to pound. She had never felt so sick before in her life. Everything seemed to be moving so fast as the men that Jake had put in charge of her safety came out. They all had their guns raised.

"I suggest you put down those weapons before I put a bullet in her fucking head!"

"Get Jake," she said, screaming out the word.

"Yeah, let's do that. Let's go and get Jake. I want a word with the little shits that have been ruining me. My men, my businesses, my everything. They think they can take everything from me."

"They have," she said. She closed her eyes and screamed as a bullet rang out. When she opened her eyes again, she saw that one of the men set to guard her had fallen.

"So The Family are back in force, hey?"

"I bet you weren't anticipating that, were you? No one messes with The Family. No one."

She would defend her man, her family, everything at all costs.

"Between your little husband, your father, I've had e-fucking-nough of this shit!" He fired off another bullet, and a guard fell, this time screaming. "You get that little fucker here now. I want Jake first, and you tell him that he's going to be without a wife if he's not here within ten minutes." He held a cell phone for her to take, and even as her hands shook, she knew Jake's number.

Dialing the number, she waited for him to answer.

"Who is this?" Jake asked.

"Jake, Damon's here," she said.

Damon grabbed the phone from her hand. He had his arm around her neck and was squeezing tightly as he talked. "Jake Carter, if you want your wife to live then I suggest you, and your fucking friends get here now, and swear your allegiance to me. You're not taking what is mine from me."

She didn't know what Jake said, but the pressure on her head was too much. She released a whimper, and he jerked her hard.

"You want to fuck with me. I will take your whore, and make sure you never see her again. I will fuck her up more than any fucking slut. I'll make sure everyone I come across will use her, taking her again, and again, and again."

"You've got fifteen minutes. If you're not here, then I start shooting bullets inside her." Damon ended the call and shot the other two guards so they were on the ground.

Then he released her, and as she went to run away, he grabbed her hair, wrapping the length around his fist, and dragged her down on the floor. She screamed as she was sure some of her hair had been pulled out. He shoved her down and kicked her in her ribs.

"You fucking slut, you fucking whore." When he went to kick her again, she caught his foot, and made sure he lost his footing.

She wasn't just any fucking woman. She was her father's daughter, and not only was she a Carter, she was also a Bracken. This man, this piece of shit had hurt men, women, and children. He had to pay for the damage he had caused, and she was going to be the one to make sure he paid.

Even as he punched her, and hurt her, she clawed at him, determined to make him hurt. She never gave up. Her father had taught her well, and when she grabbed the gun, she took aim and fired.

****

Jake had already been on his way home, his friends not far behind him when he'd told them that the coward they were chasing had his wife, his woman, his fucking soul mate. The rage bubbled up inside him, threatening to take hold.

Parking his car, he climbed out, to hear the gunshot, and then utter stillness.

"Emily!" He screamed her name, rushing through the house, going straight out the back. He found Emily standing in the grass, blood on her legs, her dress torn, coming off one shoulder as she turned toward him.

"Jake!" She cried out his name and started rushing toward him. One of his men wasn't moving, and the other three were treating leg wounds. He didn't stick around to assess their damage. He rushed toward his wife.

She wrapped her arms around him, holding him close. "I killed him. I had to kill him, Jake. He was going to hurt you, and the others. I couldn't let him do that. I killed him."

He cupped her face, pressing kisses to her lips, to her face, to her neck. "I've got you, baby. Nothing is going to happen now. I've got you."

"I killed him, Jake."

Jake looked at the ground and saw the bullet hole under Damon's chin. She had pressed the gun so close that there was nothing left.

"He was a monster, Jake. You couldn't swear your allegiance to him."

"I was never going to, babe. I was already on the way home. I was coming to protect you." Pressing his lips to hers, he silenced her cries, hoping to give her comfort.

She held onto his arms, refusing to let go.

"It's fine now. You're safe now. It's just the two of us."

"He killed Ray."

"I know." He had seen the fallen soldier on the ground. "It's over now, though, babe. He's gone. We've got The Family back. Nothing is ever going to hurt you again." He ran his hands up and down her back, holding her close, comforting her, knowing that it was over. He, Tonio, Luiz, and Donnie had finally done what they had promised they would do. They had made The Family better.

Thirty minutes later, Donnie, Luiz, Tonio, and Bracken arrived. Tulip was also there, and when she tried to take Emily, Jake shook his head. "No, she's my woman. I'll deal with her."

As his friends and parents-in-law took care of the bodies, he took his wife upstairs to their room.

He ran her a bath and helped her out of her dress. Each new bruise he saw, he wanted to tear someone's throat out. Damon he wanted to kill, but Emily had done that.

"Thank you," she said, smiling at him. The tears were gone, and she finally reached out to touch his cheek. "Thank you for taking care of me, and not giving me to my mother."

"I couldn't let anyone else take care of you. You're mine, babe. You're all mine."

He gripped the back of her neck, and pressed a

kiss to her lips.

"He was going to kill you, Jake. I couldn't let him do that."

"Thank you. I mean that. Thank you." He rested his head against hers. "I love you, Emily. Hearing him on the phone, and you cry out. I've never been so fucking scared."

"I'm a strong woman. I told you I'd stay by your side no matter what."

He kissed her lips again. "Damon is gone. The Family now holds the power, and we're united with Bracken."

"That's good to know."

"When this mess is cleaned up, I want you to pack a bag," he said.

"You do? Why?"

"We're going to finish our honeymoon. I told you the moment we got rid of the threat, I was going to give you what you deserved, what we both deserve." He cupped the back of her neck and brought her lips close to his. "I love you, Emily. Love you more than I ever thought possible. Charlene called me and said that I was a lucky guy. She thinks you're beautiful, sweet, and strong. She told me to keep you and never let you go."

"What are you going to do?" she asked.

"I'm going to do what I knew I would do our wedding night. I'm going to keep you, love you, and make sure you never have a moment of regret." He loved that smile on her lips, and once he had finished washing her, he helped her out.

He left her to dress and to pack their bags. Heading downstairs, he found everyone waiting for him outside, but Tulip was in the kitchen.

"I want you to make the arrangements for Emily and me to finish our honeymoon on your island," he said.

"If that is okay with you."

Tulip nodded. "Of course. I'll make sure you can leave as soon as you're ready."

He made to go to the door, and stopped, looking back at her. "I never thanked you for giving your daughter to me."

"It wasn't like that."

"I know it wasn't, but I wanted to thank you for giving her to me. I will love, cherish, and honor her every single day. Not a day will go by that she doesn't feel loved. I give you my word on that."

Tears glistened in her eyes. "You mean that?"

"Yes, I do. I love your daughter more than anything." With that, he made his way outside. The bodies were gone, and the soldiers that had been injured were no longer there.

"Greg, your guy at the casino, knew a guy who could fix them up."

"I have a feeling Greg needs a raise," Jake said, smiling.

"You've got a good man there," Bracken said. He blew out a breath. "This is not the first time that Emily has been in danger, but it never gets easier."

"She's a fighter. She killed Damon," Jake said.

His friends turned to him then.

"I taught her how to take care of herself. My only hope was that she was able to do it without freezing up," Bracken said.

"We're going on our honeymoon," Jake said, looking at his friends, his work colleagues, but more importantly, his brothers.

"The threat is gone," Donnie said.

"Don't worry, Jake, we can hold down the fort here," Luiz said.

"We really can," Tonio said. "You know, this is

going to be a lot of fun."

Jake moved toward his friends and embraced them. Since they were young boys they had fought long, hard, tirelessly to be strong men, better than their own fathers, and to do everything for The Family.

They had rebelled, nearly gotten each other killed, found love, and now they were back. They were in charge, and there was doubt in Jake's mind. They could live their life, they could all rule The Family, and none of them had to be like their fathers.

Jake finally felt at peace with his decision, with who he was. When someone cleared her throat, and he looked up to find Emily there. In front of their family, he went right up to her, and claimed her as his own. Slamming his lips down on hers, he pulled her in close, knowing that out of everything, he had gotten lucky. He had found a woman that loved him, and he loved her more than anything in the world.

Nothing could take that away, absolutely nothing.

## Epilogue

*Ten years later*

"Petal, George, don't push so high," Jake said, shouting out over the music.

Emily wrapped her arms around his waist and kissed his neck. Her large stomach that was filled with their fourth child pressed against his back.

"You know Andrew and Talia love it when they go higher," she said. Andrew and Talia were their kids.

Glancing around his large yard, which was filled with his friends, Donnie and Paige, Luiz and Raine, Tonio and Zara, along with all of their kids. Bracken was also there with Tulip and their grandkids. Greg and his family were there.

Wrapping his arm around Emily, Jake had her snuggled against her side as he rolled the sausages then flipped the burgers.

Ten years of happiness, and Jake looked around his yard to see the real family that he had always wanted. The Family was still going strong. Together, he and his friends fought off every single opponent, and made sure no one ever thought for a second that they were weak.

Their past mistakes were never repeated.

The Family was theirs.

He, Tonio, Luiz, and Donnie ruled The Family, and made sure their fathers' poison never again caught hold of their lives. None of them succumbed to what their fathers wanted. They were united in the belief they were better men.

"You've got that frown again," Emily said, pressing a thumb to his forehead.

"It's nothing, baby. I'm just thinking about how

happy I am."

"I told you you'd be a good dad and that you had to stop worrying." She pressed a kiss to his lips, smiling.

"You always have so much faith in me."

"Of course, I love you. I love you more than I think you will ever know."

He slid his hand down to cup her nice rounded butt. "I think I know. Question is, do you realize how much I love you? How much I adore you? How much I'm devoted to you."

He wrapped his arms around her and pulled her up for a hug.

When she had first discovered that she was pregnant, he had been shit scared that he would be as awful as his father. Emily didn't for a second believe it at all. She had known, and they had spent many nights after having sex talking about his fears. The moment she gave birth to Andrew, and he held his son in his arms, he'd known. There was no way he would ever put his son or any of his children in any kind of danger.

Jake, like his friends, was a good man. Against all odds, he had finally made it, and no one was going to take that away from him.

Staring down into his woman's eyes, with all of their family around him, he just knew life was worth living, that life was something to look forward to.

"So, Mrs. Carter, how do you like your sausages?" he asked.

Her eyes seemed to twinkle. She leaned in close so only he could hear. "I like you rock hard, pounding inside me, that's how I like *your* sausage. With the ones I eat, just in a bun."

"Damn it, woman, I love you so much." Pressing her to the front of his body to hide his growing erection, he would not only give her a sausage to eat now, but later that night, he intended to be balls deep inside her.

The End

**www.samcrescent.com**

# SAM CRESCENT

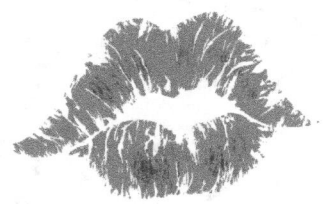

# EVERNIGHT PUBLISHING ®

www.evernightpublishing.com